Sponta...

Like paper that resists the fire at first, only to explode into flames an instant later, she met his demands with her own. Her body fused with his and she could feel the corded strength of his thighs. Hungrily, she held his face to hers, savoring the texture of his beard, drawing in the scent of his skin, learning the outline of his lips. She welcomed the invasion of his kiss. Deep tremors shook them both, and as the fire she had thought long dead seared her heart, she felt a thawing, melting weakness.

JOCELYN GRIFFIN
is a long-time resident of Michigan's Lower Peninsula who divides her career between writing and teaching English. She and her husband both love to travel, and fine summer weekends usually find them escaping from house painting, papering, and plumbing to paddle their kayak to remote islands or beaches on the Great Lakes.

Dear Reader:

Romance readers have been enthusiastic about Silhouette Special Editions for years. And that's not by accident: Special Editions were the first of their kind and continue to feature realistic stories with heightened romantic tension.

The longer stories, sophisticated style, greater sensual detail and variety that made Special Editions popular are the same elements that will make you want to read book after book.

We hope that you enjoy this Special Edition today, and will enjoy many more.

The Editors at Silhouette Books

JOCELYN GRIFFIN
Hostages to Fortune

Silhouette Special Edition
Published by Silhouette Books New York
America's Publisher of Contemporary Romance

SILHOUETTE BOOKS, a Division of Simon & Schuster, Inc.
1230 Avenue of the Americas, New York, N.Y. 10020

Distributed by Pocket Books

ISBN: 0-671-53695-8

First Silhouette Books printing October, 1984

10 9 8 7 6 5 4 3 2 1

America's Publisher of Contemporary Romance

Printed in the U.S.A.

BC91

To my parents and parents-in-law, for their love and support

Acknowledgments

The Au Sable Light Station is still closed, awaiting the restoration work Brock does on it. For access to the station, and for information, interest, and encouragement in writing this story, I'd like to thank the National Park Service at Pictured Rocks National Lakeshore. In particular, I'm grateful to Park Superintendent Grant Petersen, Chief Ranger Deryl Stone, and Rangers Georgia Dempsey and Russ Dees. And special thanks go to Leo Kuschel, Great Lakes artist. Without them, I couldn't really have told a story about such a wild and beautiful place.

Hostages to Fortune

Chapter One

*W*hat the hell do you think you're doing?''

Harsh as a north wind, the irate question caught Verity Brandon at a distinct disadvantage, and she jumped, dropping her son's pocketknife with a dull ''thock.'' One instant she had been hunched over, prying methodically at an old-fashioned door lock, the next, the whole door swung open so fast it was only a blur, while that furious male voice crackled around her ears and her spine straightened with a snap.

So much for her information that the Coast Guard stopped staffing this remote Lake Superior lighthouse twenty years ago! All too obviously it was manned again, and by the individual standing in the doorway, angry and half-naked.

To stall for recovery time, she had bent immediately to retrieve Toby's knife, yanking it from the wooden threshold where it stuck only inches from a pair of very large bare feet. Straightening again, she pushed her ruffled hair back from her face and found herself confronting a man who wore nothing but a pair of faded Levis between those feet and the towel slung hastily around his neck. And because he was more than a head taller than her own considerable height, Verity discovered her eye level was right in the middle of his broad chest.

It was a novel point of view. Used to looking most men in the eye, she simply stared in surprise as a few last drops of water slid down his tanned skin. Some tangled in the sun-bleached hairs faintly visible along his breastbone, but others rolled across hard muscles toward the low-slung waistband of his jeans, and her gaze followed them of its own accord until sanity finally returned and she managed to glance away.

Snapping the knife shut and slipping it into the pocket of her corduroy jeans, she took a deep breath and tried to ignore the sudden heat in her cheeks. Ruefully, she recognized that now she was at a further disadvantage, thanks to that bare brown chest a few inches away. But who would have thought the sight of a masculine chest would have this much effect on her? Especially when it belonged to a perfect stranger who'd just found her trying to force her way into his home. All those years of courtroom experience at keeping up a calm front no matter what happened had better stand her in good stead now!

Tilting her head to make her line of sight safer, she looked above the white towel and found rumpled red-brown hair and a redder beard, both curly and damp. The heavy eyebrows were darker, though, and one of them cocked at a forbidding angle. It said all too clearly that he was still waiting for an answer to his angry question. Well, she'd always suspected that there were times when the best defense was no defense. . . .

"Trespassing," she replied matter-of-factly. "Also breaking and entering. At least, that's what I was trying to do."

Whether or not her theory held up right now, it was at

least an unexpected response, and that was generally an advantage. Verity added to the effect by looking up guilelessly. After all, an open face like hers was a valuable asset to a lawyer on shaky ground. Besides, it gave her a chance to finish surveying the tall man in front of her.

His was a closed face. Made up of clean hard planes, it could probably have been cast in bronze and been just as expressive; on a witness stand this man would give away absolutely nothing. His mouth was long and generous, finely cut but held taut and unyielding, with deep lines incised at the corners. Over high cheekbones, his narrowed eyes could be either blue or gray, but there was no doubt about the hawklike nose. Aquiline with a high bridge, it flared impatiently at the nostrils.

Everything else about his craggy face was as still as stone, but that one tiny gesture hinted at the possibility of tightly leashed emotion. Noticing it at last with interest, Verity decided that her original impression that he had no feelings whatsoever might be wrong after all—

"Why?"

Maybe not, though! Only a single syllable, it had the same whip-crack as his first question. Candor certainly hadn't gotten her off the hook yet.

"To take shelter. The rain's getting worse."

As if on cue, the light rain that had been pattering around her as they spoke accelerated, darkening the gray-painted steps where she stood. That didn't seem to impress the man in front of her, however.

"Absolutely not." His answer was flat, and he reinforced it immediately by moving to block the entire doorway. That brought his broad chest within inches of her nose again, but this time she hardly noticed. "Not here."

"Oh, for heaven's sake," she exclaimed, her original embarrassment starting to give way to exasperation. Did he think she was going to try shoving him aside and rushing past? Deciding in an emergency to pick the lock on a building she believed to be empty was one thing, but assaulting a giant like this was quite another. Even now she wasn't that desperate! Besides, it would be so much easier if he'd just let them take refuge for a little while until the rain slacked off.

Answering rudeness with rudeness probably wouldn't get her anywhere, though, so she stifled her annoyance. It wasn't for nothing she'd learned to cut off her own feelings. Making her tone sweetly reasonable, she tried again.

"I'm sorry to have disturbed you. I thought the keeper's cottage was empty or I would have knocked, of course. But couldn't you just—"

"No."

Embarrassment disappeared completely, along with sweet reason. "But it's—" she began indignantly, and he cut her off.

"Sorry."

Of course he was! She could tell from that impervious face just exactly how sorry he was. Her usual calm control deserting her, Verity cast the man a fuming look and opened her mouth to tell him just what sort of a cold, arrogant, callous—

"Mom! Pierre's getting really wet out here."

Toby's clear young voice calling from behind her caused Verity to spin around and cut off a hasty speech that might have tested precisely how unfeeling this man was. Out of her sight now, the tiniest spark lit his narrowed eyes, as if he knew just what her next words had started to be, whether or not he cared. But his gaze passed beyond her, toward the stand of trees her figure had blocked from view.

Some fifty feet from the lighthouse keeper's cottage, just where forest gave way to cleared land, a last cluster of birch and maples edged the trail. In high summer, they'd shade the path hospitably, part of a long dappled tunnel, but now their leaves were only beginning to unfurl, the delicate lace of a late northern spring. They were lovely, but hardly much use against the rain that was starting to fall in earnest on two people huddled together underneath.

An orange parka zipped to his ears and a battered baseball cap down over his eyes, Toby himself was reasonably well protected. With a speed that still surprised her, Verity's eyes flew to him first. But it was the larger shape, barely protected at all, that would have caught and held anyone's glance.

Wearing flamboyant rags in every color imaginable, his long white hair an aureole around his head, Pierre Dumont struggled to hold himself upright with one gnarled arm across Toby's narrow shoulders and the other extended to brace him against the thin trunk of the nearest tree. For a moment he looked like some grand prophet, ancient and venerable. Led by his young disciple, he had come as a seer—

But then the illusion faded. Verity saw his hand start to slip down the wet bark on one side, while Toby shifted worriedly on the other, wrapping his short arms around Pierre's gaudy bulk. A seven year-old couldn't support all of the old man's weight, though, and neither could Pierre himself any more. His knees buckled, and he sagged toward the ground.

"Mom!"

"Coming, Toby! Hang on—"

Leaping down the steps, Verity took no time to notice that at last a flicker of emotion had crossed the face of the man in the doorway behind her. But as she raced to the trees, she knew only that the old man couldn't be left lying in the wet dirt in his condition. Beyond that, she had no clear idea what to do with Pierre while that irritable misanthrope refused to let them take shelter in his cottage.

Another mile and a half down that narrow trail, her car was still too far away for a woman and boy to try carrying him to it. But she kept an emergency tarp in its trunk—

Maybe she could hike back for that herself after she rigged some kind of cover out of branches for Pierre and Toby in the meantime. Or maybe she'd just go break a window into one of the other buildings out here! Even an old storage shed or something would give them a little protection, and that inhuman hulk would just have to tolerate it.

As a lawyer, Verity didn't usually rate vandalism high on a list of her favorite activities, but when she reached Pierre's side it started to look like the only course of action, because he *had* to get to shelter. Shifting most of his weight from Toby into her own arms, she braced herself to keep the old man from slipping any further to the ground, but he seemed unaware of her presence. Under her fingers his tattered clothes were wet and clammy, and his hair was rapidly being plastered against his skull, clinging to his leathery face in damp strings. His eyes had closed in exhaustion, and his mouth was open, his breath whistling through his lips in shallow gasps. To her touch his skin was as hot as paper about to ignite, but shudders racked his body every few seconds. Ill as he had seemed when she and Toby first found him, Pierre was even worse now.

"Pierre—"

She spoke his name anxiously, but the sunken eyes didn't open and the pale lips were still. Glancing around at the dripping trees for inspiration, Verity bit her own lip, and Toby whispered, "What are we going to do, Mom?"

"I don't know just yet," she was admitting when another voice cut in from behind her.

"Let me take him."

Peering past Toby and Pierre, Verity gaped at the tall figure approaching on the other side. The towel was gone, and he'd pulled on a navy jersey that made his hair and beard flame redder than ever. But when he met her surprised stare, his expression was as unrevealing as before.

"What do you—" she started to ask, biting off the question in the face of his bland, empty look.

Meanwhile, responding automatically to that quiet command, Toby had stepped aside and Pierre left her hold as well. Suddenly released from the burden of his weight, Verity barely got her own balance back before the old man was lifted crosswise with apparent ease. Only the flaring nostrils and a slight tightening of that long mouth indicated that it cost the bearded giant any effort at all to carry a grown man.

While Verity maintained a wait-and-see attitude, her antagonist of a minute before strode back toward his cottage. Red brick with white trim, it gleamed through the heavy rain, looking even more inviting now than it had when she first caught sight of it looming out of the mist. Wetter and wetter, she found herself hurrying toward that solid bulk; whatever that man was up to now, she certainly wasn't going to stand out here in the rain if she didn't have to.

"What's up, Mom?"

Hopping along beside her, Toby looked up inquiringly, and she dropped a hand lightly on his shoulder. A smiling shake of the head told her son that she was puzzled too. Having flatly refused to give them shelter, what was this man doing now?

Contradicting himself, it seemed. Fleetingly, she decided that he might not be such an impossible witness to face after all. With Verity and Toby together in his wake, he elbowed open the door and carried Pierre in from the rain that was coming down now in torrents.

Inside, Toby gazed around him with delight, wide-eyed at getting inside a real lighthouse keeper's cottage. Verity was intrigued too, but this wasn't the moment to ask for a tour. Leaving Toby to crane his head in every direction, she followed the other two from the kitchen they'd first entered to a light, airy room beyond.

This was evidently the room the tall man had been using

for himself. It was furnished with an odd assortment of pieces, but hardwood floors and white oak woodwork gleamed softly, while pale plaster walls and a high ceiling made it spacious and somehow welcoming. Even for a rock-hard character like him, this would be a pleasant place to spend time. And evidently he had. Beyond an upright parlor woodstove, he'd pushed a heavy old dining room table and four spindle-back chairs up against the far wall and made space for a bed and chest of drawers. Now he crossed to lay Pierre on the narrow iron bed, where the old man stirred feebly at last, drawing in a deeper raspy breath.

"What do you think you're doing with me, young man?" he demanded weakly, trying to hitch himself up on the pillow. In spite of her concern, Verity noticed with the flicker of a smile that they all seemed to be asking that question in one form or another.

"Trying to take care of you, old man."

The answer was prompt, but it came in a tone so different from the one Verity had heard before that she glanced at the speaker in surprise. He didn't return her look, however, concentrating instead on easing Pierre out of his threadbare bottle green jacket.

"I can take care of myself," the old man insisted with tired autocracy.

"Yes," the younger man agreed equably, "and probably the rest of us as well, but just not right now."

The tone was gentle raillery, but Verity recognized that at the same time it left Pierre's pride intact. Snorting a weary confirmation, he let himself become passive again, leaning forward limply. His gallant red neckerchief removed, he raised his arms a little on request so that a torn yellow vest and ragged shirt could come off too, but otherwise he slumped back into the disturbing lethargy Verity had first found him in. She forced herself to stop worrying; this time, at least, she and Toby weren't the only people at hand.

"There's clean linen in the bottom drawer."

Drawing Pierre carefully to his feet and wrapping a thick towel around him, Redbeard supported the old man against his own body with one strong arm as he threw Verity a look across the nodding white head.

"While I get the rest of his clothes off, would you please strip the bed and get it made up fresh for him?"

The raillery was gone, and his voice was politely remote. As she gazed at the two men, though, their images were printed vividly in her memory. One face was carefully blank and the other emptied by exhaustion, but in their two bodies she saw weakness held up by strength and a need answered. Nodding silently, she bent to the bottom drawer.

In a few minutes Pierre, wearing an enormous pair of striped pajamas, lay in bed. Settling him under an old-fashioned quilt, the pajamas' owner murmured, "Sleep now, if you can."

Pierre's only response was a faint grunt, his eyes already closed again. But as she smoothed the quilt with light fingers Verity saw thankfully that his breath seemed to be expelled more easily and his skin had lost its bluish tinge.

Still gazing down at him, the tall man by her side asked in the same low voice, "Where did you find him?"

Verity answered quietly, "In a tumble-down shack about a quarter of a mile from here, alone and hungry and ill."

Ending her sentence, her voice started to rise indignantly. Although his head stayed bent, the man beside her made a slight gesture with one hand, and with an effort she went on more softly.

"We couldn't possibly leave him there like that, feverish and helpless, with the roof starting to leak. I wanted to take him back to the village with us, but we couldn't get him all the way out to my car. Then Toby thought of the lighthouse here, and we decided we could at least bring

Pierre this far for shelter, if we practically carried him between us.''

Pushing her hair back with her fingers, she added a little awkwardly, ''The map we'd been using while we looked for him showed the lighthouse, but said the Coast Guard hadn't manned it since the automatic light was installed. That was why—''

''Why you took up breaking and entering,'' he finished.

She stirred uncomfortably, but instead of dwelling on that he surprised her again by offering a brief explanation of his own presence.

''As a matter of fact,'' he conceded, looking past her to the doorway, ''the lighthouse *has* been empty for years, but the Park Service decided to open it as a Visitors' Center this season, after restoring it to its original nineteenth century condition.''

Glancing around the room, Verity realized that all the furnishings were antique. In fact, there wasn't a single modern thing in sight, from the faded oilcloth mat on the floor to the kerosene lamp on the table and the carved wooden chest of drawers. Even Pierre belonged to the old days. Only she and this man were out of place here.

But perhaps that was wrong too. She might be totally twentieth century herself, but he had an oddly timeless quality to him. Studying him unobtrusively, she saw that in spite of a very immediate sense of power and presence he looked at home among these old things. With that beard, he could almost be one of the original lighthouse keepers—or a French voyageur—or even a far earlier Viking, come by some miracle of navigation to this inland sea.

Caught up in fancy, as she rarely allowed herself to be, Verity hardly registered his next sentence.

''In return for putting on the final touches, they've let me live in it this past year while I finished writing a series of articles.''

With the last words, though, his impersonal tone

became even more aloof. He hadn't moved as he spoke, still standing guard over Pierre with his russet head lowered, but flaring nostrils betrayed the control on his face. Unexpectedly, she had the strangest urge to call him, just to bring him back from whatever far and lonely place he'd gone to. Her mouth opened—and then closed again. Call him what?

Before she could find any answer to that question, Toby interrupted.

"Mom!" He clattered happily into the room, then caught sight of Pierre's sleeping form. "Ooops—sorry."

In a hoarse stage whisper he rushed on. "Isn't it great?! There's another room off the kitchen, and you can look out the windows right into sand dunes that go down to the water! And there's a whole bunch of charts and maps and stuff, and one of those desks with the sliding door that comes down, and a big old woodstove—"

"And a noisy hooligan of mine," Verity cut in, smiling in spite of herself at the abrupt change of mood Toby brought. Drawing him to stand against her, she turned them both to face the tall man.

One hand smoothed back the thatch of straw-colored hair out of Toby's eyes while she explained, "I'm Verity Brandon, and this snoop is my son, Toby, who hopes you'll forgive him for going exploring."

Not one bit abashed, Toby chimed in, "Yes, please," and grinned engagingly at the man who towered so far above his own four foot stature.

From that immense height of his, he looked down at them both, the two faces tilted to him. The smaller one was topped with pale gold hair, and the larger with dark gold, but both had the same open warmth and vitality. Almost absently, he returned, "Of course," while his eyes moved from one countenance to the other.

As an afterthought, he added, "I'm Brock Randall, by the way."

For a moment after he spoke, his glance met Verity's

directly, and she felt a sudden tension, almost a challenge, if that made any sense. Far back in her mind, something began to stir at his name, but became flustered when his gaze connected deliberately with hers. Distracted, she forgot the fleeting impression that she'd heard his name before.

Fringed by thick dark lashes, his eyes were an unusual clear light gray, cool crystal irises around gleaming black pupils, and she stared deep into them. Oddly conscious of her breathing, she wondered vaguely why she seemed to read such reluctance in him. It was almost as if he didn't want to look at her but had to at first, and afterward couldn't stop himself. . . .

Then he did. Before she herself was aware of the curiosity dawning in her face again, he had seen it and reacted. Withdrawing his scrutiny from her with an almost tangible jolt, he shifted his eyes to Toby, so that his next remark was addressed to the boy.

"What brings you both here anyway?"

The question was abrupt and disconnected, but Toby heard only its content, not its quality.

"You mean, to your lighthouse or in the Upper Peninsula?" he asked with interest.

Brock Randall's glance flicked over Verity, and she rallied to meet it again. But this time his eyes didn't linger at all, and she was left to wonder at a renewed impression of coolness. Oh, lord, was he one of those people who disapproved of everyone from the rest of Michigan and claimed that this far peninsula should become the separate state of Superior?

"Both, I suppose."

"Mom's case. She had to find Pierre," Toby answered matter-of-factly.

Looking up past Verity's slight nod of agreement to find one of Brock's dark eyebrows raised, her son added helpfully, "Pierre's niece hired Mom back home in Ann

Arbor—that's where we've always lived, since Mom was in law school.''

It was the sketchiest of explanations, and Verity might have expanded it. After all, it was the reason they'd arrived on his doorstep. But if Brock Randall had looked disapproving when he heard that they lived in the very different world of the Lower Peninsula, it was nothing to the frost in his face now. Watching it, she had a quick impression that if she touched his skin, her fingers would freeze to that icy bronze.

"I see," he said distantly. "So you're here on business, then, Mrs. Brandon?"

"Yes," she agreed, giving up on further explanations for now at least. "But it's Ms. Brandon, please—in fact, I prefer to use Verity."

"So appropriate for a lawyer, of course," he observed without inflection. Although his rugged face was completely still again, his eyes glittered sardonically.

But before she could frame an answer that would be just as coolly cutting, he added punctiliously, "I have work to do out in the shed, so if you'll both excuse me now, I'll see to that."

With those words he left the room, walking away with a long stride that took him out of sight—and hearing— before she could say anything more than "But what about—"

The outer door closed, and there was no Brock Randall to answer.

Chapter Two

In no mood to hold still after Brock Randall disappeared, Verity prowled around the room, setting a chair straight and adjusting the wick of the kerosene lamp he'd lighted. It was already filling the quiet room with warm golden light, but somehow she failed to appreciate it. Instead, she prowled some more and then finally decided to make Pierre some supper.

Sunk in exhausted sleep right now, the old man lay motionless, but presumably he'd wake up needing something hot and hearty, and she resolved to see that he had it. After all, poor nutrition was obviously part of the reason she'd found him so ill. Besides, fixing him a meal would give her something to do.

"Toby?" she called softly. "How about we see what I can find for supper? Pierre ought to eat, and it wouldn't hurt you and me either—"

Walking quietly into the kitchen next door, Verity realized wryly that she was talking to herself and let the words trail off. The room was empty, and creaking boards overhead told her that Toby had wandered off before he could get drafted into any part of this project. He'd slipped away for some more exploring, and Verity was left with no company but her annoyance with Brock Randall. Fortunately, Pierre was sleeping so deeply that even the racket she made couldn't penetrate his slumber.

Equipped again as it must have been at the turn of the century, this was an interesting kitchen. Busy, however, with thoughts of its usual occupant, Verity barely noticed. Methodically, out of habit rather than intent, she investigated the iron and enamel coal stove left from another age and discovered that it had been recently lighted. A steady warmth already radiated from it, and the huge kettle on top was steaming gently; making a simple meal ought to be easy.

She would have asked that infuriating Brock Randall for permission, of course, but he'd disappeared without bothering to stay around long enough to give her a chance for good manners, any more than for trading insults. That being the case, she banged around investigating for herself. A wooden icebox yielded bread and eggs, as well as a couple of types of cheese, and she found a cast-iron frying pan in a cupboard near the stove. Hauling everything out with a good deal of clatter, she stacked it all onto the carved drainboard beside a small sink and pumped up water from the cistern to wash her hands.

Every move could have been made a hundred years ago by earlier inhabitants of this cottage, but Verity was so busy with uncharacteristic bad temper that she paid no attention to the sense of history that surrounded her. She also failed to wonder why she was reacting so strongly to a man she had never even laid eyes on only an hour ago. Instead, she just cracked eggs with such energy that the shells shattered completely and went on to shred cheese with equal vigor.

The omelets that resulted from all this were definitely not the lightest she'd ever made, but Verity refused to care. At least they smelled good.

"Toby—come and have some supper."

Now that the meal had been made without his assistance, Toby materialized quickly, sliding onto a wooden chair at the oilcloth covered table.

"I'm starved!" he announced.

"You always are."

Taking that as a compliment, he grinned, and an answering smile lightened Verity's mood. Dividing up both omelets, she split the first one between Toby's white ironware plate and her own; the second one she set on the back of the stove. She'd take half of it to Pierre in a minute, and as for the other—well, if Brock Randall wanted it, he could darn well come and get it for himself.

In fact, he did just that. Coming in while they were still eating, he hung a wet jacket by the door and strode across the kitchen, picking up a plate and fork and serving himself, all in a series of neat economical movements. He was sitting down beside Toby, folding his long body onto another of those plain wooden chairs, before Verity finished swallowing the bite she'd taken as he appeared.

"I didn't think to tell you to make yourself at home before I left," he said, "but I see you've done so anyway."

The words were unexceptionable. Anyone else could have said them, and Verity would have felt welcomed. With this man, though, she was acutely conscious that the first phrase could have more than one meaning. As usual, his face and voice gave nothing away, but somehow she knew for sure that he was as aware as she of how ambiguous his remark was. Meeting those cool crystal eyes, she felt her own temperature soar.

Hot color flooded her face, but it wasn't for nothing she'd learned years ago to keep a tight hold on her self-control in court. Disciplining her voice, she answered equably, "Yes, thanks. I was sure you wanted it that way."

As he registered the answering ambiguity, the hand lifting his fork paused for a second before it went smoothly on. So did she.

"But rather than disturbing your meal now, I'll go help Pierre with his. You'll excuse me, of course—"

And without waiting for the answer she'd made impossible, she rose and snatched up Pierre's plate, sweeping from the room. Toby, happily unconscious of the tension crackling across the table, gave her a quick smile, and went on eating. What Brock Randall did, however, she neither knew nor cared.

Verity drew a chair over to Pierre's bedside and settled by him. She spoke his name softly, and he opened bleary eyes.

"I've brought you some supper, Pierre. Would you try to eat a little, please?"

He gazed at her without comprehension, but Verity lifted a mouthful of omelet and the smell wafted to him invitingly. The old eyes stared at her, sharpening slowly, and he struggled to say something. His lips started to frame a syllable, but it seemed to be more effort than he could manage. Shifting his gaze to the plate she held, he opened his mouth.

Murmuring encouragement, Verity offered one bite after another, and laboriously Pierre kept eating. He closed his eyes wearily after almost every mouthful, but hunger was even stronger than exhaustion and slowly the omelet disappeared. It was a long process, though, and through almost all of it Verity could hear voices from the kitchen. In spite of her avowed lack of interest in Brock Randall, she couldn't help listening for the sound of his voice.

It was surprisingly pleasant. If it hadn't been for the way he spoke to Pierre, she wouldn't have guessed from her own exchanges with the man that he could sound so agreeable. After a short silence when she first left the room, Toby—apparently finished with his own supper— set about seeing to it that Brock wasn't left in peace to do the same. Instead, he had to face a barrage of eager questions.

"How old's this lighthouse?"

Toby's piping tones carried clearly, but the lower-voiced reply was less distinct.

"It was finished in 1874."

"How did somebody get to be a lighthouse keeper?"

"In the early days, most keepers started in the Navy and then joined the Lighthouse Service. After that, the Coast Guard took over."

"Were there some really good wrecks here?"

The small-boy relish in that one was clear, even though she had to strain to catch Brock's answers.

"This was a real graveyard coast, so there were quite a few, especially at the beginning. Not so many after the light went into operation."

"I bet a lot of people went down with their ships, huh?"

"As a matter of fact, just about everybody was saved."

"Oh."

Cheerfully ghoulish like most boys his age, Toby was disappointed. Tuned to every tone of his voice, Verity heard it in that one flat syllable and smiled ruefully to herself. The surprising thing, though, was that it almost seemed that Brock Randall must have heard it too, his answer was so perfect.

"No old bones for you to pick up along the shore," he commiserated. "But there are a few planks out in the water west of the point, and if you check, you can still find lumps of coal scattered in with the rocks, washed up from a steamer that went aground just about a hundred years ago."

"Gosh!" Toby breathed happily. "Really?"

Brock's responses had been getting longer and longer,

but now his first words were lost as a chair squeaked against the floor. He must be pushing himself back from the table and settling comfortably, Verity guessed. When he went on his voice had dropped even more, so that she could only follow the changing tones. But as if that were an instinctive response to Toby's enthusiasm, they took on the sing-song rhythm of storytelling. And this from the man who was taking such pains to keep her at a distance!

Ironically amused or not, Verity couldn't seem to make herself stop listening. All through Pierre's meal, the two voices in the other room rose and fell, blending the sounds of man and boy into an age-old harmony. Finally, though, she realized with a small start of surprise that the plate in her hands was empty. With a last glance of acknowledgment, Pierre turned his head, letting his eyelids drift down and stay that way. After settling the covers gently around his shoulders, Verity tiptoed away.

In the kitchen Toby was just firing off another question.

"How long have you been here?"

Entering the room, Verity tossed Brock Randall an inquiring look of her own as she went to set Pierre's dish on the drainboard. He seemed utterly at home in this lighthouse keeper's cottage, but how long could a man who radiated such power and ability stay in a secluded place like this?

"Almost a year."

The storyteller had vanished. This answer was terse, discouraging either of them from asking, "Why?"

Even Toby recognized a sudden change. While Verity put the plate down with a thump, her son stared at the angular face across the table, his own creasing. "Oh."

His source of information suddenly dried up, Toby looked at a loss. To erase that unhappy, bewildered look from his freckled face, Verity found herself rushing to ask a question of her own, anything to bring back the relaxed atmosphere that had disappeared so abruptly.

"About us—" she began.

"What?"

That didn't sound encouraging, but she went on determinedly. "Well, Pierre is settled next door, but where should we stay?"

As an attempt to get back on some kind of comfortable footing, her question didn't seem to be much of a success. Brock Randall hadn't moved a muscle in response, but he looked again just exactly the way he had when he first found her trying to pry open his door. The gray eyes were as cold as ice, and his face was utterly empty.

Her own lips set firmly, Verity met his stare. In spite of her intentions, she was obviously right back where she started. Having Brock sit there like the great stone face wasn't any solution to the problem. Stubbornly, she broke the silence.

"Well, we do need to sleep somewhere—"

That did it.

"How about the village?" Brock suggested arctically, about to stand up and put an end to the discussion.

"No, thank you."

With a speed that was the measure of her anger, Verity moved in front of him, so close he couldn't stand without bumping straight into her. Her tone was still rigidly controlled, though, and rage gave her an added fluency.

"Not only do I intend to stay with Pierre, who obviously can't be moved tonight, but also I intend for both my son and me to live to see daylight. Although it may have escaped your notice, it's gotten dark out, and the rain is worse than ever. Even for your convenience, I'm afraid I'm not going to leave here and hike a mile and a half back to the car, just to drive it into the lake by accident."

A silence so complete they could all hear the rain beating against the windows followed that tirade. Although this time she could look down at him for a change, Verity was so near Brock Randall that she could see fine white lines radiating through the gray of those disturbing irises. She could also see the way his reddish hair and beard caught fire in the lamplight—his high cheekbones shadowed the lean cheeks beneath them—his chiseled mouth went tight. Locking glares with him, golden brown fusing with crystal, she was still somehow aware of his long-fingered hands tensing on his knees and even of the pulse that beat at the open collar of his navy jersey. It was almost audible, in fact. Or was that her own heartbeat, that erratic thumping?

"Mom, I could help. I could watch really carefully and help you stay on the road."

From the far side of the table, Toby's voice ended the deadlock. All of his earlier eagerness was gone, though, and he spoke hesitantly. Verity's eyes flew to her son and found him crestfallen and worried.

One hand went quickly to his thin shoulder, but before she could find words to reassure him, Brock spoke instead. For the second time he must have seen and heard the same things she did, and to her amazement he spoke directly to Toby, his face unreadable but his voice again a storyteller's.

"Or you could stay here and sleep in the Lighthouse Inspector's own bedroom upstairs. What do you think?"

"Wow!" Toby answered eloquently, eyes alight again. "Could I really? The Inspector's room?"

"Why don't you come up and have a look?"

This time when Brock moved to stand up, Verity stepped bemusedly out of his way. Toby jumped to his feet as well, to follow Brock out of the room, and as they left the kitchen he slipped one small hand confidingly into Brock's large one. Then they vanished from Verity's sight.

Sinking absently into Toby's chair, she heard their feet cross the hall and climb to the second story. Meanwhile their voices sounded again, the child's tones high and clear, the man's slower and deeper. But it was a genuine counterpoint, with both voices carrying their parts; Toby was clearly getting answers to a whole new bunch of questions. If she had asked any, though, stony silence would probably have been Brock Randall's only response. Why on earth was it that her son could apparently pass this man's defenses while they stayed so high against Verity herself?

Feeling oddly deflated, she sat where she was, with no company but her thoughts. And with Brock Randall's obvious distaste for her presence so fresh in her mind, her thoughts turned to David Brandon.

She seldom let herself think about her husband; in fact, he hadn't crossed her mind in months. But now—as vividly as if she'd last seen him yesterday, rather than eight years ago—he stood before her, just as he'd looked when she first met him.

He had materialized in front of her at one of the company's holiday parties, holding two glasses of champagne, and presented one to her with a flourish.

"Do let me give you something so you can join me in a toast to the most beautiful woman in the room," he suggested, standing so close to her that he could speak in an intimate undertone and still be heard over the babble of other voices around them.

The warm stare that played over her low-cut emerald dress made it perfectly clear what he meant, and Verity found herself reaching for the glass he proffered. On vacation in her last year of college, she had just stopped seeing the man she'd briefly considered marrying because everyone else seemed to be planning weddings. Now, on her own again and more than a little reckless, she joined in David Brandon's toast, laughing with him over the rim of her glass as she returned his assessing stare.

Tall and narrow-shouldered, with a perfect profile and straight platinum hair that fell across his forehead, he had classic good looks. If his lips were a bit thin and his eyes a shade close together, those were only the slight imperfections that kept him from being too pretty. Otherwise, he was outrageous and attentive and clever, staying beside her the rest of the evening and amusing her with wicked anecdotes about the other members of the family firm who had gathered for this traditional party. Entertained as well as shocked, she laughed almost continuously and refused to notice when her father's eyes rested on her with concern and on David with something more complicated.

At any rate, David took her home too, saying a protracted farewell at the door, and that was only the first of many evenings they spent together. Verity let him monopolize her time, airily ignoring all the other men who called. She ignored her father, too, when he tried to make her hold still long enough for him to suggest that he thought David might be trying to use the boss's daughter for protection from an upcoming round of cuts among the junior executives. No one could use his charm with such calculation, so she blew her father a kiss and hurried off to meet David at the races. And when he proposed six weeks later, she accepted immediately.

Chin on one palm, Verity was reliving it all when an unfamiliar noise cut through her memories, driving them away. Dropping her hand, she listened in confusion before she realized that the sounds were coming from Pierre's room and leaped to her feet.

Next door she found the old man thrashing in bed and trying with sudden energy to throw off the covers. Hurrying to his side, she caught his gnarled hands in hers to stop their restless flailings.

"Pierre, stop! Please don't—you need the warmth."

"Got to. Have to—"

His voice was hoarse and breathless; he panted while he struggled to free himself.

"Why? What is it?" She tried to make him explain, to

soothe him before he exhausted himself again and Brock heard the commotion from upstairs. "Pierre, what's wrong?"

The answer was indistinct, only a few muttered syllables that caused a racking cough. When the spasm had passed, he mumbled once more, but now the words were even fainter. Enervated, he sagged against the pillows and drifted back to sleep. His breathing steadied, and in Verity's hands, he slowly relaxed.

"Pierre?" She murmured his name very softly, but he didn't react at all.

Carefully, she eased onto the chair beside his bed. She kept the contact between them for a long time, however, loosely clasping his hot sinewy hands in her own soft cool ones, as if she could infuse her strength into him. He lay quietly now, and in the stillness she strained unthinkingly to hear any noise from upstairs.

The floorboards overhead squeaked now and again, but otherwise all she could catch were a few muffled thumps and laughs. Most of those were Toby's high-pitched infectious giggles, but some of them seemed too deep for him. Without noticing that she was holding her breath to hear, Verity listened intently, sorting out Toby's laughter from another attractive sound—not the dour Brock Randall chuckling?

Her own lips curved in disbelief at the thought. Anyone as prickly as that man had probably forgotten long ago how to laugh! If he ever knew, that was. Still, her smile widened of its own accord as bursts of contagious laughter kept drifting down.

For a while Verity thought about going upstairs to investigate for herself. Pierre seemed to have fallen into a deep natural sleep, and it was probably silly to feel as though he needed her to watch over him every moment. But his hands in hers were thin and papery, and his face against the pillows was drawn and pale— Settling deeper into her chair, Verity decided to sit by him for the time being anyway. She could stay long enough to be certain he really was asleep for the night and then say her own good-nights to Toby when Brock had gone about whatever it was he did around here.

What happened instead was that she dozed off herself, right where she was. Half an hour later Brock, walking softly into the room, found her bent forward, fast asleep on the edge of the bed. Her hands were still linked with Pierre's, but she had slumped over them. Now, face turned to the side, she slept with her cheek pillowed on his brown palm while a lock of her hair flowed between his knotted fingers.

For a long time Brock was motionless, looking at them. His leonine white mane dry again and spread around his face, the old man had a kind of grandeur, worn but indomitable. But Brock's glance passed quickly to the young woman who lay so near at hand. With her eyes closed, he could study the delicate structure of a broad forehead, short straight nose, and round determined chin. Surrounded by a halo of curling amber hair, her creamy skin showed delicate color on her high cheekbones, and her lips were still curved in a forgotten smile.

His gray gaze clung to that smile. Finally, with a shake of his head, Brock touched Verity's shoulder briefly. It was a fleeting contact, though, and she didn't react. He tried again, jogging her arm and immediately removing his fingers.

"Verity—wake up," he said briskly.

This time Verity responded. Exhausted by all the uproar of the day, she kept her eyes shut but mumbled protestingly, turning her face away from the light and into the clasped hands it rested on. Then she was quiet again, sleepily determined not to wake up.

Another pause, and Brock Randall bent down to scoop her from her chair and lift her crosswise into his arms. As her hair brushed across his hand and her fingers slipped from his, Pierre opened his eyes and looked up at Brock.

It was a completely rational gaze, meeting the younger man's directly and with full comprehension. Then, with a tiny nod, Pierre closed his eyes again, and Brock strode from the room.

As he carried her up the stairs, Verity finally stirred in his hold and recognized dimly that something had changed. Under her cheek now was fine soft wool, and beneath that in turn was solid warmth that encircled her. The welcoming heat seeped up to her skin, and she burrowed into it, drawing in a scent that seemed blended from soap and sun-warmed grass. Faint but evocative, it attracted her, and she sniffed it with a murmur of pleasure. At the sound, a slight tremor shook the arms around her as Brock reached the top of the steps.

Verity didn't really wake up, however, until she had to. Dropped abruptly onto a bed, she opened her eyes in sleepy confusion. Suddenly the warm strength and the scented wool were both gone. But Brock stood at the foot of the bed where she lay, pulling off her shoes, and she blinked at him owlishly. Before her eyes could focus properly, though, the strangely haunted look on his face had vanished, leaving it harder and more unrevealing than ever.

"This is the room next to Toby's," he announced. "He's sound asleep, and you might as well follow his example here instead of being such an idiot as to try spending the whole night huddled in that chair downstairs."

"But Pierre—" she began muzzily, propping herself up on her elbows.

"—is sleeping comfortably and will be just fine without you."

The interruption was flat and uncompromising, although he was probably right. Still, she stared at him in mild indignation until a yawn squeezed her eyes tightly shut. She stretched like a cat, and when she had recovered, Brock Randall was gone. His steps receded down the stairs; then she heard the outer door of the lighthouse close. No sound at all rose from Pierre's room, and Verity's eyelids started to droop. Groping, she dragged a fold of the quilt over her and curled up, asleep before she even had time to consider taking off her clothes.

Chapter Three

All too early the next morning sunlight filtered through the simple muslin curtains at Verity's east window and found her eyelids. For a while she escaped its inquisitive touch, as well as the muted voices and occasional clatter from downstairs, by burying her head under the pillow to shut out both light and sound. Finally, however, she mumbled to herself in defeat and pushed the pillow aside. Triumphant sunshine poured across her face in a wave of liquid gold, while the racket of feet bouncing up the stairs battered her ears.

But at least all this morning cheeriness brought with it the smell of coffee—hot and vital. Verity's nose twitched appreciatively. An instant later Toby bounded into her room, arriving beside her bed at the same time as the sound of his knock.

"Morning, Mom!" He bent to give her a hasty peck that landed somewhere south of her right eye. "I brought you some coffee."

He certainly had. Half of it sloshed around the saucer, courtesy of Toby's exuberant trip up the steps, but Verity didn't care. Thanking heaven for a child whose priorities were right, she fumbled in his direction until Toby put the cup and saucer firmly in her hands. A life-giving swallow or two, and her eyes focused well enough for her to pour the saucer's share back into the cup, nicely cooled for drinking.

Meanwhile, Toby had charged across the room to peer out first one and then the other of her windows. Spinning around again, he chortled, "Isn't it great? We spent the night at a real lighthouse, with Lake Superior right outside our windows and everything! This's got to be the best adventure anyone *ever* had!"

"Mmmmm-hmmmm."

Verity's enthusiasm was a good deal more moderate, but in the face of her son's beaming delight she had to nod in agreement. Toby barely waited long enough to see that, though.

"Guess what? Over breakfast Brock said he'd show me around the whole place so I could see the foghorn and the boatshed and even the light itself! Can I go?"

"Yes, of course," Verity nodded. "Have fun, and be sure to thank him."

"Okay! See you later, Mom!"

His voice floated back to her from the stairs, accompanied by the thud of sneakers hitting every other step. The back door banged, and silence fell again.

Left alone, Verity returned to her cup of coffee, sipping it slowly in the sudden quiet. Besides the usual early morning doldrums, she felt a bit abandoned but decided that was probably a side effect of sleeping fully dressed. Spending the night in this bed was undoubtedly a better idea than making do with the chair at Pierre's side, but she still needed a complete refurbishing today. Rumpled and fuzzy, hair on end and clothes a ruin, no one would be at her most cheerful.

A nasty possibility occurred to her. This morning's blues couldn't be a touch of simple jealousy, could they, just because Toby had taken such a liking for that irascible Brock Randall with his lighthouse and beard, his shuttered face and smoky crystal eyes—

"Oh, no!" Verity murmured out loud at the disquieting thought. She set down her empty cup and rolled onto her side, propping her head on her left hand. No, that she wouldn't allow herself. The morning grumps were one thing, but a reaction like that was quite another. When she was lucky to have Toby at all, she certainly wasn't going to let herself indulge in any such selfishness.

It was only two months ago that she'd nearly lost him, and the memory washed over her as if it had been yesterday. Around her the sunlit morning dissolved, and Verity was again at the hospital. Summoned out of court by the housekeeper's frantic call with news that Toby had been knocked off his bicycle, she had rushed to Emergency to find him.

"My son—they told me he was here. . . ."

Fifteen minutes before, her voice had been so calm in front of the jury, but now it shook with fear and breathless haste. Fighting to steady it so she could make herself understood, she locked her hands on the chest-high counter and spoke over them to a nurse who looked at her with professional sympathy.

"Toby Brandon. He was hit by a car—"

The nurse glanced down, then looked up in confirmation. "Yes, the little boy in Room 2. Let me get Dr. Hakim out here to talk to you."

With a faint rustle she vanished around a partition in back of the counter, and a few eons later Verity heard firm rubber-soled steps approaching from behind her. Whirling, she confronted Toby's doctor.

"I'm Verity Brandon, Dr. Hakim. May I see my son?"

Above a white jacket that made his dark skin darker,

intense eyes assessed her. They read her pale face and the hands clenched at her sides, but they also read her straight shoulders and the soft lips that compressed after her last word.

"Not right now, Mrs. Brandon, but do not be too much alarmed." Slightly accented, his voice was kindly as he told her the truth. "He's reasonably comfortable, but we have him sedated and he would not know you were there."

Turning, he began to pace slowly down the corridor so that she would follow automatically.

"He has no broken bones, and only a slight concussion. In that he is very lucky."

He glanced at her walking beside him and Verity nodded, relief beginning to well up in her until Dr. Hakim went on speaking in the same mild tone.

"But his spleen has been ruptured, and that must be removed. We need your permission, please, to operate."

Stopping sharply in the middle of the corridor, Verity stared at him in renewed shock.

"There are many people who have no spleens," he observed. "It is a fairly common operation, and your son will live a perfectly normal life afterward."

"And if you don't operate?" she asked stiffly.

"Then he will bleed to death."

He answered very quietly, and her face went even whiter. Searching the black eyes on a level with her own, she found both expertise and understanding. Clinging to them, she spoke again at last.

"You have my permission."

The words were hard to say, her mouth was so dry with fear, and Dr. Hakim touched her arm for a moment in reassurance.

"Good," he murmured, smiling before he turned away. "I shall send someone with the papers for you to sign, and your son will be all right."

But that was still hard to believe as she spent some of

the worst hours of her life waiting for the operation to be finished. When it was done, she was no better, either, even though Toby had been wheeled into a small ward where he was the only patient and she was allowed to stay with him all night. Standing or sitting by his bed, where he lay looking so small and bruised, so quiet and unfamiliar, she had been awake the entire time.

Dim light crept in from the hallway, while faint but pervasive smells of disinfectant and floor wax permeated the still air. Occasionally a distant siren raced nearer and nearer, ending somewhere below her with a last banshee wail that dissolved reason and filled her with lonely terror until her knuckles were white and her eyes ached. The only other sound in the room was the whisper of Toby's breathing, so soft and slow that she imagined a thousand fearful instants that it had stopped.

Each time the acrid gall of grief began to rise up in her throat, choking her with its bitterness. Then the tiny sound would come again. Limp with relief, she listened to it eagerly—and waited in dread for the next time it seemed to come too slowly. So the endless seconds limped on, and at some point in the long hours she faced the fact that her son was practically a stranger to her.

She had enrolled in law school within weeks of his birth, almost as soon as she found a housekeeper to tend both Toby and their cramped little bungalow. Then she set herself a ferocious schedule of studying during the academic year and working as a law clerk every summer, so that she was rarely in the house at all and Mrs. Parker was probably more of a mother to her son than Verity.

Graduation hadn't changed things much, either. Near the top of her class, Verity had a number of job offers. But instead of taking a glamorous corporate position she chose to spend the next two years as a public defender because that seemed important, providing the best defense she could offer to those unable to hire a lawyer of their own. It had been grueling work, though, with some of the grimmest and most tragic cases, and it kept her away from home for more long hours.

Her schedule had finally improved when she and Mark Patterson decided to set up a practice together as partners; at last she could arrange something more like normal working hours for herself. But by then Toby was in school most of each day, so Verity went on living for, and at, her job. She threw herself heart and soul into her cases—and only into them.

"You're keeping your heart in the deep freeze, Counselor Brandon."

How many times had Mark said that, laughingly at first and then seriously? His idea, of course, was that she should let him see to the thawing and change Brandon and Patterson, Attorneys at Law, to Patterson and Patterson. . . . But flippantly, Verity always held him off. The new name sounded like a tongue-twister; it would take longer to write; people would assume that they were father and son. They were silly objections, but the truth was that he was right about her heart and she intended to keep it that way.

Until that night in the hospital, when she realized that in keeping Mark at a distance, she'd kept Toby there too. In order to protect her own heart, she'd ignored his. She had already missed most of her son's short life, and that could have been all there was.

When he finally woke up, he peered at her from puffed and blackened eyes. "Mom?" he asked in faint surprise, his voice a thread of sound.

"Yes?" It was all she could manage.

"I didn't know you were here."

"All along."

"I'm glad."

"So am I."

His eyes had drooped shut, but with her words they

opened again, and he gave her a tiny battered grin. Then he fell asleep, before he could witness Verity finish making up for eight years of unshed tears.

The hospital room disappeared, and she lay blinking in Brock Randall's cottage, reminding herself of how lucky she was to have a second chance. Her case load cut back with Mark's help, she and Toby had probably spent more time together in these last two months than in all of his life before the accident. His slight shyness with her had long since relaxed, and Verity had learned what a good companion her son could be. He was sunny and outgoing —and if he wanted to take some inexplicable liking to the annoying Mr. Randall, then she should just be grateful for Toby's happy disposition.

Completely awake now, thanks to coffee and a stern lecture to herself, Verity finally threw back the quilt she'd been sleeping under and swung her long legs to the floor. It *was* a glorious morning outside, and surely today she'd be able to move Pierre into town for some proper care. Taking a quick inventory in the meantime, she found herself only a little stiff from helping him as far as the lighthouse yesterday. That was the good news. The bad news, on the other hand, was that a mirror tilting over the pine dresser showed her to be a woman who looked exactly like what she was: someone who had slept fully dressed.

Groaning softly at her reflection, Verity saw only the wrinkled tawny slacks and pullover, the tangled amber curls. But at least a flowered china pitcher on an old washstand really did hold water. Pouring some into the matching bowl, she splashed her face eagerly, scrubbed her cheeks rosy, and combed her wet hands through her hair, winding the curls around a fingertip.

All of that finished, she glanced at her image again. Oh, well—it would have to do. She shrugged. After all, Brock

Randall hadn't exactly welcomed her last night when she looked civilized, so looking rumpled today probably wasn't going to lower his opinion of her any. Contrarily, the thought entertained her. Tossing the mirror a gamine grin, she left, unaware of the classic features and fresh skin that glowed even under these conditions.

Downstairs, she peeked into Pierre's room and found him just beginning to stir. His eyes were still closed, but as she watched he moved restlessly. Slipping away, Verity decided that no matter what she looked like this morning, she could at least start by making Pierre something to eat now that he was apparently waking.

To her surprise, she found the kitchen not only empty but also immaculate. At the back of the stove the big kettle puffed softly, but nothing else indicated that anyone had even entered this room today. Toby had said he ate breakfast with Brock, but not a trace remained. The supper dishes she'd meant to get back to last night had vanished, too.

Gazing around the sunny room, Verity had to admit that Brock Randall evidently knew how to take care of himself. Strange as it was that he should have taken up residence at this long-deserted lighthouse, he was obviously just as self-sufficient as the early lighthouse keepers. Like him, they'd lived alone for months on end, often joined by their wives and children only during the summers when travel to this remote place was easy. Otherwise, they had fended for themselves, too.

Pierre certainly wasn't ready for anything of the kind, though. The mysterious Brock banished from her thoughts, Verity concentrated on fixing the old man's breakfast, and her own as well. Hunting up a box of oatmeal and several types of dried fruit, she took time this morning to notice that she was cooking in a perfectly re-created turn-of-the-century kitchen. The coal stove and kerosene lamp, the hand pump raising water from a cistern, and the icebox cooled by a slab of last winter's frozen lake were all details from a way of life her grandparents would have recognized.

Producing two meals here would have to be enough, though, she decided. She'd be returning to the eighties as soon as Pierre could be moved—and Brock Randall had certainly made it clear last night that they couldn't leave soon enough for him! But just at the moment it seemed right somehow that her efforts in an antique kitchen should be going to feed a man who probably remembered all of this first hand.

He still wasn't well enough to volunteer any information along those lines, of course. But last night's struggles seemed to be over. When Verity walked quietly back into his room, bearing a steaming bowl, Pierre hauled himself upward on his pillows so he wouldn't have to greet her flat on his back.

"Good morning," she said, seeing him for the first time without the effects of rain or fever. "I've brought you some breakfast."

"I thank you."

His voice was hoarse but the tone courtly, and she realized now that under bushy white eyebrows his eyes were edged with laugh lines. More laughter had carved lines at the corners of his mouth, too, beneath a flowing white mustache. If it was true that over the years each man earned the face he deserved, then in old age Pierre Dumont was obviously a man of warmth and kindliness, as well as stubborn independence.

But since that independence had brought him to the brink of starvation, he had to be hungry again too. The bowl in her hand redolent of hearty cereal studded with fruit, Verity slid onto the chair by his bed, thinking fast. Then, indicating the potholder she was using, she suggested, "Since this is way too hot to manage with your bare hands, maybe the easiest thing would be for me to hold it for you—"

She didn't really get away with it. A quiver of his mustache indicated that he was perfectly aware of the tact behind her suggestion, but he just inclined his head gravely, and she began to spoon up the cereal for him.

He ate nearly all of it too, while Verity talked idly about the weather, the lake, the lighthouse. As soon as he'd finished, she decided, she'd remind him about the case and make sure he remembered what she had told him yesterday. But he suddenly stopped eating when she happened to mention leaving.

"No."

"But you should see a doctor—"

"No."

The refusal was absolute, and he sagged back against the pillows, away from her. His eyes closed, shutting her out, and she realized again how true her words were. This morning's apparent recovery had faded. He lay looking ill and unutterably old, and renewed worry jolted her. Had she found him at last, and taken over caring for him, only to lose him after all?

Setting the bowl aside, she tried to insist gently. "Pierre, you're still sick, and we're so far away from help out here. There'd at least be a doctor available, if we went into the village—"

"I won't go."

His voice had risen, and Verity thought she understood the reason for his stubbornness. Trying to blend both reassurance and honesty, she offered, "But I don't think you'd have to go to a hospital. We could probably find a comfortable room in Grand Marais, and by the time you were feeling really well again, maybe the case would be settled—"

"No! I won't go stay in town. I can't go that far away—not now. I've got to wait—"

His voice rose still further, the words continuing to tumble out incoherently. Worse, Verity realized with a pang that although his eyes were open again, he didn't see her. His gaze darting around the room as if he were trying to find someone, his eyes were blank and unfocused, and he was beginning to turn and twist in bed.

"Pierre, please just—"

"Let me alone! I can't miss her!"

With a burst of energy, he went to throw off the covers and stand up, while Verity, leaping to her feet, caught at his arms. Holding on, she tried to soothe him.

"All right, Pierre—never mind. It's all right."

"I can't leave!"

"Yes, I know—"

Abruptly, he reached the end of his strength and stopped struggling, so that she was able to ease him back into bed.

"It's all right," she repeated breathlessly.

It wasn't, however. Even though he didn't try to get up again right away, he lay plucking restlessly at the bedclothes with shaking fingers, his breath coming in shallow rasps. Her hand on a bony shoulder, Verity could feel the feverish heat of his skin; fear welled up in her. She knew so little about nursing herself that she *had* to get Pierre to someplace where she could find experienced care for him. But with the car a mile and a half away, how on earth was she going to manage? She had a strong suspicion that enlisting Brock Randall in anything would be difficult, but she and Toby could never carry Pierre that far by themselves, and the old man was certainly too ill to walk that distance on his own. Even if he'd agree to go, that was!

Wrapped in her worries, she didn't even hear Brock and Toby coming back into the cottage or Toby galloping off up the stairs. When a deep voice spoke behind her, she jumped, then spun around.

"How is he?"

Brock stood in the doorway, hands in his pockets and crystal eyes fixed on Pierre. Across those wide shoulders the old black sweatshirt he wore was stretched tight; he radiated power.

"Awful."

Her voice came out on a squeak, and she threw him an annoyed look as she cleared her throat. Just what she needed when she was so concerned with Pierre was to have Brock materialize and startle her like that! He didn't look precisely apologetic about it either, surveying her from the door jamb now with a coolly inquiring stare while she tried to make her heart stop pounding.

She wasn't very successful. Instead of lasting a few seconds, like the usual burst of adrenaline, this one seemed to go on and on. But rather than let him know that her pulse was still hammering, she concentrated on Pierre.

"I don't know what to do," she admitted. "It looks to me as though he really does need a doctor, but getting him to one is the problem. My car's out at the end of the road, and that's way too far for Toby and me to try taking him. That was why we came here yesterday in the first place."

Something flickered at the back of his eyes. Then he looked at Pierre again, and she hurried on.

"But I can't think of any other way to get him out there, unless he can walk for himself. And of course, if he could, then I wouldn't be so worried about him. As sick as he is, though, I don't see how he could possibly do it—and anyway, when I mentioned leaving a few minutes ago, he flatly refused and seemed terribly upset."

Now he lay passive again, a waxen image of Old Age. Running out of ideas and momentum, Verity turned to smooth the covers over him, gazing anxiously into his haggard face. Her own overreaction to Brock's entrance genuinely forgotten, she was immersed in concern for Pierre and unaware that Brock's eyes had shifted back to her from the old man.

Almost as if he couldn't stop himself, he was studying her face, noting her eyes dark with concern, a slight frown of concentration, and teeth worrying the edge of her lower lip. When she looked up, however, his own face went blank again in an instant.

"Could you—" she began tentatively, but he interrupted before she'd even finished the question.

"No."

"You don't even know what I was going to ask!"

"If I'd move Pierre out to your car, presumably."

"Well, yes," she conceded reluctantly, "but—"

"But no."

In court that kind of brick wall was a challenge. She enjoyed hammering away at it until she finally heard some real testimony. But this wasn't a courtroom. This was the middle of nowhere, in an isolated lighthouse keeper's cottage whose inhabitant gazed at her with eyes as revealing as mirrors, and her usual imperturbability was fraying fast.

"For heaven's sake, why not?" she demanded. "You're so darn eager to get rid of us, why won't you help us go?"

"I'll help you and Toby. Not Pierre."

"*Why?*"

Blinking in a shaft of sunlight that fell across the floor, she stood directly in front of him now. Her head tilted to him, she was so close that he could see the way the sunshine caught the tips of her lashes and smell the faint daffodil scent of her hair. For a second or two he didn't respond, almost as if he'd lost the thread of what they were saying. Then he answered with sudden impatience.

"For one thing, because the only way to get him to your car in his condition would be to carry him a mile and a half, and I can't do it."

Somehow it hadn't occurred to her that even his strength must have its limits. She opened her mouth to apologize, but he swept right on, while she was stifled by fresh indignation.

"But even if I could, I wouldn't. Putting that old man

in a hospital or nursing home somewhere would kill him every bit as surely as exposure would have out in that shack where you found him. Whether or not you recognize it, the one is just as dangerous as the other. You and Toby go where you like, and do as you like, but leave Pierre out of your travel plans. He'll be all right here with me.''

That Verity certainly doubted. On his last words, Brock turned away and strode out of the room, leaving her seething at his implication that she was too insensitive to understand Pierre's needs as well as he did. Of course she wasn't planning to lock the old man up some place where everything free and vibrant in him would shrivel and die! She could see as well as Brock Randall that independence was Pierre's lifeblood.

But that blood was feverish right now, and at his age Pierre couldn't afford to ignore a serious illness like this on the assumption that it would eventually go away of its own accord. Just look at where that sort of thing had already gotten him! At the very least, he needed a great deal more rest and care—and she certainly couldn't see Brock dropping everything to sign up as a full-time nurse.

Last night, of course, Brock had gotten Pierre to bed with gentle strength, but Verity ignored that memory. With little of her usual objectivity, she forgot his tactful handling of the old man and remembered only his determination to get Toby and her out of here. The more he insisted, the less inclined she felt to go. But apparently he was so desperate to be rid of them that he'd even volunteer to take on nursing duties!—that was, if he really meant to do them.

Well, he wouldn't have to. If that's what it took, then she'd stay here and care for Pierre herself rather than leaving him to Brock. She might not know very much about illness, but at least *she* was willing. When an old man's very life might be at stake, she certainly wasn't going to abandon him, and Brock Randall would just have to make the best of it.

After a last quick check on Pierre, who seemed to have sunk into heavy sleep again, she found Brock in the living room. Seated at his desk, with the chair tipped back on two legs while he read through a handful of papers, he looked up at the sound of her hasty steps, but she spoke before he could.

"If Pierre can't leave here, then Toby and I can't either," she told him, the words tumbling out. "I was hired to look after his interests, and I'm the one who found him out here in the woods. I have a responsibility to him, and I can't possibly meet it while he's here and I'm somewhere else. Unless he changes his mind about letting me find him a place to board in the village for a while, then I'm afraid you're stuck with all of us until he's well enough again to go back to living on his own."

Out of habit, she'd begun to pace around the room as she spoke, as if he were the judge and jury she addressed and she only had to appeal to their reason. Halfway through the last sentence, though, she spread her hands in an unconscious gesture of appeal, coming to a halt near Brock's chair as she looked at him.

He met that look for only a second, too short a time for her to search his face for any expression. Then he broke the contact by dropping the chair down on all four legs with a dull thud.

"That's impossible. You can't stay here."

"Why not? I can look after Pierre, and there's plenty of room—"

"That isn't it."

"Then what is?"

Still without meeting her eyes, he hesitated—something she knew by instinct that he rarely did.

"It certainly can't be a problem with what people will say!" She laughed, trying to keep a conversation between them light for once. "After all, even if there were anyone near enough to know, we've got two chaperones."

She'd meant it to be a bit of nonsense, but he didn't react that way. His long-fingered hands lay along the edge of the desk, and in the peculiar silence before he answered she watched his knuckles whiten.

"I assure you, they won't be needed in that capacity," he said steadily, staring straight ahead. His voice grated like rocks grinding together.

Suddenly, irrationally, she was angry. "No, of course they won't," she agreed tightly, "—not for people who have absolutely no use for each other. We'd have to be here for a lifetime before that was a problem, and it's hardly likely!"

On her words, his hands loosened, inexplicably, but she was too wound up to notice. Stepping around the desk, until she was back in his line of vision, she stormed on.

"Believe me, we wouldn't be here at all if it wasn't genuinely necessary to interrupt your precious privacy— although I don't see why living at the lighthouse while you restore it should require you to act like a hermit in the meantime! But no matter how important being alone is to you, it can't be half as important as Pierre. For the sake of an old man's health, how can it hurt you to have to put up with a little company for a few days?"

Through her whole angry monologue Brock sat like a bronze statue, his face taut but empty and his eyes fixed on her without expression. At her last furious question, however, he came to life. His gaze shifted suddenly away from hers, but not before she glimpsed a pain so fierce that it pinched his lips and darkened his eyes. Watching him, Verity felt as if a fist had grabbed her own heart and squeezed it; involuntarily, she caught her breath and leaned toward him.

To distract her, though, his hands swept up the sheaf of papers in front of him and jammed them into a drawer, slamming it shut while his legs drove the chair back so hard that it squealed across the wooden floor. Then he towered above her, his face blank and hard again. The human sympathy that had drawn her to him vanished, and she stepped back involuntarily.

It seemed that he meant to answer her in angry detail. But as she retreated, he registered the motion with a sardonic lift of one eyebrow and shut his mouth without a word. Shrugging coldly, he turned and left her.

Without understanding why, she followed him for a few steps, as if he were a magnet and she a bit of metal. But when he slammed out the back door, she halted in the kitchen, watching through the window as he strode away into a small white outbuilding and shut the door behind him. Then she dropped into a chair, suddenly limp.

Absently drawing designs on the tabletop with a fingertip, she tried to figure out what had happened. She had told Brock that they would have to stay, and somehow that had been like unleashing a tidal wave. She still felt breathless. But why had he reacted so strongly? And then masked the reaction, as if a display of emotion couldn't be allowed? Or borne?

Remembering the pain in his face for that one brief second, her hand stopped its doodling, fingers tense as she felt a pang of dismay and regret for whatever it was she triggered in Brock Randall. Glancing out the window, she wondered if the hammering sounds from that shed were his way of dealing with the unbearable. Hard work had always been the best thing for her too—

She dismissed that train of thought, one hand wiping away her designs on the table. There was no similarity between her and him. They had nothing whatsoever in common.

He clearly wasn't coming back here any time in the near future, either; that racket showed no signs of diminishing. But at least he hadn't ordered them out again. It looked as if he meant to go about his business and simply ignore their presence. So be it.

Standing, she shook her head slightly, trying to shake

off the memories of a few minutes before. Then she walked to the foot of the stairs.

"Toby—"

"Yup?" Feet crossed the upstairs hall, and he peered down through the balusters.

"Come on down. We're off to the village—"

"Aw, Mom!" His face fell. "You mean we've got to go? What about Pierre?"

"Relax, Chicken Little, we aren't going for good yet."

At the delight in the small face bent to hers, Verity couldn't help smiling. Toby's reaction certainly was a far cry from Brock's!

"We have to tell them we've finally found him, as well as pick up our things and check out of the motel. But we'll be back in a few hours."

While he pounded down the stairs, Verity checked on Pierre. Still sleeping deeply, he probably wouldn't even know they were gone. Just in case, though, from the doorstep she shouted downwind toward the shed.

"Brock?—"

There was no answer, but at least there wasn't any hammering either.

"Toby and I are going to Grand Marais for our things. Pierre's asleep, but you ought to be able to hear if he calls."

She turned to leave, feeling as though she ought to say something more. But he probably wouldn't answer that either. Toby was already dancing ahead toward the dappled tunnel of the shoreline path. With a little shrug, Verity followed.

Chapter Four

$\mathcal{I}$n Grand Marais they collected their things from a shoreline motel and left word that their week-long search was over: They'd found Pierre. Afterward, quick stops at the post office, the market and the ice cream counter pretty much guaranteed that everyone else would hear the news as well. In a village of three hundred, information travels fast.

"He's all right, then, eh? Glad to hear it."

Stopped on a short sidewalk for the third time already, Verity smiled into another concerned face while Toby bobbed his head in agreement.

"Well," she explained, "he'd developed a terrible cold and fever before we caught up with him, but I think he'll be all right now. A week or so of rest with someone to keep an eye out for him—"

She let the phrase trail off, and her current questioner finished it for her. "Be good as new, he will. That old man's a tough character."

His own face as seamed and weather-beaten as drift-wood, he shook his head on an admiring chuckle. It was infectious, and Verity smiled again in response. With a wave, he ambled away before she'd even mentioned that Pierre was at the lighthouse now.

As a matter of fact, somehow she hadn't mentioned it to anyone. She'd just let people assume that she and Toby were staying out in that tumble-down shack where they'd found Pierre, rather than mention the lighthouse—and Brock Randall. She couldn't have said why. . . .

But it wasn't really important anyway. Attractive and mysterious, contradictory and intriguing as he might be, he was still just someone who was tolerating them for a few days until Pierre was well enough to be rational about coming into the village. Then they'd get out of Brock Randall's way, and he would undoubtedly forget them as quickly as possible.

That wasn't a particularly satisfying thought, and Verity shook it away. For now, anyway, they were going to stay with him, and her only other errand in the village was a call to Brandon and Patterson. Standing at one of the three public phones in the village while Toby poked along the harbor's edge nearby, she dialed her office.

"Mark, it's Verity." After a quick update on some pending cases, Sally had put her call through to the office across the hall from her own.

"Hallo, love."

A lazy baritone drifted along the wire, and she could almost see its owner. Tilting his swivel chair back, he'd be setting one elegant shoe on the edge of the desk. The idle sybarite was a pose he cultivated carefully, but behind it was a brilliant legal mind. Opposing lawyers, however, were apt to discover that only in court, after they'd written him off as a dilettante.

"Decided to check in with the working stiffs, hmmm?"

Verity grinned at the unlikely picture of Mark as a

member of that group. "I might if I knew one!" she fired back.

Her target dodged the shot with an easy laugh. "How's it going up there in the hinterlands?" To Mark, any place without a dozen theaters and at least a four-star restaurant or two was almost the back of the moon. Still, he was interested. He always had been, in everything Verity did.

She hesitated. Like the bright-colored fragments in a kaleidoscope, images of the last day and a half flickered through her mind: Pierre lying helpless in that ruined cottage; Toby trying to hold him up in the rainy woods; Brock Randall at his door, bare-chested and furious, or in Pierre's room with the old man in his arms, or on the stairs with Toby's hand in his. . . . How could she possibly tell Mark about it all?

"Fine, finally." She settled for the play on words and heard Mark's chuckle of amusement. "We caught up with Pierre yesterday, and it's a good thing that happened when it did. He was alone and sick, so I'm afraid it'll be a while before he's really himself again. But I can go ahead with the case in the meantime—"

"Do," Mark encouraged. "That way you can come home sooner."

"That's your profound legal advice?" she asked teasingly.

"My very best, counselor. I'm already tired of being discounselate."

He brought out the awful pun unhesitatingly, and any serious conversation was over as she wailed a protest.

"For that you should be disbarred!"

He laughed unrepentently. "Barring disaster, hmmm?" he suggested.

"That does it," she announced firmly, trying to keep her tone serious. "I'm getting off this phone before you commit any more barbarous assaults on the English language!"

It was a good exit line, and she hung up quickly while Mark's rich laugh still rang across the wire. Another time she might have stayed and matched him pun for pun until they were both finally desperate enough to agree on a truce. But somehow today wasn't one of those times. Maybe because she was concerned about getting back to Pierre? That must be it. Five minutes later she and Toby were driving out of the village.

Even so, it was late afternoon when they walked that last mile and a half to the lighthouse, leaving their car at the trailhead where the road ended. Each of them had a small suitcase, and Verity balanced hers with a bulging briefcase so familiar it was almost an extension of her arm. But the load was still light enough so they could enjoy the walk.

Strolling through the slanting light, she and Toby could watch shifting patterns of sun and shade and smell the faintly spicy scents of earth still damp from yesterday's rain. An old dirt track, their path meandered along the shore through ferny thickets and stands of lofty trees. Up ahead the season's first tiny insects danced like dust motes, their whirring nearly lost in the rustle of new leaves, and on the left the lake spoke softly to itself.

Visible here and there through gaps in the trees, it was falling quiet as the wind died toward the end of day. Waves that had pounded the shore for hours now began to calm down, barely brushing the rocky ledges. It was like a mighty orchestra, choosing at the end of some long tumultuous piece to play its last low notes on a breath of sound, and listening, Verity was caught up in the ancient music.

Even Toby padded quietly along beside her, his bright head cocked to hear. Occasionally, they caught each other's eye and traded smiles, but otherwise they walked in wordless harmony. Savoring it, Verity was conscious of how little this tranquil time was like the battles with

Brock Randall she'd had since they first came this way a day ago.

"Mom, look!" Toby's whisper was hoarse with excitement, and he stopped dead. "Over there!"

Her own steps arrested, Verity followed his eyes. Only about twenty feet ahead of them at the side of the trail were a fox and her kit. Motionless in the sunlight, their fur glowed a vibrant golden red and they stood poised, the vixen with one forepaw still raised. For a timeless interval all four gazed at each other with curiosity and a sense of communion. Then the foxes stepped into the ferns, silent and unhurried. A few fronds quivered, and they were gone.

"Gee—" Toby let out his breath on a sigh of wonder, and Verity nodded agreement. Side by side, they walked on through the woods.

Like the lazy afternoon, the lighthouse was quiet when they reached it. The boatshed still stood closed, but no more hammer blows echoed from it. Maybe Brock had finished exorcising his private demons—or just found a less noisy way to do it.

Pierre, too, lay sleeping without a sound. With Toby crowding beside her, Verity peeked in from the doorway, then retreated.

"Shhhh," she whispered. "Let's just sneak on by."

Nodding, Toby took the lead and pointed out each squeaking board with elaborate care as they crept upstairs with their bags. Around them, even the cottage itself seemed to doze quietly.

An hour later, however, all that serenity began to change. Verity sat beside Pierre while Toby sprawled on the floor nearby, poring over a book of Brock's about lighthouses in the old days. Using a long pad of legal paper from her briefcase, she'd been taking notes about the old man's situation. In the lazy silence, though, her notes trailed off into doodles and tiny sketches of his sleeping face. Then as the evening settled in, Pierre began to stir, and she set aside the pad.

"How about a glass of juice, Toby?" she asked softly, standing up. "I'd like to get Pierre to take something. While I'm at it, would you be interested too?"

"Mmmm-hmmm!" He nodded until the silky forelock slipped over his eyes, and she grinned. Where food was concerned, predicting Toby's answers was easy.

Predicting Pierre's condition was turning out to be quite difficult, though. He'd seemed to be resting so comfortably, but as he woke he went straight from sleep to delirium. Tomato juice set aside and forgotten, Verity hovered near his bed. A hand on his forehead told her that his temperature was rising fast, and worriedly she remembered that fevers often worsened at that time of day.

Pierre's certainly did. In what seemed like a matter of minutes, he was burning up and more ill than Verity had seen him. His face was flushed, and cold sweat plastered his hair to his skull as much as yesterday's storm. Breath harsh and labored, he shook constantly with a chill, so that the blankets Verity heaped on him slipped off again and again. Even more frightening than the fever itself, though, was the raving.

At first he only muttered to himself, rolling his head on the pillow while she hovered nearby and murmured reassurances. But very quickly the hoarse and broken syllables rose in volume.

"Not going. Can't leave here. . . . No!"

As if it were that first morning again, he thought she wanted to take him away. Leaning over, Verity tried to calm him.

"It's all right, Pierre. You don't have to go anywhere. No one's going to make you leave."

Close to his ear, she spoke with all the conviction she could muster, but still he didn't seem to hear. He didn't struggle with her again; he just retreated farther and

farther from reality and that was worse. Throwing himself
back against the pillow with a sudden fierce movement, he
turned his head aside and stared blindly at the wall.

"No!" he barked. "I will not hear of it. You are not
allowed."

Arrested by the unexpected strength of his voice, Verity
stood silent, searching for words. Was he speaking to her?
Had he remembered why she came here and decided to
reject her help? But if ever a client needed help, this
dispossessed old man was one. Somehow she had to
convince him—

Before she could think of a new tactic, he spoke again
as if someone else had answered, pleading.

"Never! You will not while you live under my roof!"

As the echo faded, he lay perfectly still, rigid with
rejection. Then, very slowly, by endless tiny degrees, the
harshness passed. Like ice melting to water, his old face
lost its sternness while tears ran down the furrowed
cheeks.

Turned unseeingly to her, he asked, "Not here? Anywhere?"

Bewilderment quivered in his voice, but Verity—her
own eyes filling—couldn't answer him. Powerless at his
side, she knew only that he was reliving some terrible part
of his past.

"Marie," he said brokenly. "Marie?"

Getting no reply, he began to toss restlessly again,
repeating the same name over and over. It made him
cough, so that he fought for breath but kept on calling,
drowning out Verity's attempts to soothe him. Finally he
started to struggle out of bed, and this time she couldn't
hold him back. No matter what she and Brock Randall
thought of each other, she was going to have to ask him
for help.

"Toby—"

Backed up out of the way, he still sat on the floor,
watching with widened eyes. "Uh-huh?"

As she tried to catch one of Pierre's flailing arms, her own voice was breathless, but she steadied it to keep from frightening him. "Go on out to the boatshed, would you, and see if Brock can come give me a hand? I can't seem to get Pierre calmed down—"

"Okay."

He scrambled to his feet and edged away; two seconds later the door banged.

It was only two or three minutes more—although it seemed like hours—before it banged again. In the kitchen Brock's voice suggested matter-of-factly, "Why don't you go ahead and fix yourself some cereal for supper, Toby, while your mother and I take care of Pierre?"

It wasn't a very exciting prospect, but then again the other room was probably a good deal too exciting right now. Toby agreed cheerfully, and Brock was beside her.

His crystal eyes seemed to sum it all up right away: Verity, winded and dishevelled, trying desperately to hold onto Pierre, and Pierre himself, swaying on uncertain feet as he searched wildly for the clothes that Brock had taken away the night before.

"What's this, old man?" he asked, steadying Pierre with one hand on a bony shoulder.

The effect was astonishing. Responding to voice and touch together, Pierre abruptly stood still. Verity let her tired arms fall to her sides and took a deep breath, looking from one man to the other in amazement. One was thin and somehow shrunken, but the other's height and breadth gave him a kind of mountainous strength. Just his very presence was heartening.

"I have to go," Pierre muttered confusedly. "I can't miss her—"

"Yes, of course you do," Brock agreed. "But it doesn't have to be right away."

Pierre began to protest, but Brock went on immediately. "I won't let you miss her. I'll check for you, and if she comes, I'll tell her where you are. Will that do?"

The deep quiet voice rang with reassurance. Verity felt it herself, and Pierre nodded slowly. "Yes—" he said, vague and disoriented. Head turning shakily, he gazed around the room as if he'd never seen it before.

"Good. In the meantime, then, let's get you back to bed so you'll be healthy when she comes."

Nodding again, Pierre's head dropped on his chest, and he stumbled in weariness. Catching him, Brock lifted the frail body into bed with a single motion.

Over his shoulder he spoke to Verity, "His temperature's soared. Bring me a large bowl of cold water and some towels, would you? There's a stack of them folded in the bathroom cupboard. We've got to get this fever down."

She was gone in an instant, thankful to be given something to do and even more thankful Brock Randall seemed to know what should be done.

Slipping back into the room a few minutes later, she handed him damp towels to pack around the old man's burning body, and for the next two hours she kept on with her task, while Toby put himself into his own bed. In bowl after bowl of chilly water, set on the chair by Pierre's side, she soaked towels and wrung them out, folding the wet fabric into cold compresses and passing them to Brock. But as fast as she handed them over, others came back, already warmed against Pierre's scorching skin.

It seemed to go on for so long that, alone, she would have been frantic with worry. Pierre still lay burning with fever, drawn and flushed against the white pillows, sometimes muttering incoherently. But Brock simply went on working. Those huge, gentle hands laid fresh compresses in place and occasionally turned Pierre into a new position. They bathed the old man's cheeks and forehead, too, and held cold water to his parching lips. And all the while Brock kept up an easy stream of talk.

"Let's see how that does, eh? Best water in the world, that water. Clear and icy, pure and fresh as crystal, drawn from the lake in rainclouds and dropped back down in storms that'll fill the cistern here in less than a day. . . ."

Smooth, undemanding, the deep voice rolled on as Brock strove to let the old man know that he was never alone.

Brock paid absolutely no attention to Verity. She might have been nothing more than another pair of disembodied hands, useful when he couldn't do everything at once. But on her side, she was almost unbearably conscious of him, following his every move with her eyes and wondering about him. Each time she decided that he was cold and inhuman, his compassion proved her wrong.

He'd begun by refusing them shelter and gone on to say that even if Pierre stayed, she and Toby had to leave. When she called him a hermit, he had reacted with a flash of anger, stalking icily away. All afternoon he'd been barricaded in the shed, apparently resolved to ignore them.

But he had also carried Pierre in here yesterday, seeing him settled in bed with tact and understanding. He'd given Toby the run of his entire lighthouse and answered a thousand eager questions. And he had even taken her upstairs last night, rather than leave her huddled wretchedly in a chair for hours. Now, coming to her rescue, he was caring for Pierre with warmth and skill, and Verity watched him in bewilderment.

Bent over Pierre, his enormous height was more noticeable than ever in contrast to the old man's frailty. The hands that tended him were massive too, broad in the palm and blunt tipped. But they were also long fingered and sure, moving with a delicate strength that she had never seen before. How could one man be so full of contrasts?— anger and emptiness, care and callousness, power and gentleness. As the anxious minutes wore on, Verity found her gaze clinging to those sensitive hands as if they could somehow comfort her too.

Her back had long since begun to ache and her own

hands to cramp in the icy water before she realized that Brock's hasty motions had finally slowed. He was no longer passing her another compress to soak again every minute or so; in fact, he'd straightened up and stood looking down at Pierre with an expression of satisfaction on his usually impassive face.

"How is he?" she asked, letting the last towel drop back into the bowl.

"Much better." He kept his eyes on Pierre but answered without the usual flatness. "The fever's finally turned, and he's fallen into a real sleep. The worst should be over now."

"Thank heaven!"

Relief echoed in her tone, and he glanced over at her. Caught drying her hands inelegantly on her jeans, she gave him a quick sheepish smile when she felt his gaze. At first it probably made her look just like Toby, but then the resemblance faded, along with her smile. Her hands paused in midair and even her breathing slowed, because Brock's eyes were still meeting hers. As if a visible line linked them, she seemed to be held by a silken cord, and it was taut at both ends. For an instant she knew that, willing or not, neither of them could look anywhere else.

Then Brock did. The harsh lines of his face hardened, and his whole body seemed to tense with effort. Wheeling away from her so he *couldn't* hold that stare, he asked tonelessly, "Could you put fresh sheets on the bed again while I get Pierre into dry pajamas?"

He was lifting the old man already, and Verity steadied herself with one groping hand on the chair back. She felt off balance, as though a support she relied on had suddenly collapsed. But Brock didn't look at her again, and she made herself let go of the chair. Head high, she gathered up the discarded towels and bowls and carried them away.

When she turned back the fresh bedding a few minutes later, Brock laid Pierre between the sheets and drew the covers up around him. One big hand lingered on the old man's shoulder, then Brock walked quietly out of the room. After a last check of her own, Verity followed, to find him standing by his desk next door.

She couldn't have said why she did it. But besides that strangely intense contact five minutes ago, they'd just worked together so long that on some wordless level there was a link between them now. Half conscious of it, she went after him, thinking vaguely that she should thank him for his help.

At first she could hardly see him in the shadowed room. While they were tending to Pierre, night had fallen around the lighthouse, and only a faint glimmer crept in from the kitchen. But it showed her the outline of his broad back, turned to her. Stepping softly, she walked over and touched his arm.

"Brock—"

He hadn't heard her coming. For a split second his entire body froze, then an iron hand clamped over hers as he spun around to face her, almost as if he were a soldier reacting to a sneak attack. Instead of the enemy, there was only Verity, eyes wide in the shadows and lips parted in surprise, the words stilled in her throat.

Coming at an angle, the dim light made her hair only a faint corona around her head and slipped across her upturned face like golden mist, gathering at temple and cheekbone and the corner of her mouth. There shock made the pale skin quiver with unsaid syllables, and Brock's eyes—following the light—came to rest on that tiny movement. His fierce grip on her fingers relaxed, but he didn't let go and the fingers stayed where they were, only stirring a little in his hold.

For a long time they stood like that. Around them the darkness lay in corners like an affectionate black cat, and outside the night breathed softly. Wind stole across the dune grass, rustling fragile stems against each other, and blowing minute grains of sand along to build new dunes.

Below, in black and silver, the lake waters lapped at the shore, advancing and retreating in an endless dance. And everywhere there was a feeling of expectancy, of waiting and potential.

Poised in front of Brock, Verity waited. Around her, the cool green scent of water blended with the lighter fragrance of spring leaves and the faintest tang of shaving lotion. Over the quiet obbligato of the night, her breath blended in harmony with his, growing ragged to the muffled drumbeats of a heart. And above her, Brock was a tall shadow.

He bent toward her as he released her fingers at last, using both his own hands to draw her toward him. With dreamlike clarity, she seemed to see him coming in slow motion, but she made no move to stop him. She only closed her eyes as his beard brushed her cheek with silky softness and his mouth found hers.

Chapter Five

For the length of time it took their lips to warm to one another, it was a tentative kiss, delicate and exploratory. But as heat flowed to heat, a groan rumbled deep in his throat and his hands shifted, wrapping fiercely around her until her body clung everywhere to his. His mouth opened hers, searching, insisting, demanding.

She was passive in his arms for just a few heartbeats. Then—like paper that resists the fire at first, only to explode into flames an instant later—she met his demands with her own. Her body fused with his, straining against him so she could feel the corded strength of his thighs and chest beneath her own taut muscles, while her hands rose to twine in the hair at the nape of his neck. Hungrily, she held his face to hers, savoring the texture of his beard, drawing in the scent of his skin, learning the outline of his lips. She welcomed the invasion of his kiss, sharing his gasping breath, and met his tongue with her own. Deep tremors shook them both, and as the fire she had thought long dead seared her body she felt a thawing, melting weakness.

Then without warning he tore himself from her embrace. Wrenching his lips and hands from her, he strode away to the far side of the room, halting there with his head bowed and ragged breath still audible. Her arms dropped to her sides, and she stumbled, dizzily, on legs that shook beneath her. Catching herself on the edge of his desk as her mind began slowly to function again, she peered into the shadows, searching for him, searching for the vanished moment of passion.

It was just proximity, she thought hazily. That must be it. Otherwise—

Suddenly, her mind was racing, hunting for rationalizations to explain away the irrational. He was here, and both their emotions were tuned to a frantic pitch by the strain of tending to Pierre. They had been under such pressure that the kiss was just spontaneous combustion, nothing more. After all, far from caring about her, Brock didn't even want her here. And on her side, she'd never even met the man until yesterday. Even if she were willing, she couldn't possibly feel anything but simple physical attraction for him this quickly—and she of all people knew how dangerous that was.

That was it, of course. Proximity. She drew in a deep, steadying breath and realized how loud it sounded. He was utterly silent now, and even the noises of the night seemed to have withdrawn; the stillness in this room was so thick it tasted powdery and old. It pressed down on her, and intuitively she knew that it pressed even harder on him.

In the shadows at the far side of the room, he didn't speak, offering no explanation for either the embrace or its ending. As she found the dim outline of him, a flash of pure empathy told her that he couldn't explain himself right now, even if he wanted to. Something about the bowed head and set shoulders spoke to her of confusion or dismay, and of their own accord her hands stirred at her sides, wanting to reassure, to comfort.

To quell that impulse, she slipped both hands in her pockets but at the same time rushed to break the silence at last. With words, at least, she could end the tense stillness and tell him one idle kiss was no calamity.

"Well, we did it!" she said brightly, trying to convince him that she considered the kiss nothing more than congratulations for a job well done. "And thank you from the bottom of my heart for helping out."

He swung toward her, and she rushed on to talk about the old man, as she'd originally meant to do.

"Now we've got that fever down, things have got to get better for Pierre. Of course, I don't see how they could possibly get any worse! Do you know, before we finally located him yesterday, I'd been trying to find him for more than a week?"

She'd been babbling, but as she remembered, her voice rose in real indignation. She didn't wait, however, for an answer that might or might not have come.

"After his niece hired me, Toby and I drove up here almost immediately, but no one could tell us where he was. Everyone smiled and said, "Old Pierre, eh? Why, he's the nearest thing to a living legend around here. Remembers the old days when this was a boomtown and has stories all the way back to the voyageurs.' "

Part actress, like every good courtroom lawyer, she caught the local inflection perfectly, starting to pace near Brock's desk as she spoke. Even in the dim light, he could see her hands come out of her pockets and move too, sketching out her words.

"But no one knew where he lived—he just showed up once in a while for supplies and hadn't been in for days. All they could tell us was that he moved around the woods from one abandoned place to another, because the government had condemned his cabin and torn it down. But

Pierre never told anyone where he was, because he was too busy keeping ahead of the federal officials sent to move people outside the boundaries of this new park they're creating.''

Across the room Brock stepped over to a small round table. Faint groping sounds built up to the rasp of a match, and a kerosene lamp began to glow. As he set the chimney back in place, light radiated upward to cast his face in sharp relief, emphasizing the angles and hollows. Every line was as sharp as if he'd just fresh-carved a block of wood to make a mask of detachment. But Verity hardly saw him, because it was safer to see again the way Pierre had looked when she and Toby had finally discovered him yesterday.

"We didn't find him until we reached the very last one of those old places marked on the map. And when we finally got there, it was a tumble-down wreck you could almost knock over with your hand. Bushes and weeds had grown up around it, so we had to fight our way past to the shack. The porch was almost separated from the cottage and the boards so rotten we had to step around the holes. Half the windows were broken, and the roof leaked!''

She let her indignation punctuate that line and then continued.

"He had a few bits and pieces with him, of course, but he'd run out of food and been too ill to walk into the village for more. When we found him, he was so weak he couldn't even move his cot out from under the drip that started with the rain. He barely had the strength to listen to us about coming to take shelter here, much less to walk any kind of a distance. And that was what the government had reduced him to—all for a park!''

Coming to a halt, Verity let both hands drop and finally looked over at Brock. Caught up in her description, she wasn't even aware of the angry tears that glittered in her eyes in the lamplight. Brock must have seen them, though. He walked toward her, one hand half raised to brush them away.

But when he was still three feet from her, the hand fell to his side, while his face turned hard and unrevealing again before she was even sure that she had glimpsed warmth and sympathy there. Abruptly, he turned toward the desk instead of her. Reaching it, he lit the lamp that stood there with quick precision. Only when this second light poured out into the room, making Verity blink automatically, did he speak at last.

"The fact is, of course," he said coolly, "that someone always has to suffer."

The words were like a slap. Outraged, Verity dashed the moisture from her eyes without ever noticing that it had been there and glared at him.

"Absolutely not! I refuse to accept that."

"Whether you accept it or not, it's still true."

"It doesn't have to be! Everything worthwhile doesn't have to be paid for in human misery."

It was a cry from the heart, but his answer came detachedly.

"Not always in misery, perhaps, but distress, discomfort, inconvenience. In a world as bad as this, the best you can try for is the greatest good for the greatest number."

"That isn't enough!" she protested. "Not when the individuals get really hurt. Not when people like Pierre lose practically everything they have. When the government condemned that house of his because it stood inside park boundaries, they took the only thing he really had!"

Calmly, Brock adjusted the flame on the desk lamp with lean adept fingers. "His loss is society's gain. He gave up a bit of private property so a magnificent stretch of shoreline could be saved for the whole public to enjoy."

"The public had no greater right to it than he did!" she flared.

"True, but they had the same right, in greater numbers!"

This time he sounded as ardent as she did. Almost as if they were both redirecting the passion of a minute ago into safer channels, they continued arguing.

"They had the same right Pierre did to know the lake as it is—beautiful and unspoiled—to see how the sun hesitates before it drops into the water at night—how the banks march endlessly along the shore, growing and dying—how the storms whirl in to carve new castles in the cliffs." Brock's face was alive, intense with conviction. Distracted, she faltered, and he pressed home like a dueler.

"What would you advocate instead?" he demanded, twisting the verb. "That the whole lakeshore stay in private hands, so owners can do as they choose with it?—like putting up 'No Trespassing' signs. Or perhaps selling out at a huge profit to some fast-food chain that will come in and build a few pizza palaces on the dunes, so plastic forks can grow in the sand and Styrofoam boxes drift in on every wave!"

The two pictures he'd just painted contrasted cruelly with each other, and Verity shifted her ground.

"Of course not," she conceded. "I don't oppose creating the park—"

"How could you?"

"But at least the government could have bought up all the land and then given it back to its current owners on lifetime leases, instead of condemning it outright. Then people like Pierre could have lived out their lives here, treasuring the land as they've always done instead of being forced off it!"

"And that's what has happened in some cases," Brock agreed. "But Pierre's property wasn't some isolated little cabin, well off the beaten track and easy to overlook for the rest of his life. It was a cottage and three outbuildings, right along the shoreline road and at the edge of a spectacularly beautiful birch forest."

That was where it had been? Like every other visitor to

the area, Verity and Toby had gone to see those birches. Their graceful columns were so white that they seemed to have been left from the first days of the world, standing in a sun-drenched idyllic dell like the pillars of Eden.

"All right, maybe it had to go." Yielding one point, she fought for another. "But if it did, then he should have been given enough cash settlement to buy land just outside the park. Its value has gone up a bit too, but that way at least he could have stayed in the area he loved, instead of being forced off at any price the government chose to tell him he would take!"

"It wasn't 'any price,'" Brock pointed out precisely. "The government offered what the land has traditionally been worth."

"But it's worth a great deal more now!"

"Certainly, *because* of the park guaranteeing the continued beauty of this area. But I gather you'd like to see people paid the exorbitant prices the fast-food chains would offer!"

"That's not realistic, of course," she admitted. "But neither is the settlement they gave him, if it won't buy another cabin like the old one!"

"Then he didn't have to take it. People don't have to accept the first offer if they think it's too low. The government's automatically authorized to add a 10% increase in a case like that, and if the owner still refuses to sell, the whole thing goes to a jury trial. Whatever the jury determines, the government has to pay. If you've already done any research at all for this case," he added, "then you know that's the procedure."

"Of course I do!" she fired back. It rankled her that he was implying that she came up here without even doing preliminary research on the case. But what rankled her even more was that she'd let herself get so carried away that she said something as sloppy as that "any price" comment. Arguing with a man like Brock Randall, she'd have to be as accurate as she was in court.

More carefully, she continued. "But Pierre didn't know it, so he took their first offer. His niece told me that when those federal officials came to him they just said they had to have his land for a new park—nothing else—and he finally agreed."

"If he agreed—" Brock began sternly.

"He did agree," she conceded before he could finish the sentence. "But that doesn't—*shouldn't*—mean a thing here. He's an old man, and he's spent his whole life in a place this remote. What does he know about the federal government? It never even occurred to him he might have a right to challenge what they said! And they didn't tell him a bit about any of his rights. They just put him down as a 'willing seller' and then broke his heart by making him leave so they could tear down his cabin."

"He could have had relocation assistance from the government," Brock observed. "That's a standard program."

"Not that standard!" she disagreed. "No one ever bothered to tell Pierre about that, either. They just amputated his whole life, and then didn't even get around to offering relocation assistance as a Bandaid!"

It was a vivid charge, and she took a deep breath, scenting victory. Let Brock Randall counter that one! But instead of arguing right back, he changed directions entirely, almost as if he were shying away from the sketch she drew.

"What does Pierre himself think about it all now?"

Her feeling of triumph evaporated. "I'm not sure," she admitted. "When we found him yesterday, I told him why I came up here and he signed his name on all the papers I need to go to court, but I'm not sure he really understood. . . ."

Brock shot her an incredulous look, but before he could speak she rushed on, to avoid losing all the momentum she'd gained in this argument.

"That doesn't really change anything, though! I can

always explain again when he's not sick and half-starved. But now I've finally found him, I *am* going to court, and one of my best points is going to be the appalling conditions he was reduced to by his own government because they didn't take the time to—"

"Mom, what's all the racket about?" Toby's sleepy voice cut her off, and they both turned to find him standing at the door, hitching up his pajamas with one hand. "Is Pierre upset again?"

"No, he's fine. Much better now, in fact." With an effort Verity dropped her voice to its usual calm pitch. "Brock and I were just discussing him."

"Sounded more like fighting to me," Toby observed with interest.

"I don't fight," Brock stated.

She threw him a quick glance. All of the earlier heat was gone from his tone, and he was as remote as ever. Before Toby could risk a snub by asking the obvious "Why not?" she put an arm around him and swept him out of the room.

"And you apparently don't sleep, young man. But you'd better . . ." She made her tone threaten dire consequences otherwise, and he giggled.

.On the steps, however, he pointed out, "I was asleep, but you woke me up."

"Sorry. Since I never got to say good-night before, how about I make it up to you now by putting you back to sleep?"

A skeptical grin made it clear that he saw the catch in that one, but upstairs he let her tuck him in. Tipping his face up for a good-night kiss, he whispered, "I love you, Mom."

The kiss lingered while she swallowed hard. When she answered, her voice wavered a little. "I love you too, tadpole."

"I know."

He snuggled down and she left the room, closing the

door and bowing her head against it. Limp, she marveled wearily at the emotional gamut she had run in the last hour. Worry, passion, anger—they'd all seethed inside her. And love. No payments in misery, she thought imploringly. Brock was wrong. It wasn't necessarily true; the world didn't have to be that bad for everyone. Not for Toby.

And not for Pierre. Standing straight again, she promised herself that she'd stay here as long as she had to, and see to that. She'd take his case to court and she'd win it so that gallant old man could stop living like a fugitive. Apparently Brock Randall cared too much for the "greatest number" to care about an individual like Pierre, but she didn't.

Two days later Verity drove to the federal district court in Marquette. She hadn't tried again yet to remind Pierre why she was there, but she'd decided to chance going ahead with his case anyway. She couldn't promise him results, of course. But surely, when he was well enough to think it all through he'd still be willing to risk having her at least go to trial. After all, what did he have left to lose?

Homeless and alone, he was already so badly off that nothing could possibly be worse than this. And she might be able to win him something a whole lot better, even though she'd have to admit from the start that he had agreed to be a "willing seller." But she knew that she could argue effectively that he'd sold only because he hadn't understood his options, thanks to the government's failure to tell him what they were.

His cabin was gone; there was nothing to be done about that. But Verity was confident that she could convince a judge that it had been worth more than the government paid. To Pierre, in fact, it had been priceless. But as she told Brock Randall, she was determined at least to win the old man enough money so he could buy a home outside the park boundaries. That way, rather than flee through the

woods like an animal driven from one den to another,
Pierre could live out the rest of his days in some decent
cottage that was still right near the area he'd always
known and loved.

None of this was going to happen very quickly, though,
and she knew it. At best, it would be a minimum of
several weeks because the federal district court sat only
periodically, when enough cases warranted bringing a
judge to that far northern city. Then, inevitably, everything took time because there were a number of cases to
get through. But she'd set the wheels in motion anyway,
no matter how long it took, because she *wouldn't* let Pierre
pay with his misery for someone else's park.

In the meantime, whether or not Brock was right about
the greatest good for the greatest number, he had been
right about Pierre's fever. It still climbed late each
afternoon, so that the old man was confused and far from
well enough to move, even if he would agree. But the
night that they had tended him together apparently saw the
last of his delirium.

Going to Marquette, then, would be no problem on his
account. Pierre slept most of each day, only waking for
meals, and would barely know that she was gone. And
Toby would be delighted to spend the time pottering
around the lighthouse grounds or tagging after Brock. As
for Brock himself, Verity wasn't sure what he really
thought of her trip—or anything else.

Ready to leave for court the first time, she gathered her
papers into her briefcase, picking up her bag and a pair of
disreputable old loafers as well. They definitely weren't
the thing for a courtroom appearance, but the elegant
heels she had on for the moment weren't designed to hike
back and forth to her car either. Knowing that she was a
good deal better off to carry an extra pair of shoes than to
break an ankle in the middle of the woods, Verity added
them to her load. Predictably, though, by the diamond-

paned window on the stairs, the loafers slipped from her clutch.

"Damn!" she muttered, peering in the direction they'd vanished. Retrieving them without dropping anything else would be quite a juggling act. But before she could free a hand, Brock appeared at the bottom of the steps, holding her vagrant shoes.

"Yours, I presume?" he inquired dryly, one eyebrow cocked.

"Mine," she confirmed, tossing him a rueful smile of thanks as she came down the last few steps with more care, her own eyes fixed on her feet.

When he first spoke, she'd almost thought there was a gleam of amusement in his tone. But when she reached the ground floor and looked up at him, his face was closed and shuttered as usual. Finishing a protracted survey that took in her hair swept into a neat twist, gold earrings and fine neck chain, trim blue-gray suit and pale blue shirt above a pair of high-heeled pumps, he finally met her eyes, and his own were opaque.

"I'll get your suitcase," he said. "Or would you rather drop that down the stairway too?"

"No, of course not."

Both eyebrows lifted this time, and she clarified. "I don't plan to drop it anywhere, and you don't need to bring it down for me either, thank you. We aren't leaving. I'm only going to Marquette to see about filing the papers on Pierre's case."

"I see. That explains the metamorphosis."

Without being vain, she knew that she looked good; she'd learned years ago how to dress for court, and that professional but feminine style became her. But as his gaze flicked over her on the last word, she caught an almost hostile quality to it. For some reason, he preferred to see her in jeans and sweaters. That is, if he had to see her at all.

Occasionally the mask he kept over his face blew aside

for an instant. And she was learning to catch glimpses of the man beneath. Without knowing why she bothered, it was to that man she said, "Only a temporary one, for working hours. As soon as I get back, I'll turn into a caterpillar again."

"Do as you like. It doesn't matter to me."

He clearly meant that to refer to her clothes, and to her trip as well. But the impression she caught was that it *did* matter to him that she was going outside the narrow world of his lighthouse. It was almost as if it wasn't just the Lower Peninsula he disapproved of, as she'd thought at first, but *every* place except this isolated point, although she hadn't the least idea why. And now Brock certainly wasn't going to confirm or deny that notion—or anything else. The mask was firmly back in place.

Shrugging, he just perched the loafers on top of her pile and turned away, his broad back making it clear that he'd put her completely out of his mind. But Verity, finding him very much in her mind for much of the long trip out to Marquette and back, wondered why the man intrigued her so.

Handling the car with automatic skill while she puzzled about Brock Randall, she gave only minimal attention to the peaceful winding dirt roads that led away from the lighthouse. A gravel stretch across the Kingston Plains didn't catch her eye either, and the lonely stumps scattered across that empty landscape, eerie reminders of the early logging days, barely got a glance. Once she finally reached the paved road, she paid even less heed to the miles of countryside rolling past her windows. The pale stone bulk of the post office building in Marquette was no more than a vague impression as she climbed to the court clerk's office on an upper floor and filed the necessary papers for a trial on Pierre's case. Everything she did was done automatically, because her thoughts were so fixed on Brock.

Heaven knew, that wasn't because she had nothing else

to do but think about him! Looking after Pierre and drawing up his papers had taken hours already. There was time to spend with Toby, too, and the meals to see to, since by tacit agreement she'd taken over cooking for all of them. But somehow she still found herself thinking an inordinate amount about the enigmatic Brock Randall, just as she was now doing again as she headed back from Marquette.

As if he were a puzzling legal case, she analyzed the little she knew about him. He'd been at his remote lighthouse for almost a year, apparently living alone and managing for himself. He said he was writing, although as far as she knew he'd only worked at his desk that first night they arrived. He guarded his solitude and resisted having them disrupt it, but he was capable of both generosity and understanding. He kept that empty mask to the world, but she'd seen it slip and give her glimpses of an entirely different person, one who could protect Pierre's pride, sympathize with Toby's enthusiasm—and kiss her with explosive passion. Remembering the kiss, and her own unexpected response, her cheeks flushed and her methodical analysis broke down. She reached the lighthouse at the end of the day knowing that she was a long way from being able to make a mental note that the case was closed on Brock Randall.

As for Brock himself, both before and after her first trip into Marquette, he made it abundantly clear that as far as he was concerned their one wild embrace might never have happened. He studiously didn't mention leaving again but came and went around the lighthouse as if she wasn't there. Her presence was just a temporary inconvenience, to be ignored as much as possible.

But it wasn't always possible, for either of them. He could work outdoors when she was inside, and indoors when she was out. He could eat his breakfast before she woke up, and his lunch and dinner so belatedly that she'd set them on the back of the stove. He could look in on Pierre when she was busy somewhere else, or send Toby to ask her when he needed to know anything vital, like whether she had enough kerosene for the lamps. But no amount of planning could forestall the accidental meetings, and then it was difficult for either of them to ignore the other.

One reason was that she was overwhelmingly conscious of him. After that single devastating kiss, Verity told herself firmly that distance was the best cure for the effect his proximity had on her. He was bent on avoiding her, and she'd be happy to oblige.

It was a perfectly simple plan, but over and over again it failed. All she had to do was bump into Brock without warning and rediscover just how dangerously attractive he was, even when he was streaked with dirt. . . .

Rather than ask him, she let Toby show her around the lighthouse grounds the next afternoon, much to his delight. And in four days he'd managed to learn an impressive amount about it.

"This one's the Assistant Keeper's cottage," he announced at their initial stop, puffing with importance. "Brock says it was built first, but then they added to it when they built ours."

That last pronoun sounded odd in Verity's ears, but Toby was already walking around the side of the cottage, and she just murmured, "Oh?"

"That little round thing—Brock says—is where they stored the oil for the light, and this big one's the fog signal house. They used to use bunches of dogs that were trained to bark in the fog, but then they decided to build a steam whistle."

"Oh, come on, Toby!" Verity teased in smiling disbelief. *"Dogs?"*

Toby answered with authority. "Yup. Brock said so."

That settled it. Wryly, Verity guessed that she was

going to hear a lot of that phrase. The boatshed was closed, though, so they skipped that one and even missed the lighthouse tower itself when Toby rediscovered his softball, lying forgotten by the door. He pounced on it and lobbed it to Verity, and in a minute they were playing catch.

"Sorry, Mom!" Toby hollered a few throws later, his baseball cap tilted back to watch the ball shoot sideways and drop toward the water.

"Playing for the Lakers, hmmm?" she teased and was rewarded with a pained look of masculine scorn.

"They're a *basketball* team, Mom!"

"All right, all right. Heaven forbid you should grow up eight feet tall," she returned equably. "Now hold on while I try to find out where the darn thing went."

Stirring through the long grass and wild blueberry bushes, she hunted for it without success, barely conscious of a muffled thudding sound, separate from the roll of waves hitting the sandstone ledges below the lighthouse. She was nearly down to the water, slithering along an embankment below the fog signal house, before she realized that the sound was Brock, sinking postholes to extend the retaining wall that held the bank in place. Turned at an angle to her, he was rhythmically driving a posthole digger into the ground and scooping dirt from the narrow hole at his feet.

While she watched, strangely unable to look away, the pile of dirt beside him grew gradually taller, and he bent deeper over the hole. Verity, rooted where she was, absorbed every detail—the powerful stance, muddy workboots planted wide and solid; the faded jeans low over lean hips and strained by bulging thighs; the stained shirt, taut across the shoulders and rolled up over muscled forearms but unbuttoned almost to the waist—

"Mom! You find it yet?"

At Toby's voice, calling her back to herself, Verity

started and tore her eyes away from Brock—only to discover that the softball had rolled down to perch right at the edge of the rocks below him. What was worse, by the time she'd picked her way down after it, he had stooped and picked it up himself. Tossing it idly from one hand to the other, he watched her approach him.

Bare arms and legs tanned to pale gold, she was wearing only brief khaki shorts and a lemon yellow top, its shirttails tied above her waist. As she reached him, his eyes rose slowly to meet hers, passing very deliberately up the paler skin of her midriff and lingering over the three shirt buttons she hadn't bothered with. Her cheeks heated under his stare. Why on earth hadn't she tucked that wretched shirttail in and buttoned every single button? She might have known she'd bump into him if she went out practically undressed like this!

"Is this what you want?" he asked, extending the baseball at last.

A streak of dirt ran across one angular cheekbone, and his hair and beard were ruffled in the wind, his bare chest shiny and face wet from exertion. For one appalling moment, the only thing she wanted was to touch him, to push aside the limp collar of his shirt and set her hands on his shoulders so that her forearms lay along the damp strength of his chest, tickled by the bronze hair matted along his breastbone. Near enough to catch the rustle of his breath and the heat of his body, she was uncontrollably drawn to his primitive vitality.

"Mom? You down there?"

In spite of the sun pouring down over them, she shivered as Toby broke the spell.

"Yes," she answered, but it came out in a husky croak. Clearing her throat awkwardly while Brock watched her, she tried again. "Yes, Toby! Be right up."

This time the words were audible more than two feet away, and she reached out to take the softball from Brock.

Inevitably, her fingers brushed his, small and clean against the dirt-stained breadth, and a flame seemed to shoot up her arm. As if that vitality of his were an electric current, it seared her skin, and she snatched her hand away before it could be burned—or ignited—any further. Turning hastily, she scrambled up the bank, not sure if she was escaping from Brock or herself.

Chapter Six

$\mathcal{T}$heir next meeting did nothing whatsoever to make her less conscious of Brock, either. Working at the kitchen table after supper the next night, she'd sent Toby to get ready for bed but, distracted, had not followed him up for nearly an hour. Finally, rubbing her eyes wearily as she looked up from the abstracts of some cases like Pierre's, she heard the stolid tick of the shelf clock over Brock's desk in the next room and remembered what time it was.

Hurrying up the stairs to say good-night, she rushed in the doorway and slammed into Brock before she'd even had a chance to recognize the sound of voices—much less to hear the echo of Toby saying sleepily, ". . . 's a neat story. Thanks, Brock. Kiss Mom g'night for me?"

She collided with him so hard the impact of hitting that broad chest rocked her back a step or two off-balance. But his hands shot out and gripped her shoulders, steadying her automatically and pulling her forward again. Then,

Toby's words sank in, so that she caught their sense as well as their sound, and she looked up at Brock.

For once he was unguarded, relaxed and smiling faintly. But just as she realized that his hold was almost an embrace, his eyes met hers and the smile faded. The mask was still off, though, and she could see a flash of greeting, as if he'd been waiting for her.

Then his openness faded too, while tension took its place. Searching her upturned face, his gaze halted at her lips, while his thumbs moved absently, hypnotically, along her arms. She was so close that she could feel his breath stir the wisps of hair at her temple. They feathered along her cheek, while her lips went soft and full of their own accord. Independently, they seemed to recall his touch—and to long for it. His eyes were clear pools, lakewater on a bright, hazy day, and she was slipping into them, deeper and deeper, leaning insensibly toward him. It would be so easy for him to do as Toby suggested. . . .

"You can kiss her for yourself. Here she is."

His words cut through the mindless yearning that welled up in her. Her own eyes widening, she met his for a second more and saw them drained and arid. Then his hands fell to his sides and he swung away; his footsteps rang on the stairs.

Left behind, Verity had no choice but to say good-night to Toby and return to her papers. Brock's face kept drifting across the pages, though, looking as it had for that one unguarded moment and her concentration was broken. Bemused, she could only feel—again—the lassitude, the longing that had drawn her toward him.

Faintly in the back of her mind, a tiny inquisitor ranted at her.

Proximity! it announced shrilly. You're just overreacting to proximity again! All those years of keeping to yourself, and now all you have to do is spend a few days sharing a cottage with some complete stranger who happens to be decent-looking, and bingo! Right away you start to think you care about the man!

But the inquisitor's voice—all that seemed to remain of her objectivity—was remote, and Verity ignored it.

Only once did an accidental meeting fail to cause the usual tension. Two nights later, with supper over and Pierre dozing while Toby entertained himself poking along the shore, she found herself at loose ends. For half an hour she'd struggled to keep her mind on her work, wondering why it should be so hard to concentrate in a place this peaceful. But the golden stillness was beginning to steal across the water, and her mind kept wandering from the papers she'd spread on the kitchen table again. At last she gave up, stuffing them away and slipping out the back door.

Even outside she prowled restlessly, catching up a broom to sweep sand from the steps and walkway. Then she pinched off the first spent blossoms from the pink roses that grew wild by the door. But somehow those little jobs didn't have their usual peaceful quality, and the evening's calm only made her feel more unsettled. Unconsciously, she glanced around for a tall broad-shouldered form, but Brock was nowhere in sight, and finally she wandered down to join Toby at the water's edge.

Hearing her steps crunch in the stones, he looked up and gave her a pleased smile. "Hey, Mom—look what I've got!"

Both hands plunged into his bulging pockets and came out overflowing. "Aren't they great?"

Laughing at his enthusiasm, Verity cupped her hands under his, trying to catch the tumbling stones. "Well, they're certainly plentiful!" she agreed. "But what's so special about them otherwise?"

"Lots of things!"

Catching a skeptical gleam in her eyes, he grinned and stuffed most of his loot back into the abused pockets, keeping out only a couple of examples to explain.

"For instance, this one's coal from an old shipwreck Brock told me about."

Round and sand-blasted to a low luster, the gray black lump lay on Toby's palm. It was almost identical to the twenty or thirty other lumps heaped in the corner of his closet, but Verity didn't let on that she'd ever stumbled across his secret hoard. She just stared at the blackened fingers that held it, agreeing dryly, "Yes, I can see it is."

Toby read her tone perfectly but just grinned and pocketed the first lump, holding out the second in his other hand. "And this one's an agate."

"Really?"

Lifting the stone, Verity peered at it. She knew Superior was famous for its agate beaches, but never having found any agates for herself, she peered doubtfully at the small dun-colored rock. Dry, it had only the faintest traces of color, but when Toby took it back and dunked it in the lake it suddenly sported rings of brilliant amber and rust and cream.

"See?" he crowed.

"All right, I'm convinced," Verity yielded. "That's got to be an agate."

"Of course." Toby agreed matter-of-factly. "Brock showed me how to find 'em."

Longingly, he added, "He said I might find a whole bunch sometime, too, if there's ever a seiche."

"A what?" A Michigan resident for years, Verity still didn't recognize the word.

"A seiche—S-A-Y . . ." Starting to spell it for her, Toby hesitated and stopped. "Well, it's a wave, anyway. Sort of, at least. It's when the water at one end of the lake goes way up all of a sudden, and the other end goes way down. If the water went down here, I could walk all the way out there and look for agates."

He gestured expansively, halfway to Canada, and Verity contradicted him right away. "Oh, no, you couldn't, my pet,'' she said firmly. "Not by yourself anyway. You know the rule about staying out of the water.''

"But I wouldn't be *in* the water, exactly, just where it usually is,'' Toby ventured, pocketing his agate wistfully.

"And where it might come back in a hurry! No, not a chance. Understood?''

She met his eyes sternly, and Toby gave a reluctant nod. "Okay,'' he agreed on a long sigh. "Brock said the same thing when he told me about 'em yesterday,'' he admitted.

Verity couldn't help grinning at his disgusted tone, even if Brock's name somehow wasn't exactly what she wanted to hear—repeatedly!—just now. She gave Toby a quick hug, though, to seal their bargain and announced on an impulse, "I'm going up the tower. Want to come?''

She suggested it partly as a distraction from the tantalizing subject of seiches. But having already been up the tower with Brock that first day they were at the station, Toby had already satisfied his voracious curiosity about the lighthouse. Seiches, on the other hand, were something new.

He cocked his head to consider the top of the lantern, soaring so far above them, then stared along the beach. "If a seiche happened, could we see it from up there?''

"I don't know for sure, but I think so.''

That evidently wasn't good enough. Toby wavered only a moment more. "If I saw one from down here, could I come and get you?''

"Absolutely.''

"Then I'll stay here and watch for a while, just in case.''

Suspecting he might have to watch much longer than he thought, Verity smothered a grin.

"All right,'' she agreed and touched a kiss to his round, sun-burned cheek with one fingertip. Scrambling away up the sand, she left him hunkered down on the rocks, watching the water level with one eye and using the other to hunt for more agates the usual way.

Walking toward the tower, Verity let her eyes play over the graceful shape. Banded at the bottom in gray, it was a faded column of white-painted brick, soaring more than twice the height of the keeper's cottage to the actual lantern itself. A landmark by day and a beacon by night, it had warned vessels for a hundred years of the rocks at Au Sable Point; if they struck and sank anyway, it had sent out lifeboats and sheltered the weary survivors.

And now it was doing the same again, she mused. Like a casualty of some long-ago shipwreck, Pierre had taken refuge here from a storm. So had she and Toby, for that matter. Brock, too—all at once she knew with complete certainty that whatever had brought him here had also been a storm of some kind.

He hadn't simply taken up residence in this isolation because of his writing; there were far more accessible places where he could have found peace and quiet for that. But there were few places where he could find such solitude as this. Whatever had happened before he came here, it had apparently driven him away from the rest of the world. That is, until she and Toby and Pierre annoyed him so by bringing it back to him.

As she was thinking, she'd been climbing a graceful wrought iron stairway that circled up the inside of the tower, hardly noticing as she passed three arched windows on the landings. Then suddenly she was at the top, and every other thought was driven from her mind.

Scrambling through a small trap door, she came out onto the narrow catwalk that circled just below the lantern itself almost a hundred feet from the ground. For safety's sake, a railing edged the walk, but it was made of some light metal that was durable and thin. Through it, above it, and beyond it stretched the whole panorama of lake and shoreline.

Behind her lay the familiar path cutting through the

woods along the shore, west of the lighthouse. To the north, sandstone ledges sloped out into the water, mottled cream and rust that faded into the crystalline green of the lake. But—most spectacular of all—away off to the east she saw for the first time how the land climbed beyond the point. The trees drew back and the land rose into great swelling banks that soared almost three hundred feet above the lake, then slanted sharply to the water. Touched here and there with a stripe of green where some hardy trees had taken a toehold on the steep sandy soil, the banks were otherwise a palette of muted colors. They gleamed in the last of day, showing topaz and ivory, amber and pearl and bronze, the colors fading as they arced around a shallow bay and receded into the distance.

"Oh—"

With the little breath Verity had left after the climb, she murmured in delight as she leaned on the railing.

Far below her, Toby gave up on both agates and seiches. Skipping a few last lazy stones into the water, he ambled into the cottage, but she lingered, knowing that he'd be content adding to his coal hoard and counting over the messy treasure.

Her own restlessness seeping away, she gazed out at the beauty spread before her. Timeless, the shore was both unthinkably old and forever young; sand and water had met here for eons, but their meeting was always new as the banks advanced and the lake swept them away. For them, permanence itself was change, and even while she watched the scene was changing.

While crickets sang and the breeze blew gently, the sun at her shoulder sank lower. The lake lost its color, giving up the blue of day for the molten silver of sunset. At the same time, the banks gained color, catching fire as the sun turned red and the clouds reflected distant flames. Finally, the sun was only an ember, and then it vanished entirely, while the banks cooled to ashy paleness at the edge of a charcoal lake.

Spellbound, Verity watched it all. Only when twilight began to wrap around the lighthouse did she come back to herself—and find Brock on the far side of the tower. She had been about to descend but was circling the lantern first when she saw a darker shadow in the evening shadows.

His back against the brick, he sat on the catwalk with one long leg drawn up and hands clasped around the knee. Between the darkness of hair and beard, his face was only a dim blur, and the gray sweater he wore blended with the shadowed whiteness of the bricks. She might have fallen over him, but he spoke first.

"Verity."

He just said her name, his voice echoing quietly in the darkness, and she turned to the sound, a shadow herself. Ordinarily she would have jumped at a disembodied voice in the night, but somehow this one was no more surprising than the whisper of wind across the water. It spoke softly, and she was drawn to it.

Remembering her intuition about his need for solitude, though, she hesitated, silent herself. Here of all places was the most distance from the rest of the human race; if she had to break in on his privacy in the keeper's cottage, at least she could leave him alone up here.

She could hardly be more visible in the darkness than he was himself, but he seemed to see her hesitation. Unexpectedly, he shifted sideways, making room for her to join him in the lee of the lantern, and she dropped down beside him.

Tucking her feet beneath her, she murmured, "I didn't know it was this beautiful."

He turned to her, his eyes dark hollows in the dimness of his face, and she realized ruefully what an opportunity she'd just given him. It would be so easy for him to counter that remark by pointing out this was the beauty being protected by the creation of the park that had dispossessed Pierre. She could almost hear him already, his voice edged and sardonic.

But when he spoke, she heard neither of those things. "And completely untouched by the outside world," he said, and she could catch only a deep-seated thankfulness. "Even the Indians generally left it alone, as a home for spirits, not men."

He turned back to look across the water, and his face was lost in the shadows, so she couldn't tell for sure if the mask was gone, leaving his emotions open. But his voice had rung with relief, and she wondered again. What had happened in the outside world to make him leave it so far behind, and so resist its touch?

His silent form beside her didn't offer any answers, only—for once—a wordless companionship. And Verity, who spent her life ferreting out answers, found that companionship worth even more. She asked no questions but just sat beside him while the lake murmured below and the vault overhead turned from aquamarine to indigo. Finally, though, the light flashed on automatically, piercing through the stillness every six seconds as a warning to the world of men, and beside her Brock moved. Their shared solitude was broken, and she stood up, obeying an instinct she didn't doubt.

"I'll go check on Pierre and put Toby to bed," she said quietly and slipped away, climbing down through the trapdoor and onto the stairs before he could put an abrupt end to this truce with one of his usual acid comments.

Only a day later, though, that serene hour might never have existed. Coming back again from Marquette, Verity reached the clearing on the point just in time to see Brock ease his big body out of one of the small windows in the light tower. Stopping dead, she watched him inch his way out feet first onto a small rectangular metal platform. It was obviously a painting platform, designed for jobs like this faded tower, but as it rocked beneath his weight it looked about as substantial as a few lengths of pipe and some chickenwire.

Verity's heart flew to her mouth, and the bag of

groceries she held sagged in her slack hands. It slipped down her body, and she set it on the ground without even noticing what she did. "Brock—" she said urgently, as if she could warn him about the risk.

Thirty feet away and sixty more in the air, he didn't hear her. But Toby must have been nearby, because at the sound of her voice he charged over and skidded to a stop beside her.

"Mom, Brock's painting the tower! Isn't that something?!"

That Verity could agree with: something awful. Climbing up inside the tower and sitting outside on the catwalk at the top—that was one thing. But dangling along its sheer sides, high up off the ground—that was entirely different!

"Mmmm-hmmm," she nodded feebly, while her stomach muscles clenched in apprehension. If that flimsy arrangement let go, Brock would plummet more than five stories to the ground. . . .

Free from any such fears, Toby chattered happily on. "He says in the old days they used to put in all kinds of stuff to make the paint stick—white glue and molasses and sugar and ash and things like that."

The relish in his tone made it sound like the recipe for some delicious treat, but those ingredients!—Verity gave him a revolted look, and Toby laughed reassuringly.

"It's okay—now he's just using some special kind of paint that sticks all by itself."

"Glad to hear it," she murmured.

Toby grinned, and of their own accord her eyes found that tall figure on the tiny platform again. He'd put on some kind of hard hat that glowed a brilliant yellow-orange, and above that spot of color, a section of the tower already sparkled in fresh white paint, too. Reassured for a minute at least, she realized that he knew what he was doing.

Just as she thought that, however, letting out her

pent-up breath in an unconscious sigh, Brock went to adjust the height of the platform. Reaching out for a red-handled lever, he gave it a tug. But instead of sliding smoothly down a few feet, the platform suddenly dropped like a stone for a full fifteen before it seemed to reach some kind of check point and catch again, jolting to a halt.

"Brock!"

Verity's shriek ripped out, echoing across the clearing while the platform still bounced up and down at the end of its fall. Everything else was motionless. Pressed to her side, Toby stood frozen, and Verity's own muscles had lost the power to move. All she could do was stare at the platform until her eyes burned, watching as it came to rest at last and hung against the tower, as still as a stopped pendulum. But even when it was immobile, there was no sign of Brock.

Years had passed before their straining eyes found any signs of life. Then finally the platform jiggled a little, and Brock hauled himself upright and into their sight. They both raced to the bottom of the tower, standing off to one side so they could crane their necks upward.

"Brock, are you all right?"

Verity held Toby to her with a hand on his shoulder, as much to steady herself as to reassure her son.

"Mom?—"

Toby sounded unbearably frightened when Brock didn't answer immediately, and Verity's hand tightened its grip. But finally Brock waved one arm over the side of the platform so they could see it from below.

"I'm okay." Rasping, his voice drifted slowly down to them.

"Really? You're sure you're all right?"

"I'm fine! No problem."

His terse second answer came much faster. Evidently he was in good enough condition to be impatient. Verity's rubbery legs gave way beneath her, and she sagged to the ground, letting out her breath in a rush.

"Whew!"

Looking down at her, Toby's eyes widened even more, overwhelming his small face, and Verity forced a shaky smile.

"Now that," she said melodramatically fanning herself with one hand while the other lay over her heart, "*that* was really something."

Catching the reference, Toby managed a shaky grin of his own. "I'll say!" he agreed fervently and plopped down beside her. A minute later, though, he leaned back to peer up at the tower again. "I wonder what it felt like?"

Curiosity was replacing fear, and Verity knew that his world was right side up again. Her own, however, was still a bit tilted. After all, it wasn't every day that she saw a man nearly get himself killed. Whether it was Brock or someone else, she'd be bound to feel a little weak with relief after a close call like that.

"Horrible!" she decreed on a shudder, noticing that her stomach had taken up residence just below her ears. "And don't let me ever hear of you trying to find out personally."

Even insatiable curiosity wouldn't lead him that far. "Uh-uh!" Toby's head shook widely, and she knew he'd remember those few sickening moments almost as long as she would. But overhead Brock was painting again, smooth strokes sweeping across the bricks of the tower. Even at this distance his silent absorption made it clear that he considered the incident over, and Verity pulled herself together. Scrambling to her feet, she retrieved her abandoned bag of groceries and carried it into the cottage.

In the kitchen half an hour later, though, she realized that for all his apparent unconcern Brock too might have been more affected by the fall than he let on at first.

Leaving Marquette that afternoon, she'd stopped on her way back for a few supplies. After all, there were three more people eating up Brock's food now, and the least she could do would be to refill the larder once in a while.

She'd also added a small portable radio to her pile of groceries, catching sight of it and thinking that Pierre might enjoy listening to it as he got better. Even a place as remote as the lighthouse ought to be able to catch a few stations at night.

Her stomach back in its usual place at last, she was just unpacking the radio from the bottom of the bag when Brock strode in the back door, generously splattered with paint, but safe.

Looking up at the sound of his footstep, she gave him a quick smile. "It certainly is nice to see you back on level ground! You gave Toby and me an awful scare."

Genuinely relieved, she was also remembering that before all this commotion, they'd managed last night to meet each other for once without any of the usual fireworks. What a waste it would have been for him to go swan-diving off the tower when they were just starting to be civil to each other! But instead of commenting or even returning her smile, he was staring at the little radio in her hand, his face dark.

"What's that?" he ground out savagely.

"A radio, of course," she answered, puzzled. "I just got it in Marquette."

"Why?"

"I thought Pierre might enjoy it in the evenings now that—"

"Get rid of it."

"What?"

"Get it out of here!"

Confused, disbelieving and irritated, she set the radio down with a thump. Of all the ridiculous commands! Circumstances might be keeping them here temporarily, but Brock Randall wasn't their jailer, and he certainly couldn't order her to get rid of something that might give Pierre pleasure.

About to tell him off, she took a deep angry breath and then choked back the words as her knowledge of human nature caught up with her. This was the man who'd nearly broken his neck falling from the tower a little while ago. After an experience like that, he wasn't apt to be interested in pettiness right away.

He wasn't, either. His face was stony, as unexpressive as ever, but it had a white tension she'd never seen before. His nostrils flared, and his shoulders were rigid. While she watched, he jammed his hands into his pockets as if to get them out of sight, but even through the fabric she could see the hard ridges his knuckles made, fists clenched. His whole body was taut, and she read it with the skill she seemed to be developing where Brock was concerned.

This wasn't an autocratic whim or any other trivial response. Whatever the cause was, he genuinely loathed that radio, and if nothing else, basic human decency said he shouldn't have to tolerate it.

"All right," she said quietly. "I'll put it away for now and take it back the next time I go to Marquette."

For just an instant, his eyes shut in relief as she lifted the radio. Laying it in the bottom of the bag, she found him watching until it disappeared from sight, while the tension eased slowly out of his body. Then he nodded silently and walked out the back door again.

She couldn't get him out of her mind, though, even after the image of that platform swinging empty against the tower began to fade. All that afternoon she kept seeing Brock's clenched hands as they stretched the fabric of his pockets. The groceries put away, she changed into shorts and a striped tee shirt, then swept the kitchen floor, washed out clothes for herself and Toby, and visited with Pierre.

Gradually getting stronger, he was awake now a good deal more, and Verity had slipped into the habit of stopping by for a few minutes every so often. This time, hunting for a distraction, she stayed longer than usual.

"Brock's starting to paint the tower," she told Pierre, and the old man cocked a bushy eyebrow inquiringly.

"That too, eh? He's going to have this place looking just like it did when I was a little kid."

"I guess that's the plan," she agreed, "to make everything the way it was then."

Unexpectedly, Pierre grinned. "Right up to that revolting paint mix, hmmm?"

She'd been remembering that, and it must have shown on her face for Pierre to read. Pleased that he was well enough to bother teasing, she grinned back. "No, thank heaven! Toby tells me his new paint will stick without all that extra help."

The old man chuckled, and Verity knew that he really was getting better. In fact, he was recovering so well that it would have been a good chance for her to speak to him about the case, but she didn't even think of it.

All the time she was talking to Pierre, her thoughts kept wandering back to Brock; whenever that happened, the best she could manage was rather disjointed bits and pieces of conversation. Finally she excused herself and left the room, unaware that Pierre watched her go with shrewd old eyes. His strength might not all be back yet, but his perception certainly was.

In the kitchen again, Verity shuffled aimlessly through the papers she'd brought from Marquette this time. She had a good deal of reading to do about the progress of cases related to Pierre's, but right now it didn't seem interesting, or even important. Finally, she gave up and went to look for Brock. She had no idea what she could say to him, but she wanted to see him again—to see him and be sure that terrible tension was gone.

He must have stopped painting for the day, because he wasn't anywhere near the lighthouse tower. He wasn't down by the embankment, either, but for once the boatshed door stood open. Maybe he'd gone there again to work off whatever that was the radio had stirred in him? Scraping, brushing noises drifted out of the door, and so did Toby's high-pitched giggles.

"More, Brock, more!" he laughed. "Put 'em all over you?"

Walking toward the sounds, Verity thought again how grateful she was that, even though Brock almost never relaxed his guard around her, Toby probably didn't know that he *had* a guard.

From the first her son had somehow slipped past Brock's defenses, following him around in the appropriated role of Lighthouse Inspector. Toby poked through old record books, cadged stories about the early days, and supervised Brock's work on the embankment, thriving in the masculine company he'd never had before. Even if she couldn't say anything to Brock about the radio, maybe she could thank him for his easy kindness to Toby. If he'd give her a chance to say anything, that was!

Still searching for words, Verity stepped into the doorway of the boatshed and then stopped short in surprise and delight.

Inside the narrow shed, perched on metal ways that ran the length of the building toward the water, was the hull of a perfect little sloop. Only about twenty feet long, it had the sleek lines of a seagull, and it was nearly finished. The small cabin, barely large enough for two, was in place, and the deck planking had been laid. Apparently Brock was in the process of sanding it to the same satiny smoothness as the rest of the wood.

His back to her, he'd stripped off his shirt to work, so that the sawdust was thick on his hard muscles. He must have been drawing warstripes on his tanned skin for Toby's amusement, because on the far side of the boatshed her son was doubled up and shouting with laughter. Verity's own responsive chuckle died on her lips, though. Brock's arms and chest might wear foolish stripes, but his back was marked by a horrifying network of livid and puckered scars.

A brutal contrast to the sleek interplay of skin and muscles on his right side, they drew up the flesh of his left side, beginning at his shoulder blade and vanishing under the low-slung waistband of his jeans. Tracing those jagged purple lines over knotted flesh, Verity sucked in her breath on an involuntary gasp of shock and pity.

It was only a tiny sound, but Brock whipped around as if it had been a scream. His own laughter vanishing in an instant as he took in her frozen face, he snarled, "If it bothers you, *Ms.* Brandon, then get out!"

And Verity got out.

Chapter Seven

By suppertime Verity had regained control of her betraying face. It had taken half an hour spent barricaded in her room, however, pacing around as she tried to cope with the sick horror and distress of seeing Brock's mangled back again and again.

"If it bothers you, then get out!"

His furious words still echoed in her ears. But while she could get herself out of the boatshed, she couldn't get the image of Brock's terrible injury out of her mind. When she closed her eyes, it leaped into sight—that perfect torso viciously scarred. A hand to her lips, she guessed at the agony of that tearing of skin and muscle, sinew and flesh. The healing, too, must have been nearly as painful, as severed tissues rejoined slowly, then still more slowly regained their strength and function.

Even with her eyes defensively open, the image hardly faded, and she wished urgently for a kind of oblivion—to forget not so much the ugliness, as the suffering it caused.

Finally, though, she gained a shaky calm by reminding herself that however terrible the injury, Brock *had* survived and seemed to have recovered completely, at least in body.

As for his mind—she had no way of knowing just what mental effects it all might have had on him, of course. She couldn't help suspecting that his isolation here might be a consequence of being so cruelly hurt. But that was one of those questions she wouldn't ask; Brock had made that all too clear already.

"Hi, Mom! What's for supper?"

Coming in to eat, Toby said nothing about what had happened either. If he'd missed Brock's few brutal words to her, he might never even have noticed that she was in the boatshed for those few awful moments. And Brock himself didn't eat that night.

When he didn't show up with Toby, she set his plate on the back of the stove, in what had become the usual place. But instead of coming in at last—the usual way— he never came at all. When she finally went to bed long after midnight, he still hadn't appeared, and in the morning his meal was a congealed mass, which she tossed away.

His bed had been slept in, though, and not yet made when she glanced inside his room. Sounds from the embankment indicated that he was working out there rather than painting the tower in cloudy weather, and heading for Toby's room with the clean sheets she'd brought for his bed, she slipped into Brock's instead.

He must have moved up here that night he gave Pierre his bed in the dining room, but it was the first time she had been inside this one remaining room of the cottage. Even though she'd taken on the other housekeeping chores, she had never ventured into this last sanctuary, instinctively leaving him the only bit of privacy she could. But now, driven by impulse, she edged through the door, still clutching her armful of laundry.

It was a completely impersonal room. Furnished like the other bedrooms with an old-fashioned washstand and wooden chest of drawers, a straight chair and sturdy metal bed, it had no personal touches whatsoever. The bed was a tangle of rumpled sheets and blankets, pulled completely awry, but no shirts lay across the chair, no hairbrushes on the chest, not even a book by the bed. If she had half-consciously wanted to see this room for the information it might give her about Brock, then at first glance she could only be disappointed. A second look, however, made her realize that the very emptiness of the room where he slept told her about him. Even here, his defenses were up.

Discouraged, Verity backed quietly out, wondering which was worse: seeing Brock and being kept at a distance or not seeing him at all. Still, now that they'd been here more than a week, leaving the lighthouse outright no longer occurred to her, even though Pierre was much better and might finally have agreed. Somehow, staying here had become almost a habit with her, although Verity admitted ruefully that she was far from a habit with Brock. All she seemed to get from him was a quarrel or silence.

Whichever was worse, though, she didn't have much choice. He went on spending nearly all his time outside the cottage, so that Verity had no chance to mention the scene in the boatshed, even if she'd decided to face his anger. She didn't, and the truth was that she didn't know what to say.

More than once she wondered urgently how to tell him that she hadn't been looking at his mutilated back in disgust but only in distress for his pain. But whether or not it was a consequence of that pain, he wouldn't let her close enough these days to tell him anything at all, even if she found the words. With or without Toby at his heels, Brock stayed away, and she buried herself in working on Pierre's case. Only one thing broke the silence about Brock, and it wasn't words.

Deep in the abstract of a similar case from another park, she was sitting in the kitchen again one evening when Toby called from the living room. "Mom, you got a pencil?"

"Mmmmm?"

"Have you got a pencil I could use?" Clutching one of her legal pads that he'd appropriated, he appeared in the doorway. "I'm trying to make a map of the lighthouse station," he explained.

"Sorry, Toby," she murmured with an absent smile. "You made off with my last one a couple of days ago, remember?"

"Ooops."

He looked guilty, and sweetly she suggested, "Maybe you should make a map indicating the location of the lost pencils?"

"Aw, Mom!" She couldn't help laughing at his pained expression, and disgruntled, he wandered away while she found her place in the abstract.

It was about ten minutes later that he spoke again from the other room. "Mom, come look!"

Stretching cramped muscles, Verity had just let the abstract drop to the table, and she heard the excited note in his voice. He must have turned up one of those missing pencils and finished his map; with a private smile, she prepared to admire a diagram made entirely of triangles, Toby's favorite shape.

But it wasn't a diagram at all; in fact, the pad was still empty. Sitting at Brock's desk, Toby had the top drawer open and a sheaf of photographs in his small fists.

"Look, Mom—it's Brock without his beard!"

It was, she could see that at a glance, but right now she had to be more concerned with something else.

"Toby Brandon, where did you get those pictures?"

she asked sternly, bending so she was face to face with her son.

Eyes dropping, he shifted in Brock's chair. "In the drawer, right here on top."

"And what were you doing in Brock's drawer?" Gently but firmly, she tilted his chin so he had to look at her again.

"But I had to find a pencil!"

"Did you ask him if you could go digging through his desk?"

Since urgency hadn't worked, Toby tried another tactic. "We-el-ll, no, but—"

"There isn't any but, tadpole, and you know it."

"I bet he would have said yes if I *had* asked—"

Straightening, Verity made a wry mental note not to take her son to court with her. He might enjoy seeing where she worked, but he obviously knew too much already about equivocation.

"That may very well be true, but you don't know it yet. Now hop out of that chair and go find him right now. You can at least get permission retroactively."

That last word wasn't on Toby's list, but he handed her the pictures and hopped, peeking sideways up at her to see just how angry she was. Catching the look, she tried to scowl ferociously, failed, and settled for pointing sternly toward the door. "Now scat!" she said, and touched a kiss to his snub nose before it vanished out the door.

The stern finger dropped, but as Verity went to slide the photographs from her other hand back into Brock's drawer, they spilled from her hold and cascaded onto the floor. Annoyed, she bent to pick them up; a moment later she was kneeling beside the desk as she gathered them up.

Black and white pictures, they were all informal shots, natural and unposed. In a square of endless cobblestones, a pair of lovers said farewell. A boy in uniform played his mandolin, head bowed over the instrument, a blank wall behind him. In the blackened ruins of a building, children danced in a circle. Knotted hands linked, an ancient dark-skinned woman peered out through a broken window. . . .

They were of many different moods and far more different subjects. But Verity realized slowly as she sorted through them what their common theme must be. In each one the photographer had somehow caught an intensely human vulnerability; in each, the emotions of a lifetime were distilled into an instant, as if that were all there could be.

Turning them over with care, Verity came at last to the final photograph, the one of Brock. As Toby had said, it showed him without his beard. Gazing at the clean, hard jawline, the cleft chin that had always been hidden, she felt a flash of recognition. Not that she'd ever seen Brock Randall clean-shaven before; she couldn't have. It must be just that those strong features were the kind he ought to have.

But her feeling that he somehow looked the way he should wasn't what held her there on the floor, sitting back on her heels to stare at the photograph in her hand. It wasn't the lines of his features at all; instead, it was the vulnerability in them.

Candid like the other pictures, this one had been taken in haste. The images were slightly blurred at the edges and a little too light, but nothing diminished its power. It showed Brock with one strong arm supporting a younger man. Hardly more than a boy, he wore a tattered uniform, and his face was contorted with grief as he stumbled beside Brock. Holding him up, Brock looked off at an angle, as if he were watching for danger, and on his own features was alertness and strength and shared pain.

Gazing at it, Verity didn't know that her fingers began to quiver. But she knew that her heart contracted as she stared at that honest face, a mirror of Brock's compassion, and wondered where all his unconstraint had gone. What had happened to that ability both to feel and to let the feeling show? And who had caught the man he used to be with such power and clarity?

She couldn't have said how long she stared at the photograph, but finally she put it gently with the others and slipped the entire stack into Brock's drawer. Back in the kitchen, she struggled with her abstract again, but the words flickered on the pages before her unseeing eyes. At one point, trying to shake off that blindness, she asked herself why she couldn't seem to shut out distractions and concentrate anymore. But no one answered, and like the abstract, the question too slipped from her mind, as she went back to staring sightlessly.

Worse, the same sort of thing happened again in Marquette the next day when she visited the judge's chambers to get his decision about hearing Pierre's case. Book-lined and dark, his clerk's office was stuffy, and even Judge Clark's larger office seemed airless when she was shown into it. Her mind kept slipping away to the lighthouse. There the air would be fresh and cool, as always. It would be eddying through Pierre's room, and probably ruffling Toby's flyaway hair as he trailed after Brock. And Brock himself? What would he be doing? . . .

"This is the willing seller case?" the judge inquired.

"Right, sir," his clerk confirmed. "Pierre Dumont of Grand Marais."

"Hmmm. Interesting. Yes, I think we can do something with this." Judge Clark ran his eyes over the sheaf of papers spread across his wide desk, then glanced up at Verity.

"Well, Counselor Brandon—" he began and paused, tilting his head to look over the silver spectacles that perched on his nose. She was standing in front of his desk, but her gaze was fixed and she hadn't reacted to her name.

"Counselor Brandon," he repeated in a sterner tone of voice. "If I might have your attention—"

This time his words caused Verity to snap to attention as she tried to control the hot embarrassment that stained her cheeks.

"Yes, Your Honor, of course. I'm sorry."

"I was about to give you your court date," he announced and named a day only a little more than a week away.

He had her full attention now. "Thank you, Your Honor," she said with cool professional detachment, and then gave him a delighted smile.

Mollified, Judge Clark took off his glasses and began to clean them carefully. While he was still at work, she murmured a polite, "Good afternoon, sir," and was gone from his office.

Her pleasure in his decision didn't stop her, however, from railing at herself on the long drive back to the lighthouse. Judge Clark had decided to let her bring Pierre's case to trial all right, but it certainly wasn't because of the way she'd just acted. Instead of letting him see how committed and well prepared she was, she'd simply stood there, day-dreaming! And the stuffiness was no excuse. No experienced lawyer allowed himself to be so distracted by *anything* that it interfered with his ability to practice, wasting his time and the judge's. She'd known that for years, and prided herself on caring deeply about her clients without losing her perspective. So why was she letting it happen now?

Granted, looking after Pierre, sharing the keeper's cottage with him, meant that she knew more than ever just how important this case was to him. She'd seen first hand what losing his property had done to him. If she and Toby hadn't found him when they did, it might even have cost him his life. But she'd dealt with other desperate, heart-rending cases. Why was this one affecting her so? The answer, of course, didn't really have to do with the case itself at all—but it was the next night before Verity let herself acknowledge that.

Having lain awake restlessly until well after midnight, she was disoriented at first when she woke up a few hours later. Her eyes opened suddenly, and she lay blinking in the darkness, wondering what had stirred her from sleep. Shadowy but familiar, her room seemed the same as always. Like some friendly guardian lion, the dresser crouched against the far wall, while the washstand watched at one window, half-concealed between fluttering curtains.

Vaguely reassured, Verity curled up again and closed her eyes, only to be jolted fully awake a moment later. An explosion of white light so brilliant that it showed through her lids had filled the room, followed by a continuous rumbling that almost bowed the walls. It brought her to a sitting position in a single convulsive movement, her heart pounding and breath accelerated, before she realized that it was a storm over the lake.

After a mild day, the evening had been fair, and when Verity went to bed the sky was studded with stars. But as her pulse gradually slowed she remembered that Superior was famous for its sudden fierce changes of weather. Sweeping in from the north, this storm must have been what woke her originally, and now it was right overhead. Like opposing armies that fought for possession of the lighthouse, the clouds shifted back and forth across the point, while lightning flared and thunder crashed almost continuously.

Her eyes filled with scarlet afterimages and her ears nearly numbed by the din, Verity was still exhilarated. Slipping out from under her quilt, she caught it up around her shoulders and padded barefoot across the room so that she could stand at the window and watch the wild beauty of the night.

Torrential rain and fog had closed the lighthouse station into a narrow circle of visibility. But within that small scope she could watch white spray from the lake shoot into arcing arrows that battled the falling rain, then sank beneath it. She could see the trees and bushes near the lighthouse fight against the wind, twisting and turning frantically to evade its power. And overhead she could see the low clouds charging by, as they massed around the pale, gallant light from the lantern.

Caught up in a combat that seemed to echo some war within herself, Verity didn't notice when the quilt slid from her fingers and dropped to the floor, or even when a gust of wind drove rain in her open window and soaked the front of her skimpy nightgown. But during a brief lull in the storm, she did hear an inarticulate cry that rang through the lighthouse. The storm forgotten, she spun away from the window and ran to answer that terrified call.

It didn't come from Toby's room. Hurrying in to reassure her son, Verity found him sound asleep, the covers bunched up around him and his head burrowed under his pillow so that only his nose poked out for air. Hibernating happily, he was completely unaware of the commotion, and Verity smiled as she closed his window against the rain. In the morning he'd be indignant at having missed the excitement, but for now he was dead to the world.

Pierre certainly wasn't, however. The cry sounded again, and this time she could tell it came from downstairs. Flying down the steps on light feet, she rushed to him and didn't even think to stop for slippers or a robe. Not until she bumped into Brock, that was.

"Brock!"

He must have been coming from the living room to check on Pierre. The lamp on his desk was burning, and he stepped into her path just as she reached the dining room door. Startled by his unexpected appearance, she couldn't stop abruptly enough to avoid hitting him, and managed only to turn a little, so their shoulders collided.

Like hers, his was bare. Maybe insomnia had brought him down to work at his desk in the middle of the night, because his hair and beard were ruffled, as though he had tossed and turned on a pillow, and he was wearing nothing but pajama bottoms. Ricocheting off him, she put a hand out to steady herself against the door frame just as he stepped back to catch her.

"I'm sorry, Brock. I didn't see you—"

She did now, though, and it was another of those disquieting times when more than her eyes was involved. She felt as if she had no bones, no muscles, but only sight and touch, making her physically conscious of every detail of his magnificent body. The tousled hair that would spring against her fingers if she went to smooth it down, the hard shoulder whose skin was improbably soft against hers and left her aching for more contact, the worn blue pajamas that hung faded and thin from a narrow waist . . .

"Oh—"

With an audible gulp, Verity suddenly remembered that Brock wasn't the only one to rush in here without stopping for a robe.

A quick glance down reminded her that this was the shorty nightgown that barely reached past her hips. She'd bought it because it was so tiny it took up next to no room in a suitcase; besides, it was handy in case of hot weather, when its sheer fabric was a relief. Now, however, clinging damply to her breasts, it was anything but.

Thanks to the storm front, the air was cool, but around Verity it seemed to heat up fast. His back to the living room lamp, Brock stood with his face in the shadows, so she couldn't tell at first where he was looking. But she was acutely conscious of waves of warmth flowing up her body in a tide of embarrassment.

"Yes?" he answered at last, very slowly.

She could have turned around and bolted away. She

could have rushed into the kitchen and snatched up a tablecloth to wrap around her, or at least crossed her arms over her chest for a little concealment. But instead she stayed rooted and silent where she was with Brock motionless before her, while the color spread across her skin like sunrise on white roses. As inevitably as that sunrise, he followed it with his eyes, and neither of them moved.

"The sound—those noises—" Pierre muttered thickly, and at his voice Brock turned away with a jerk. Released, Verity still stood weakly where she was.

"It's all right, Pierre, it's only a storm," Brock answered reassuringly, walking to the old man's bedside.

Still only half-awake, he protested, "But the noise—"

"Just the thunder rolling around the rocks. You're here at the lighthouse."

"Brock?" Finally Pierre's eyes opened all the way, and he peered around the room while lightning augmented the glow from the lamp.

"Yes, I'm here. And Verity too."

Just collecting her wits to slip away, she stepped forward to stand at the head of Pierre's bed, where she could keep herself out of his line of sight but lay a warm hand on the old man's shoulder.

"Right here," she murmured, and he reached up gnarled fingers to pat her hand.

"Thank you, my dear," he said simply.

His own hand dropped to the bed again, and he sighed. "I'm sorry. I don't mean to be such a nuisance to either of you."

"You aren't a nuisance—" Verity began to object before Brock could speak, but Pierre cut her off with a brief wave of his hand.

"I am when I take to getting sick or shouting in the night like this."

Verity knelt at the head of the bed while his eyelids fell, and he seemed to gather his thoughts. "It's Marie," he explained then, opening his eyes again to gaze blindly across the room. "She's why I'm so stubborn about this place."

Stepping away a few paces, Brock folded himself unself-consciously into one of the dining room chairs against the wall. The dim light turned his bare skin to the gold of a lion's pelt, as he rested his elbows on his knees and clasped his hands in front of him. "I know, old man," he answered quietly.

"It's the only link I have left, and so little to hold on to." On the next words a slight shrug lifted Pierre's shoulders in a Gallic gesture the voyageurs would have used. "At my time of life, there isn't much to want, but a few things get more important instead of less, and she above all."

"But she was always important to you."

"Ah, yes, but I don't think she knew. I didn't tell her much except no."

"She would have known anyway—"

Brock's comment offered an excuse, but Pierre didn't make use of it. He continued in a low voice that wrung Verity's heart. "Maybe, maybe not. And that's my greatest fault. That's the one I've had to live with, and it may even be that I'll die with it."

He lay still, but on top of the quilt his hands clenched in a brief spasm of pain. Seeing it, Verity wished helplessly that she could offer some comfort, some hope. Not understanding even now who Marie was, though, Verity remained silent at the head of the bed. But Brock stood up, rising from that low chair to his full height, and came to set one huge hand over each of Pierre's.

"It may be," he agreed quietly. "But it may also be that you'll have a chance yet to tell her yes and everything else. Now isn't the time for dying but for living, old man, and living leaves time for forgiveness."

Bent over Pierre's bed, he gazed compellingly into the

old eyes, while Verity bowed her head and dashed away the sudden tears.

At the same time her heart ached for Pierre, though, she couldn't help wondering ruefully what was happening to her. Not only was her concentration in rags, but so also was the iron control she always kept over her emotions. Except for that night in the hospital after Toby's accident, she hadn't cried in years.

When she looked up again, Pierre was still meeting Brock's stare. As she watched, the old man nodded once, slowly, almost as if he were responding to a command. Then he closed his eyes and deliberately settled himself for the rest of the night.

Brock stayed where he was, and in a few minutes Pierre's breathing deepened. He was asleep.

Soundlessly, Verity eased to her feet and crept away, while Brock straightened up at last, one hand rubbing the back of his neck as he looked down at the old man's sleeping form. He caught up with Verity in the shadowy upstairs hall, however, and any thoughts of sleep for herself were driven completely from her mind.

Hearing the soft brush of his bare feet behind her, she turned to say good-night. He was following her so closely, though, that she turned right into his arms. They locked around her, and he bowed his head to search her face in the darkness, his breath warming her skin until he found her answering breath and stopped it with his lips.

Startled, she only received his kiss for an instant, while thunder rumbled off to the north and west again like a drumroll. Then of their own accord her hands rose to his body. One gripped his shoulder, clinging to the solid framework of his collarbone, while the other slipped around to the back of his neck, plunging into the thick hair at his nape to press his face to hers as she gave him back his kiss.

Wildly, hungrily, she met his lips with her own,

shifting and searching to find him at every angle. One breath served them both as her mouth opened beneath his, and she savored the taste of him. Their tongues touched behind the line of her teeth, moving and twining around each other while their bodies bent and curved together.

Like chemicals that meet only to create fire, they reacted to the contact. Yearningly, desperately, she pressed against him, as he crushed her breasts against his bare torso and his thighs strained beneath her hips. The springy hair along his breastbone brushed against her skin, and she freed her lips to lower her face and rub a cheek in the tangled mat, while her ragged breathing drew in the hot male scent of him. It had been a hundred years since that one brief kiss in the lamplight by his desk, and she had told herself a thousand times that the searing magic she remembered hadn't been there. She had never known it before, and it wouldn't happen now. But she was wrong.

Weakened by desire, her hands lost their hold and slipped down his upper arms onto his chest, before finding their way again at his rib cage with a knowledge beyond thought. Meeting the symmetrical ridges of bone beneath warm flesh, her fingers glided along them, tracing each rib toward his spine. As her gentle touch ventured around his sides, he shivered once in her arms but stood motionless, his uneven breathing suspended.

A sudden different tension crackled between them, but with wordless certainty she kept her fingers moving. Behind his back her left hand slid easily over smooth skin, but her right found the hard and knotted tissue of his scars, caressing the puckered flesh with infinite tenderness. Along the whole length of her body she felt his answering shudder, and a stifled cry burst from his lips before they found hers again as he clutched her to him fiercely.

Holding her an eager prisoner of his body, he rained kisses on her lips, her eyelids, her cheeks, before trailing his mouth down the column of her neck. At the base of her throat, he placed his lips in the hollow of soft flesh that pulsed fervently beneath his touch, while his enormous hands followed the line of her collarbone. Reaching the thin straps of her nightgown, he brushed them gently aside, setting a kiss where each one had been while the straps slipped off her shoulders and the wisp of fabric floated down her body.

At her breasts, it clung for an instant over the budded tips, then drifted reluctantly away, unveiling her nipples and below them more satiny skin. It rippled over the firm roundness of her hips and buttocks and down graceful long legs, finally settling in a billow around her feet, so that she was left naked to his eyes in the soft shadows of the hallway, a dim ivory statue with open arms.

She was pliant and yielding in his hands, though, when he swept her up, holding her to him with arms and eager lips as he shouldered open the door of her room and kicked it closed behind him. While lightning began to flicker faintly again in the distance, four strides took him over to the bed, where he flung aside the sheet with one impatient hand and lowered her gently to the mattress. Sinking into it and away from him, she made an incoherent sound of dismay and hunger, and he followed her down, covering her with himself to answer her aching need.

Bowing his head to her, he found her breasts in the darkness, searching out first one and then the other with his lips. They began in the scented valley and climbed each tremulous height to discover the tender quivering peak. Kisses saluted her nipples, as his breath spread simmering heat across her skin and she gripped his shoulders with urgent fingers. And the heat blazed up into towering flames when he took each nipple in turn into his mouth, flicking it with his tongue and kneading it with lips drawn over his teeth, while she moaned and her head rolled wildly on the pillow in a tangle of dampened curls.

The sweet torment of his touch seemed to pierce deep

into some hidden essence of herself, carrying the fire with it to lick at her vitals, melting her into the huge hands that held her buttocks. They writhed in his hold, searching for the ease that only he could give, and her legs twined eagerly with his. The only fragile barrier between them was the worn fabric, strained by his desire, that her hungry hands found as they stroked the hard flanks moving against her with hypnotic heaviness. Mindlessly, she tore at the thin cloth, while whimpering sounds came from her lips as she tasted the hot wet skin of his heaving chest above her.

His breath came in ragged gusts too, and vaguely she felt them blow across her glistening flesh, unaware of the other wind that snapped the curtains at her window again, or the sudden eddies that filled the room as the storm rolled back in. Thunder rumbled near at hand, but it could have been their heartbeats, thundering through the storm that shook them. Only the lightning had to lie beyond their embrace.

It flared around the lighthouse, washing her room with unearthly white brilliance, just as she slipped desperate hands beneath his waistband to caress his desire into fulfillment. At her touch his body moved convulsively on hers, and he made a hoarse primitive sound of longing deep inside his chest, his eyes flying open. The eerie light fell across her, illuminating her moist skin that gleamed like satin, a graceful spine arched with passion, pale globes of breasts that rose and fell rapidly, full from his kneading. Her head was thrown back, a jumble of silvered curls spreading across the pillow, her eyelids closed, her lips moist and open, and he went suddenly still as the storm light vanished. Even his wild breathing halted, and at the silence her eyes fluttered open.

"Brock?—"

Drugged with desire, she peered at him hazily, her hands stirring on his flesh. But he had turned to stone beneath her fingers, and they hesitated. In the shadowed room, he was only a blacker shadow above her until lightning pierced the darkness again. In its glare she saw burning desire transformed into tortured recognition that made the planes of his face as sharp as broken glass. An instant later he wrenched himself free of her, crashing across the room and out. Heavy footsteps stumbled down the stairs, and the back door banged behind him as he sought refuge from one storm in another. Behind him, Verity still shook with longing, but it was nothing compared to the tears that wracked her as her passion died to ashes.

Chapter Eight

$\mathcal{F}$ace buried in her pillow, she cried uncontrollably while the storm raged overhead with renewed fury, drowning out the sound of her sobs. Heaped beside her were the covers Brock had thrown back to lay her on the bed, but now it held only Verity. She was alone, as she had been for so many years, and she wept without restraint, twisting and burrowing in the crumpled sheets as if she sought some secret passage out of all this pain.

There wasn't one, so she cried until she was limp. The pillow was drenched, and her hair clung to her salty cheeks in tendrils before her tears ran dry and her choked sobs subsided to gulps, then steady breathing at last. Straightening cramped limbs from her huddled position, she shuffled to the window as if she were a thousand years old.

Around her, everything was quiet. The storm had finally passed off to the south and east, murmuring faintly in the distance, and the first glimmer of dawn was beginning to light the underside of low clouds. The air was freshly washed, and beneath her window the lake was a pewter plate under a pale gray sky. Dark with moisture, the sand had been hammered by the rain, and each leaf or blade of grass bore gleaming droplets.

After the storm, only serenity remained outside, but here in her room misery seemed to lurk in the corners, gritty and pervasive. Suddenly wild to escape, she turned from her window and fumbled with her clothes from the dresser, dragging on jeans, a jersey and sweater with awkward haste. A brush raked through her hair, she held it back with a headband and caught up her shoes, hurrying from the room.

In the hall her nightgown still lay where it had fallen, sad as a forgotten gift; sweeping it up, she flung it back toward her bed and rushed on without looking to see where it landed. A glance at each door showed her Toby and Pierre slept undisturbed. Otherwise, the lighthouse almost echoed with emptiness. Slipping out through the kitchen, she left it behind for the tranquil fullness of the sunrise.

While the eastern sky turned from gray-blue to celadon to gold and rose, she headed across the yard. Brushing through the wet grass until she was soaked to the knees, she made for the shore beyond the lighthouse and picked her way aimlessly along the rocks. As she walked, Verity began to think.

Outside, it was somehow easier to recognize the truth. With granite solid beneath her feet and the ageless lake-song singing to her left, it was easier to see beyond the moment Brock left her, to the realization that remained. She was in love with him. It was that simple—and that stunning. After keeping her heart locked away for so long, she had somehow fallen in love with Brock Randall.

Abruptly, Verity sat down on the nearest boulder while

small waves lapped at her feet unnoticed. *That* was why she'd given up any idea of trying to persuade Pierre to leave. It was why her concentration was in shreds and her emotions keyed up; it was why she forgot what she was doing and cried easily. If she hadn't decided years ago that it was far safer to feel nothing than to risk loving, she would have recognized the symptoms sooner.

Innate honesty made her wonder if she would have avoided them, and she stirred uncomfortably on her rock as some niggling voice of self-preservation reminded her how painless the last eight years had been. Uncommitted and uncaring outside of court, she'd poured her only emotions into her cases, where professionalism kept her safe. Longing, jealousy, doubt, even desire—she had desperately locked them out. And felt nothing much at all.

That was the price, of course, a braver voice observed. Her heart might have been safe, but it was shriveled too. Years passed, and she missed so many other emotions besides the ones she avoided. Along with much of Toby's childhood, she missed the joy and discovery, exhilaration and fulfillment she could have had then. She was only learning them now because a teenage girl with a new driver's license cut too close to his wobbling bicycle. The morning air was suddenly chilly, and she shivered. She'd gotten a second chance with Toby; was Brock a second chance too?

Sheer panic flared along her nerves at the thought of risking her heart again. Loving Toby was dangerous enough. That one small body, fragile flesh and blood, already made her subject to so much worry and grief. In a world with accidents and illness, separation and death, how could she possibly risk loving Brock too?

But how could she not? It was already too late. Fear fell silent, and her lips curved in a sweetly reckless smile as his image rose before her. Brock, with his towering height and lean grace, his broad shoulders and compassionate hands. Brock, with his stubborn, masklike reserve and his scarred, magnificent body. But she'd seen behind that reserve, and she'd begun to know that body. Like wax in the sun, he could melt.

She was moving again. Without even knowing that she'd hopped off her rock, she was clambering gracefully from one boulder to the next, poised for a second and swooping off again just for the joy of movement. When the sound came the first time, she assumed vaguely that it must be a loose stone, squealing against the next one, or the branch of a tree, rubbing against another trunk. But when it occurred a second time, it was a thin, tired wail, and the frightened sound cut through her reveries.

Racing along the shore now, she slithered and slid on the wet brown rocks, trusting the rubber soles of her jogging shoes to keep her from breaking a leg. But no one should be that terrified, not a loon caught in some half-submerged net or—

A child. Scrambling over a massive boulder, she slipped down the far side and toward the battered remains of an old wooden fishing boat, while the sight before her printed on her brain like an instant photograph. Bow in, the boat was wedged between two rocks. The oarlocks were empty and its propellor bent, jutting twisted and useless at the stern while incoming waves broke past it. At least eighteen inches of lakewater already sloshed lazily back and forth in the bottom of the boat, and soon the hull would be resting on the rocks four feet below the surface. But lashed to the forward seat by a line tied to his tiny orange life preserver was a child of about five.

He must have been trapped there for hours, until he'd just about given up any hope of rescue. Small sneakers pulled up onto the seat, he crouched, huddling with his head bowed in exhaustion while the cries came even more faintly than when Verity first heard them. How long he might have been calling, and what must have happened before that to the boat's owner, were prospects Verity couldn't even bear to think about. She just reacted on pure instinct.

"Oh, my lord—" The exclamation burst forth as she dropped into chest-deep water beside the boat, reaching to steady it against her body.

"Poor lamb, poor baby, hang on—" she murmured despite the shock of Superior's chilly waters. "Let's get you out of here, sweetie, hmmm?"

At the sound of her voice the child looked up and struggled off the seat, splashing into the water in the bottom of the boat.

"Daddy!" he croaked, trying to reach Verity with a last burst of energy. But the boat rocked sluggishly, and the small figure fell against one of the stern seats, sobbing forlornly. "I want my daddy!"

Daddy. That heartbroken wail knifed her, but Verity knew that she couldn't make any soothing promises like "Daddy's waiting for you." The fury of last night's storm had probably claimed him as yet another of the countless souls Superior had taken over the ages. All she could hope to do was keep this child from the same fate.

"Come on, love," she encouraged him through teeth that chattered reflexively. "Come on over here, so you can just step over the side into my arms."

But the child had reached the limits of his strength. "I c-c-can't," he cried, clinging terrified to the seat while another wave washed in over the stern. It caught him across the face, and he sputtered helplessly. "I can't!"

Fleetingly, fervently, Verity wished that Brock were at hand. How she needed that calm strength! But he wasn't there, and any minute the boat could sink completely or break up on the rocks. Taking a deep breath, she set both hands on the boat's gunwales and flung her weight onto them, straightening her elbows and kicking off from the lake bottom.

The action forced down the side of the boat, tilting it so that much of the water it was carrying slopped in her face. But at the same time the child slid down the angled seat toward her. With another kick, Verity balanced on her right arm and used her left to scoop up the little boy and haul him across the gunwales as the line to his lifejacket parted. Then her right arm collapsed under their combined weight, and they both dropped into the lake, while the boat jolted away from them.

Hitting the water, the child shrieked and thrashed. But Verity, ignoring a stinging pain in her right elbow, got her feet under her and gathered the struggling body tightly to her own.

"Ooof!"

A wild kick caught her in the side, but then as he realized that she had him, his two small arms wrapped tightly around her and his face pressed into her neck.

"There you are, lamb," Verity panted, "safe and sound."

That wasn't entirely true yet, of course, and she knew it. Somehow she had to get them both back on shore and then to the lighthouse. But adrenaline was still coursing through her, so she turned and started forging her way home, leaving the boat to sink or break up or drift to safety by itself.

Twice she lost her footing in the water, picking her steps laboriously as she looked for a place where she could climb out with both hands occupied. Before she finally found her way to shore, she was as exhausted and bedraggled as the child in her arms. She was breathless, too. Not until they reached dry land did the stranglehold around her neck ease slightly, so Verity could at least draw a few deep breaths. And even then, the cold little face against her skin stayed where it was.

Verity didn't try asking her burden to walk for himself, though. Mute and bewildered, he needed to be held and cuddled more than she needed relief from his weight. Getting a better grip on the small figure in its bulky lifejacket, she plodded on, crooning nonsense in a husky voice.

By the time they reached the lighthouse, she was so winded that she'd fallen silent, and even getting the back door open was a problem. Able to free only a few fingers, she lost her hold on it the first time. Half-open, it slammed shut again. The second try worked, but by now their entrance had been announced.

Partway across the kitchen, she glimpsed Brock raising his head from his hands and standing up at his desk in the next room. At the same time the thud of bare feet heralded Toby on the stairs, and even Pierre came slowly from his room, walking carefully and rolling back the long sleeves of Brock's pajamas.

"What was that?"

"Mom!"

"My God, what happened?"

At their voices, she looked up thankfully, just as they reached her. Loaded down and breathing hard, however, with her clothes plastered to her and her hair in damp curly tendrils, she couldn't have been a reassuring sight.

"You all right, my dear?" Pierre asked. "And the child?"

A nod was all Verity could manage past the boy in her arms, but the old man gave her a smile of approval, lowering himself into a kitchen chair. "Well, then."

Meanwhile, Toby patted her left arm anxiously, crowding close to convince himself that she really was all right. On her other side Brock was more practical, big hands gently unwrapping the limpet grip on her.

"All right, champ," he murmured. "Let's give you a higher perch."

One deft move that Verity watched with pleasure as well as relief and a small sneaker dangled over each broad shoulder, while short arms wound around Brock's head like a turban. On a tear-stained face, faint interest flickered at this novel view of the world. Below that, the second face was harder to read.

"What happened?" Brock repeated, steadying the wet sneakers with his hands.

"He got stranded in a fishing boat driven onto the rocks by the storm," Verity explained. "I was out walking about an hour ago and heard him calling, so here we are."

Smiling over Brock's head, she downplayed her rescue efforts and didn't mention her fears about the boat's owner. She didn't say why she'd gone walking at dawn, either, and Brock registered all the omissions. He didn't meet her eyes, but a complex expression flickered across his face.

"Taking shelter," he concluded in a peculiar tone. "Why don't you go get yourself dry, while Toby and I see if we can do the same for your friend here?"

He patted one sneaker, and high in the air a small head nodded in hesitant agreement.

"Sure, Mom," Toby chimed in. Deciding that he was almost an adult in comparison to the child on Brock's shoulders, he suggested earnestly, "My clothes'll be way too big, but I bet we could tie them around him somehow so they wouldn't fall down—"

"Sounds good, Toby," Verity concurred gravely, and looked away before Toby could see her eyes dance, tired as she was. Her glance crossed Brock's, and for a split second they gazed straight into each other. Like sparks, silent laughter flashed from her brown eyes to his gray ones. Then the contact was broken as the child on Brock's shoulders sneezed three times in quick succession.

Brock raised a hand to steady him through each lurch, and Toby, impressed by the volume of sound coming out of that little body, said, "Wow!—I mean, bless you. Gosh, we really *had* better get him dry, huh?"

He hauled at the hem of Brock's navy sweater to lead him away, and the three of them vanished up the stairs. Left behind, Pierre and Verity traded smiles.

"And you, my dear," he suggested, "are you going to change those wet clothes before you start to sneeze too?"

"Yes, of course—" she agreed.

"Otherwise, you'll be sick, and then who'll look after us all?" His face was gravely concerned, but above the white mustache his shrewd eyes twinkled.

On her way out the door Verity acknowledged the hit with a laugh, realizing gladly that Pierre's kind of affectionate teasing was a measure of how much better the old man was. Clearly, he was well enough again so that sometime soon they really should sit down together and discuss his case. This didn't seem to be the ideal moment, however, when she was dripping wet. Obedient to Pierre's suggestion, she left the kitchen. Upstairs in her own room she also discovered that she herself was a bit worse off than she'd realized.

After kicking off her shoes that left wet prints with every step, she shucked her soggy jeans and went to peel off her sweater as well. But starting to raise and bend both arms brought a jab of pain in the right one; it was so stiff at the elbow she could hardly use it.

"Ouch!"

Lowering her arms, she peered toward that right elbow, trying to see the trouble. The sweater seemed to be torn, but she couldn't tell any more without getting it off, and that was the problem. It took several minutes of careful one-handed contortions to drag off her sweater and the jersey beneath it.

Both let go with a sticky tug at the elbow that revealed a three-inch gash. Inspecting the damage in her mirror, Verity remembered the oarlock on that boat, catching at her as she hauled the child out of it. Her reddened sleeve had mopped up the worst results, but the cut still bled slowly. She was going to have to clean it and bandage it up.

Starting to shiver, though, she scrambled out of her clammy underwear first, working her way awkwardly into dry panties and corduroy slacks that felt blessedly warm against her skin. That left her naked from the waist up, however, and ruefully Verity recognized that the next steps would be a good deal more difficult. She could do without a bra, but somehow she was still going to have to cope with both a bandage and her shirt, one-handed.

With clean clothes piled on the rumpled bed in front of her, she was trying to work it out when someone knocked on her door.

"Verity?"

It was Brock, and her heart leaped. "Yes?"

"Are you all right? You've been up here a long time."

And was likely to be a good deal longer! "Never mind—I'll be fine," she called, a little breathless with suppressed laughter and something else.

He must have heard the odd tone in her voice, though, as well as her actual words, because he didn't simply go away. "I'm coming in," he said flatly, just as she snatched up the shirt with her good hand.

It was the first time she'd seen him alone since he left her here the night before to cry until her tears ran out, and to realize that she loved him. As he walked in with that lean grace of his, she couldn't help feeling a surge of pure excitement at the sight of him. After all the empty years, she'd fallen in love with this enigmatic, passionate man, and elation swept away dawn's first panic.

That didn't change the fact, however, that she was standing there in front of him half-naked. Reflexively, she clutched the shirt to her bare breasts, while color flooded her skin. She might have been wearing a great deal less last night, but not in full daylight and—more or less!—full control.

Brock closed the door behind him and strode across the room, his face impassive and his eyes their usual crystal. But they had to see Verity's own golden gaze, full of warmth and embarrassment and laughter, the wild rose pink suffusing her cheeks, the satin skin of her bare shoulders and—just partly hidden by the plaid shirt she held with one hand—the soft fullness of her breasts that rose and fell with the turmoil of her emotions.

He crossed the room to her and watched how her breathing accelerated and a tiny shiver ran across her skin, both evident on those creamy breasts. By the time he stood directly in front of her, his eyes were turning a molten silver. But then he caught sight of her blood-stained arm and they changed again, suddenly becoming opaque.

"What happened?" he asked, taking her wrist in one big hand so he could rotate it gently and see the extent of the damage.

"The boat, I think," she explained vaguely, feeling his touch as she never had the oarlock. It washed over her skin like hot water, spreading in ripples up and down her arm, and she quivered. "I didn't really notice at the time—"

Running his fingers lightly past the cut as he checked to see how deep it was, he made an unidentifiable sound. His head was bent and he stood at an angle to her now, but she tried to figure out what that had been. A snort of disbelief or impatience, maybe? That must be it.

She pulled herself together. "It's nothing much, though. I just need to get a Bandaid on it—"

"Well, you won't have much luck with it by yourself."

The answer was flat and uncompromising. Remembering the trouble she'd had getting this far, she knew that he was right. But she darn well wasn't going to ask him for help when she had next to nothing on. He didn't wait to be asked, however.

"Sit down," he said, and it was a tone that brooked no

argument. Her eyes wide, she stared at him, but he met the look unyieldingly. A dull ache was beginning to throb in her arm, and suddenly she gave up trying to cope on her own. Docile for once, she sat, perched on the edge of the bed.

A glinting look acknowledged this unusual obedience before he turned and walked to her washstand, gathering up soap, a damp facecloth and her towel. Crouching beside her, so that his burnished head was only a few inches higher than her own, he steadied her arm in one hand and used the other to swab at the blood that had dried on her skin.

His touch was light, and she was so distracted by his nearness that she barely noticed. All she was conscious of was the texture of his hair and beard, the faint heat that seemed to radiate from his tanned skin, the scent of him.

But he just continued working. Turning the cloth, he cleaned the cut itself too, standing up when he finished. Then he left the room for a minute while she simply sat where she was, bemused, until he returned with gauze and adhesive tape. Unfortunately, he also had bottles of alcohol and iodine, and the next step was harder to overlook.

When he finished, her skin was as white as the bulky bandage on her arm, and the plaid shirt was a crumpled wad at her chest, held in clenched fingers. More of her than ever was visible, but she was past caring. Nevertheless, as he set aside his supplies and stood at last, she looked up to thank him with a quick gallant smile. It was as much as she could manage, and she ducked her head again, her free hand shaking a little as she loosened her clutch on the shirt.

Gazing down at her tangled curls and slight shoulders with an expression she couldn't see, he said abruptly, "You can't handle that for yourself, can you?"

"No." She was too drained for stubborn independence, and the admission came in a small voice.

"Give it to me."

That brought her head up again, and she searched his face intently while color flared and faded in her cheeks, leaving them whiter than ever. Rational thought was beyond her, but what she saw in him reassured her insensibly. Without a word, she handed him the shirt.

"Can you stand up?"

"I think so."

Levering herself from the bed with her left arm, she missed the depth of emotion that transformed his face at the fragile, trusting beauty of her. Urgently, he blanked it out, and by the time she stood upright before him, swaying slightly, nothing remained but that flare of the nostrils.

"Lean on me," he said.

Without question, she did so, resting on his chest with her face turned so that her cheek was against the broad expanse of his sweater and she could hear the measured thud of his heartbeat. It might have been faster than usual, but she was too tired to be analytical. Her eyes closing, she just knew dimly that it was good to have him care for her.

She felt him move a little and heard the tiny rustle of fabric as he gathered up a sleeve of the shirt, about to ease it up her right arm. Halfway, however, it stopped at the thick bandage that protected the gash at her elbow. Too tight to fit over, it caught, and she breathed an involuntary murmur of pain.

"Damn!" His comment was a rumble beneath her cheek, and the ghost of a smile flickered across her lips. She didn't move, content to let him decide what to do.

A pause, and he held her off from him a few inches, keeping her wrapped in one long arm while the other did something else. Then he switched arms, and some object dropped softly to the floor while he kept on working at another. Finally, fabric slipped easily up her arm over the bandage, warm to the touch, just as he shifted her again.

Her cheek settled back on his chest, but this time no wool met her skin, only skin, matted with hair.

The other sleeve slid into place while she registered slowly what had happened. He'd stripped off his sweater and given her his own shirt, still warm from his body. Even though it hung on her, the shirt's intimate heat gave her a sense of possession, of belonging to him in some primitive way. Still unbuttoned, it billowed from her shoulders with no barrier to separate her from him, and her bare breasts were crushed against him. It was as if he'd never left last night, but stayed until—passion spent—she lay exhausted in his arms. With a wordless sigh she nestled wearily closer, drawing in the scent and feel of him.

For once he didn't pull away, and a sweet eternity passed by. Slowly she grew heavier against him, though, as comfort slipped into sleep. She was hardly aware when he freed a hand to smooth her tumbled bed and then slipped an arm beneath her knees, lowering her into it. Nor did she know how long he stood beside her, seeing exhaustion smoothed from her face and the soft rhythm of her breathing grow deeper.

Chapter Nine

She slept dreamlessly for five hours, not waking until early afternoon. The dark green shades at her windows had been pulled to keep out the sun, but the room was flooded with a dim golden green light, like some underwater cavern. Swimming up to consciousness, she yawned and began to stretch, stopping with a smothered yelp at the warning jab from her right elbow. Lowering it cautiously, she found the pad of bandages protecting it and cradled it in her other palm while memory drifted back.

Brock had cared for her, mending her torn skin with tender hands and wrapping her in his own shirt. Now it lay folded across her chest, her fingers discovered, lingering to twirl a button absently. He'd come in to check on her . . . after seeing to the child she brought home . . . from walking at dawn when she first realized she loved him.

Whatever his past, wherever he'd come from and

whatever haunted him, she did love him. He was mysterious and contradictory, explosively passionate one moment and withdrawn the next, but she didn't care. Whatever doors he'd slammed in her face before this and might yet again, he had still kept them open this morning to hold and comfort her when she needed him. For the first time he had shown her too that vast compassion, and she loved him. After all those hollow years she was alive with loving—dangerously, magically alive, and she didn't mind the risks.

Sliding from her bed, she raised the windowshades, letting in a wave of golden sunlight to fill the room the way it already filled her heart. Brock's shirt flapped around her, but she didn't even consider taking it off. One-handed, she fastened most of the buttons, smiling at her disreputable image in the mirror. For decency's sake, though, she inched her way into a loose red jacket that confined the billowing folds. With a few clumsy strokes of the hairbrush, and dry loafers she could just slip on, she looked reasonably presentable.

Downstairs, she found Pierre and the two boys in the kitchen. While the old man finished a cup of coffee, Toby was busy gobbling sandwiches. A milk mustache on his upper lip, he had the peanut butter and a loaf of bread close at hand and was clearly in no danger of starvation. The child she'd rescued from the rocks, however, was another case.

On the plate in front of him was another of Toby's culinary achievements, a bulging peanut butter sandwich. But it had been abandoned with only its edges nibbled, and beside Toby's sturdy form, the younger boy looked smaller than ever. Swathed in Toby's clothes—as big on him as Brock's shirt on Verity—he was nearly invisible in them. Above his minute bare feet, the jeans were rolled at the ankles and folded at the waist, while the red and white striped jersey had shoulders that reached his elbows and sleeves that flopped down to cover all but his fingertips.

Over everything was a shock of black hair and two enormous dark eyes, liquid with tears.

"Mom!" Toby caught sight of her in the doorway, his voice echoing with relief.

"Verity, my dear, how are you feeling?" Pierre asked, rising slowly.

"Fine, thank you—almost as good as new, in fact." She smiled warmly, adding conviction to her words, and he sank back into his chair with a satisfied nod.

Meanwhile, Toby had bounded to his feet, rushing over to drag her into the room—luckily, by her left arm. "We thought you were *never* going to wake up, but Brock wouldn't let me see you."

Silently, Verity wondered how on earth Brock had managed to deflect her son. But Toby was still talking, words tripping over each other, and she got her answer.

"He said I had to stay with Nick—he doesn't talk, but his life preserver says his name is Nick—and make sure he really is okay. We got him dried off and dressed, but he won't eat anything. Mom, what are we going to do?"

Running out of breath, Toby paused expectantly. Her hand still linked with his, Verity looked past him to the waif beyond, and her heart turned over at the contrast. Inwardly, she prayed that that lost and hopeless look would never dim her son's bright face too, the way it had done to Nick. But right now she had to answer Toby's question.

Releasing his warm fingers with a squeeze, she nudged him back to his chair and walked toward the one next to it. "Well," she said matter-of-factly, "I guess we'll have to decide about that."

Without waiting for a reply, she went on, "If you don't mind sharing your chair, Nick, we might as well just sit here right now and figure out what's next."

"You can have my chair, Mom—or Brock's," Toby offered, puzzled.

"Thanks, Toby, but I'll be fine here, if Nick says it's all right."

An uncertain nod gave her permission, and she slid onto the seat beside him, using her left arm to swing him up on her lap as if it were the most natural thing in the world. For a minute the small figure sat rigid, then it curled into her body. Across the table, Pierre's tiny nod acknowledged her tactics while beside her Toby stared from one adult to the other.

"Oh-h-h—I get it!"

Verity shushed him with a laughing look over Nick's head, and he subsided, grinning.

"So what *are* you going to do, Verity?" Pierre inquired, and she grew serious again, just as the back door opened.

Brock stood in the doorway, and before she could venture an answer, he supplied one for her. "As soon as she feels up to it, she's going to take him into Grand Marais and try to find his people," he announced categorically.

Through the surge of joy that seemed to flood her whenever he appeared, Verity heard the brisk tone of his voice. Far different from the way he'd spoken while he bandaged her elbow, it was as clear as a billboard telling her things were back on their usual footing, as if the past twenty-four hours had never happened. Wryly, she reminded herself that just because she'd realized that it wasn't worth living without the risk of loving didn't mean he had too. Then she made herself concentrate on what he'd said.

"Yes, of course," she agreed. Remembering her car's automatic shift, she added, "I can do it this afternoon, if you think—"

Breaking off, she didn't voice her fears that Nick might not have any people left, if his only family had been on that boat in the storm. Unconsciously, she held him more tightly as Brock strode to the stove, poured himself a cup of coffee and dropped into the empty chair by Pierre. His mind must have been running along the same lines as hers, however, because he spoke to the old man next.

"Can you think of anyone in the village who might have a child about this age?" he asked. Setting his elbows on the table, he linked both hands around his cup while Pierre frowned thoughtfully, running a meditative finger along his luxuriant mustache.

"Yes, I think so," he answered. "In spite of the young people who move away to find work and don't come back till they've retired, there are still some families with small children in the area."

With a regretful shake of his snowy head, he added, "The trouble is I'm afraid I don't know everyone well enough anymore to be sure which family it would be."

But at least there might be a mother, even brothers and sisters—

Encouraged, Verity spoke up. "Even if you could just give me a list of some possible names and addresses, Pierre, that would be a good start."

For the first time Brock glanced directly across the table at her. A shaft of sunshine falling into the room turned her hair to molten gold, and hope lighted her mobile face, in spite of the faint smudges that still lingered under her eyes. She hadn't tried to change her clothes yet, either. The brave red jacket only hid part of his shirt; it lay open at her throat to show the pulse that beat in the delicate hollow of her collarbone. Beside her Toby was a smaller replica, as warm and candid as his mother, while on her lap was another child, the opposite of them both. As dark as they were fair, as frightened as they were fearless, Nick nestled into the crook of her good arm. While Brock watched, Nick burrowed deeper, and she cuddled him to her. Then all three turned toward the men across the table.

Facing Pierre and Brock, Verity realized that this was the first time they'd all sat there together. With a child beside her and another on her lap, she had a half-formed thought that they were almost a family—one made by accident instead of intent, but still a sort of family. Before the idea could finish taking shape, however, Brock spoke again. He'd lowered his head all of a sudden, so he could see little more than the inside of his coffee cup, and his voice was as coldly withdrawn as it had ever been.

"Fine," he said distantly, standing up. "If Toby will gather up Nick's clothes, I'll find something for Pierre to write on and then walk you out to your car."

Impelled by him, they were heading toward Verity's car in a matter of minutes. Leaving her with nothing but her car keys to carry, Toby clutched a plastic bag with Nick's own soggy clothes in it, and Brock carried Nick himself, perched astride the broad shoulders again.

From that vantage point, Nick probably had the most enjoyable walk along the shore, although Toby also seemed content as he trudged along. But for the first half of the hike, Brock seemed blind to the beauty of the trail, lost in thought and looking neither right nor left as they walked. Verity, too, was distracted. Acutely conscious that this was the farthest away from the lighthouse she'd ever known him to come, she could almost feel the effort it cost Brock to do so.

It wasn't that the distance was so great, or the burden of Nick's few pounds so heavy. But with every step they took toward the outside world, she could sense Brock's reluctance increasing. He'd had to come, though, given that Nick was too tired to walk the whole distance and that she couldn't carry him so far with only one arm. If Brock wanted to reunite Nick with whatever family he might have, this was the only way. But the haunting question was whether he cared more about returning a child to his people or about getting yet another unwelcome guest out of his cottage.

Like so many questions before it, she had no answer to that one either. It went on her list of puzzles about Brock, and she thought with frustration that she hadn't had many cases as tough as the mysteries about him—or any cases at all that she cared about as deeply as she cared about him. Not that caring had taught her any more about him yet!—With an explosive little sigh, she gave up wondering and settled for admiring.

He'd gotten ahead of her, and she watched him go. Nick on his back and Toby chattering beside him, he moved in and out of the shadows that dappled the trail. Walking with a smoothness that seemed almost contradictory in a man so big, he covered the ground with long strides, while she feasted her eyes on the lithe, animal grace of him and listened absentmindedly to the sound of voices drifting back.

"Y'mean there really *is* something called a loon?" Toby was asking incredulously.

"Of course. Why not?"

Like everything else he'd said since they left the lighthouse, Brock's answer was hardly expansive. Clearly, he was still prey to whatever thoughts those were that made her feel such an intense reluctance in him. But that sort of thing had never discouraged Toby before, and it didn't this time either.

"Well, everybody says 'loony' and 'crazy as a loon' and stuff like that," he conceded. "But I didn't know there was any such thing."

"Sure. As a matter of fact, you can see them around here fairly often. They're handsome big black and white birds that fish offshore."

"And *are* they?"

Nick didn't seem to be paying much attention, and Brock was still aloof, but Toby was as cheerfully persistent as always.

"Are they what?"

"Loony," Toby repeated. "Are they?"

Whatever Brock had been thinking about must have

faded away. He started to chuckle, almost reluctantly at first, but relaxing into a full-fledged laugh, rich and contagious. "Sorry!" was all he managed for a minute. Then in the face of Toby's patient interest, he got his amusement back under control and explained, "I think 'loony' is from 'lunatic', Toby, and no, they're perfectly sane. I have to admit they don't always sound like it, though."

Easing up, his voice had completely lost the earlier tension. It still carried an undertone of laughter, and Verity listened to it in delight. Toby, however, paid more attention to Brock's actual words.

"Huh?" he inquired concisely, and even Nick's otter-sleek head bent a little to hear.

"They've got a call pretty much like this"—Brock demonstrated the laughing cry of a loon—"and if you call back to them, they'll keep on answering you, over and over again for as long as you can stand it."

"Honest?" Toby was entranced. "I could go like that, and they'd *talk* to me?!"

"Uh-huh," Brock confirmed, and Nick nodded in agreement.

"Oh, boy!"

Head thrown back, Toby immediately started practicing a reedy version of Brock's call. When he paused for breath, Brock hooted another demonstration, and in seconds the trail echoed with demented mirth. Verity, straggling along behind because she was almost too convulsed with laughter to walk, decided it didn't matter; lunatic might be the root word, but these loons at least were clearly loony. But she'd never heard Brock play before; he was as silly and unself-conscious as Toby himself.

All too soon, though, they reached the clearing where her car waited beside the dirt road, and the laughter died away, leaving only constraint in its place. Verity felt it descend on them like starch, and Brock must have been equally aware. The reason they were here came rushing back, and even Toby fell silent.

For an instant she almost thought Brock was going to say something to Nick anyway—good-bye, good luck, *something*. She saw his hands give the small figure on his shoulders a quick squeeze and heard him take a deep breath. But then the impulse died. Swinging the little boy down from that great height, he handed Nick over and just said briefly, "I'll leave you now. I'm off to go get Pierre's things."

With those words he turned his back and vanished into the woods, while Verity caught her breath at last. Hand in hand with Nick, she led the way to her car, wondering what Brock had almost said—what he'd been thinking about before Toby brought up loons—why it was that he'd been so determined to send Nick back to the village today. . . .

Settling both boys in the front seat, she was sure of nothing except the one fundamental fact that she seemed to love Brock Randall more each minute, so that all he had to do was walk away into the woods and she felt as if the sun had suddenly disappeared. An hour later she was entering Grand Marais, hoping to find the first few answers about him. Before that, however, they had to solve the problem of Nick: who he was and where he belonged.

Driving slowly into the village from the west, with Nick beside her and Toby beyond, she was just going to reach for Pierre's list of names, lying on the dashboard. She had her right hand raised gingerly when, without warning, Nick batted it from in front of him with a banshee screech. "DADDY!"

Transformed from the numb, silent child of the light-house, he was a whirling dervish, shrieking and scrambling over Toby so he could dive from a moving car. Trampled, Toby somehow retained enough sense not to let Nick go, catching him by the back pockets of his jeans, while Verity pulled over. But the instant she'd come to a stop, Nick wrenched himself from Toby's grip and slid out the open window, without even waiting for the door. Then he took off, his small bare feet racing.

Still shouting, he charged toward a haggard man coming despondently out the door of the nearest house. At the racket, that bowed figure straightened with a jerk, dropping the red gas tank he'd been carrying, and snapped around to stare in their direction. Then he gave a hoarse answering cry as he caught sight of Nick's flying form and began to run heavily. The space between them vanished, and Nick threw himself into his father's arms.

For a long time the two clung together, motionless. In the car Verity had leaned over beside her own son to watch, and they sat quietly too. Pressed against her, Toby whispered, "I guess we found Nick's dad, huh?" Silently, Verity nodded her agreement, knowing that she couldn't speak past the lump in her throat. She knew what it was to get a child back. . . .

Finally the two who held each other in a green side yard broke apart and rejoined, while Verity and Toby climbed from her dusty automobile. Hoisted high in his father's arms, Nick babbled a blue streak as they approached the car but fell silent instinctively as all four met.

A lean brown man a year or two younger than Brock, Nick's father held his son with sinewy hands whose knuckles were still white. As dark as Nick, he had the narrowed, far-seeing eyes of a fisherman, and they searched Verity's face while he hunted for words.

"Thank you for my son," he said huskily at last, and the simple words were as eloquent as the moisture that glistened on his high cheekbones.

"We were pulling in the nets by moonlight last night when that storm came out of nowhere. I tried to run for home ahead of it, but got knocked overboard, and when my line to the boat snapped I thought I'd lost Nick too."

His voice cracked, and impulsively Verity put a hand on his arm. She let it drop when he managed a crooked half-smile before going on. "I came to way down the banks, with no idea how I got there and no way to see but the lightning. I hunted for hours, then finally had to give up and follow the shore home when I couldn't find any trace of Nick. Before they came in for gas just now, even the search party this morning could only find one oar—"

His hands clenched again around his son, and Verity picked up for him. "Because Nick and your boat were up in the rocks near the lighthouse. I went out for a walk early this morning and heard him calling, cold and wet and frightened, but otherwise no worse for wear."

She said nothing about the danger Nick had been in when she found him, but the man in front of her could read between the lines. Past his son's slight body, he gave her an acknowledging look. She met it with a warm straight glance, then apologized. "I'm afraid we left the boat to fend for itself, though, because we'd both had enough exercise for one morning."

He shrugged that off. "I'll walk out and have a look tomorrow, but Nick is the only thing that matters."

The intensity of his voice reinforced the words. He must have heard it too, because with an effort he toned it down, almost as if he were afraid of feelings that strong.

"My name is Sam Fox, by the way, and Nick and I would be honored if you could both stay and have a meal with us."

"Verity Brandon," she returned, smiling in answer to his old-fashioned courtesy, "and this is my son Toby— and we'd be delighted to stay."

Beside her Toby beamed in agreement. Nick wriggled free of his father's arms, sliding to the ground as he shouted, "C'mon, Toby!", and the two boys charged out of sight around the corner of Sam's neat frame house.

More sedately, the adults followed them to the door. Sam held it open for Verity, then hurried to the phone with a murmured excuse, dialing with fingers that still shook a little.

"Charley? Sam. He's found. Nick's here, safe and sound—Right."

Across the receiver Sam met Verity's eyes in a look of profound relief as he explained, "He went on the rocks out toward the lighthouse, and some folks found him before he got into any real trouble. But Charley, listen— thanks. And thank the men for me? Tell them it's all right. . . ."

His voice went deeper, and Verity glanced away until the receiver was replaced on the hook. Then Sam turned the tap on full and bent over the kitchen sink, splashing in the cold water for a minute before he groped for a towel. When he reappeared from the terrycloth folds, his brown face had lost its strain; in half an hour they were sitting down to a fresh salad, fried potatoes, and Lake Superior whitefish he'd grilled to perfection. While the boys wolfed their food and communicated mostly by whispers and giggles, their parents relied on less arcane communication.

"There's just Nick and me now—that's why he goes everywhere with me," Sam explained through the savory steam rising from a platter in front of him. "His mother left a year ago."

Verity made a sympathetic sound, and Sam shrugged resignedly.

"We got married when I was in the service in Texas, and she couldn't stand the winters up here. After Christmas the snow's so deep we all get cabin fever. Along about the end of February, in fact, it's so bad that everyone's just spoiling for a fight!" A quick grin made it graphic before he sobered again. "But coping's got to be even harder if you weren't brought up with it."

Even down in Ann Arbor, hundreds of miles to the south, Verity remembered, Michigan winters had gone on until everyone was nearly driven to distraction. Sam's

Texas bride must have been frantic to leave her husband and son and go. But Sam was still carrying on, as if he didn't get many chances to talk.

"Times around here haven't been real good, either. My folks've always been in logging, but I figured I'd try my hand at fishing on the side, even though it's not as good as the logging anymore."

He glanced at Nick's vivid face, turned to Toby, and then added almost to himself, "I guess if I'd had more experience out on the big lake, we wouldn't have gotten caught like that last night. Anyway, with the fishing off, that's why a lot of people around here are glad to have the park coming in: It's bringing some jobs and more visitors." With a quick shake of the head, he'd made his voice matter-of-fact again, and now he asked, "Didn't I hear in town that you came up here on something to do with all that?"

His straightforward interest was a far cry from Brock's prickly attitude, and Verity found it easy to tell him what she was trying to do for Pierre Dumont. Without realizing it, though, she gave him a much more balanced summary of the situation than she would have offered a couple of weeks ago—and didn't recognize that it was a result of her fiery discussion with Brock.

"So you're all at the lighthouse, eh?" Sam concluded. Those far-seeing eyes of his had noticed the oversize shirt she was wearing, but instead of making any comment on it he just pushed his chair back from the table and chuckled. "Well, I envy you."

Finishing her last bite, Verity looked puzzled, so Sam explained. "Not the trouble with Pierre or the court business. I'm glad to hear he's better, and glad it's you not me handling all that legal work. But as a kid I would have given everything I had to live in that lighthouse. Heck, I'd have hocked my parents and not thought twice!"

While Verity laughed, he added, "I tried to grow up quick so I could join the Coast Guard and get stationed out there, but they put in the automatic light while I was still in grade school, and there went my chance.''

He still looked rueful, and before she could change her mind about it Verity asked, "How did Brock Randall wind up there, then, Sam?''

Surprise flickered in Sam's eyes, but with that natural courtesy of his he didn't comment on her ignorance. All he said, lighting a cigarette, was, "I really don't know.''

The smoke wreathed in front of him, and he stared into it meditatively. The upward lift of his last words sounded as if he had more to say, though, so Verity stayed quiet while the boys carried on in their private language. And in a minute or two he started talking again.

"I've never known Brock all that well, even though he grew up here too." Eyes narrowed, Sam didn't see Verity start—or didn't show that he saw. He just went on thoughtfully, "He was a couple of years ahead of me in school, and I always kind of looked up to him, but we didn't get to be good friends. He may not have had a lot of time, of course. After his parents died when he was a little kid, he lived with his grandfather, and they spent hours and hours together building boats. I remember hearing they did it all by hand, the way folks used to do before those fiberglass boats started turning up everywhere—'' Sam shook his head, watching the smoke drift, while Verity remembered the perfect sloop in Brock's boatshed.

"I guess the old man got to needing a lot of care toward the end, too. Anyhow, his grandfather died about the time Brock graduated from high school, and he went off to college somewhere out of state. After that we only heard about him indirectly most of the time. He got a degree and started working as a TV reporter with one of the big networks. By the time I got out of the service, he was turning up on the evening news a lot, broadcasting from whatever hotspots seemed to be making the most trouble.''

A reporter? Something clicked into place, and Verity

remembered the pictures Toby had found in Brock's desk. Humane, insightful, they were all the sort of shots only the best of news teams would take. And the one of Brock himself— She'd felt a flash of recognition then but decided it was only because, beardless, his strong features seemed right for his personality. Now she knew that she really *had* recognized him, known him as a voice that always spoke out of international chaos with courage and integrity. No wonder she had been drawn to him so quickly. . . .

But Sam hadn't quite finished yet. Knocking a cigarette ash into the saucer under his coffee cup, he wrinkled his forehead, trying to remember. "Then—maybe eighteen months ago, say—we stopped seeing him, and last September he turned up here again for the first time in years. No explanation, no nothing. He didn't really have anything to say to anyone around here. But he set up out in the lighthouse, and we heard he'd made some deal about fixing it up with Ben Hall over in Munising—he's the Chief Ranger for the Park Service here, as well as the one friend Brock apparently did keep in touch with. Ben might even have some idea what's been going on in Brock's life. What brought him back all of a sudden, though, nobody else knows."

And that, in the end, was the answer Verity wanted most. All the others told her about his past, when what she really wanted was the key to his present. Finally she understood his fierce love for the unspoiled beauty of this area; his skill at shaping a boat from simple lumber; his tact and knowledge of Pierre; and even her own immediate attraction to him. But those had all come from the past, and none of them explained the paradox Brock had become now: a newsman who avoided the news; a cosmopolitan man who withdrew from the world; a passionate man who rejected his emotions.

When Sam and Nick saw them off in the slanting light of late afternoon, Verity drove back to the lighthouse

absorbed in everything she had learned—and not learned
—about Brock. The miles slipped away slowly beneath
her wheels, and she responded absentmindedly to Toby's
chatter, barely noticing the green and golden tunnel their
dirt road wound through. The car stirred up an aura of
gilded dust that drifted between the lengthening shadows,
but Verity didn't pay any attention.

With bits of Brock's past like tiny tiles before her eyes,
she was trying to create a mosaic of him now, but the
picture was incomplete. It showed a man who could easily
manage to live alone at the lighthouse, but not one who
would choose to do that at this stage in his life, dropping
out of a successful and important job.

Granted, those articles he said he was writing could
well relate to his life as a newsman. But otherwise he
seemed to have cut off all contact with the world of
international events he must know so well, forbidding
even that little radio she brought back from Marquette. So
what could possibly have made him cut off his life's
work?—and apparently his heart as well.

She was still trying to make the picture whole when
Toby darted ahead of her, shouting, "Brock, Pierre!
We're back—and Nick's got a father, and he's fine, and
we ate with them—"

With a start Verity realized that she'd gotten all the way
from the village to the lighthouse without thinking of
anything but Brock. He was all she saw at first, too.
Stripped to the waist, he was only wearing boots and
sawdust-streaked jeans that hung on narrow hips and
strained over the muscled strength of his thighs. His hair
and beard curled damply, while sweat shone on his bare
skin. Like a magnet, he drew her toward him and she
came without resistance, pulled forward by the need to be
near him again, to see him, to touch him—

Turned to Toby's words, he caught sight of her behind
her son and reached automatically for the denim shirt he'd
discarded. She came the last few steps toward him, and

their eyes met. Hers were clear and golden, his opaque
and pewter; but before he turned back to his work, he
tossed aside the shirt without putting it on. Neither of
them had said a word, and even Toby's voice telling Pierre
about their adventures came faintly to Verity's ears. But a
sense of homecoming blossomed in her, hopeful and
life-giving.

It faltered only when she finally saw beyond Brock.
Behind him the boatshed stood completely open for the
first time, and he was laying out ways from it to the water
while Pierre and Toby coached. Inside, the little sloop
stood poised in her cradle, and she was nearly finished.
With wide eyes fixed on the beautiful boat, Verity tried to
ignore a sudden irrational pang.

Chapter Ten

Sam's boat proved to be salvageable too. In the morning he and Nick found it just below the rocks, bow in the sand and rolling sluggishly on each incoming wave. Bailed out, with the propellor straightened and its engine working again, it was nearly as good as before. That still left it an elderly veteran of a fishing boat, of course, but Sam brought it past the lighthouse late the next afternoon anyway.

When he came by, Brock was finishing the metal ways that ran like track from the boatshed to the lake. Gathered around him, Pierre was busy consulting, Toby chattered happily, and Verity just admired, content for now to watch his broad shoulders and corded forearms strain the faded denim of his shirt. The ways aligned, he drove in long steel spikes, stretching and bending as he smashed down the sledge hammer with controlled violence.

Suddenly a hail rang across the water.

"Hello there, lighthouse crew!"

Sam's pleasant baritone had a treble echo. "Hiya, Toby!"

"Sam—hello!"

"Hey, Nick!"

Cutting his engine so it died on an asthmatic cough, Sam let the boat nose in against the L-shaped dock that ran along shore below the embankment and then out into the lake. While he stepped onto the dock and steadied the bow, Nick hopped out and scampered up the rocks, clutching a brightly colored bundle against his life preserver.

"I got your clothes!" he announced to Toby, handing over the jeans and jersey he'd worn at the lighthouse. Neatly washed and folded one moment, the next they were trailing like banners as the boys ran them to Toby's room.

Sam watched them go with a rueful shrug, then grinned at the other three. "That's one reason we came by, besides just saying hello. Pierre, Brock—good to see you both."

"And you, Sam Fox—with your son by your side again."

Before he turned and walked slowly off, the old man's greeting was heavy with sudden feeling. In contrast, Brock's was terse to the point of rudeness.

"Sam," he said flatly, returning to his interrupted work after he noted the warm look the other man was giving Verity.

The barely leashed power of his movements said volumes, but Sam didn't read them. As oblivious of the message as Brock was himself, Sam just gestured to his old boat with a flourish. "And Verity—we wanted you to see us back on an even keel."

While she chuckled at the turn of phrase, he explained, "Found the old girl down below the rocks and gave her some bailing out and sprucing up. New oars and a little work on the engine just now, and she's in business again. And that's thanks to you as well—if I hadn't had some idea where to look for her, she probably would have been battered to pieces before I found her.''

The flourish dropped away and he added quietly, ''I really owe you everything, Verity—my son and my livelihood both.''

''More to good luck than me, Sam, and dinner already made up for my part in it.''

She met his gaze evenly but set limits to his gratitude right away. And Sam, who saw so much with those narrowed eyes of his, understood everything she was saying. As Nick scrambled back down to the dock with Toby at his heels, his father gave Verity a crooked grin and a small one-handed salute of hail-and-farewell. Then with both hands, he scooped up his son.

''Okay, Nickles-and-Dimes, hop aboard!''

Giggling, Nick landed in the forward seat, and Sam stepped into the stern, pushing off from the dock. With an uneven roar, the engine caught raggedly, turning the boat toward the open water.

''Bye, everyone. Take care.''

''Good-bye, Sam, Nick!''

''So long, Toby—see ya 'round!''

Nick waved wildly from the bow, and Sam lifted a hand once from the stern. Then he set his face to the lake and didn't look back. Even when his old engine backfired without warning, making a sound that echoed over the water like a pistol shot, he only bent to the controls and didn't glance behind him—to see Verity and Toby flattened on the dock. They'd been waving good-bye, but in one split second the sharp report of Sam's engine reached them and a blow across the shoulders had knocked them both to the dock.

It was all so fast that Verity lay with her cheek on damp wood before she knew anything had happened. Then the lake was slapping just below her ear, and the green scent of the water was in her nostrils. A foot away Toby sprawled, gazing at her with eyes like saucers. "Mom?" he asked in a voice that wobbled.

"It's all right, tadpole."

She reassured him automatically, but her own voice wasn't very steady either. Trying to figure out what had happened, she realized that there was a weight across her back and craned her neck to see what it was. Brock lay with his elbows on the dock and his hands clasped at the back of his neck, his long body arched over both her and Toby like a curving shield.

While she watched, the hands released, dropping away from his bowed head so she could see his face. His skin was ashen and his eyes closed as he rolled away from them, gathering himself slowly to stand. Toby scrambled to his own feet, and opening his eyes, Brock reached down to pull Verity to hers. His grip was solid and she rose easily, but through their linked palms she could feel a deep tremor in him. Dropping her hand, he took an audible breath.

"I'm sorry," he said tightly. "I thought it was gunfire."

For an instant his eyes were defenseless, and she could look deep into some well of unforgotten horror.

"Brock—" she began, heartsick and wild to reach him.

Then she was closed out again. With no further explanation, he turned on his heel and walked away. Still shaken by what she'd glimpsed, Verity made no attempt to follow. Even Toby was subdued for once, sitting back down on the edge of the dock and watching his toes skim the water. She gave one narrow shoulder a squeeze and sat down beside him.

"And had Mr. Dumont been informed that relocation assistance was available to him?"

Facing Judge Clark's bench, the Assistant U.S. Attorney for the northern district of Michigan looked uncomfortable.

"No, Your Honor," he admitted. "I'm afraid that was somehow overlooked in this case."

"And your client, Ms. Brandon, had no idea it existed?"

"None, Your Honor," Verity confirmed. "He didn't know there was anywhere to turn."

"What has he been doing, then?"

"The only thing he could think of, Your Honor: living like a fugitive in the woods."

Judge Clark turned to the witness stand at the right of his bench. "As a matter of interest, what sort of conditions would a person encounter in those circumstances?" he asked.

Hitching up one leg of the gray trousers that were part of his uniform as Chief Ranger at the National Lakeshore Park, Benjamin Hall crossed an ankle over the other knee in his chair behind the stand.

"Bad ones, I'm afraid, Your Honor," he said slowly, running a meditative hand along his bearded chin. "In a case like Pierre Dumont's, the situation could get pretty terrible."

"Could you be specific, Chief Ranger Hall?" the judge asked.

He gave Verity a brief nod, and she walked back to sit at her table before his bench, hearing the rustle of people settling to listen. Sitting down at a matching table beside hers, Jim Feenstra folded his arms across the chest of his light gray suit and tried to listen impassively. Behind them both, in carved white oak pews, a score of spectators sat motionless or fanning themselves quietly. Brown and wrinkled or fresh and smooth, each face was turned to the witness stand.

"Right, Your Honor," Ben Hall agreed. "Well, when an individual accepts a payment for property condemned by the government, of course that property is gone and he loses all legal standing as owner. But if he won't or can't go too, then we have to consider him a trespasser if he tries to continue living in the area, just as a park visitor would be.''

While the court stenographer tapped his words into shorthand, Ben absently adjusted the pens in his shirt pocket with one hand. "Obviously, then, he has to avoid contact with the park personnel, by trying to leave no signs that he's around. He can't keep more than a few clothes and some bedding, a cooking pot or two, and something to store canned food in—no more than he can carry with him quickly.''

Vividly, Verity saw again the pathetic little heap that was all Pierre's possessions. As he'd said he would, Brock had brought them back to the lighthouse that day she found Nick. . . . But this was no time for her to let her attention wander again while Ben was still talking. Verity concentrated on his words.

"In the meantime, structures on condemned property are dismantled if they're in areas visible to the general public, or allowed to molder if they're more remote.''

He paused, but Verity stayed still and didn't interrupt. Neither—somewhat to her surprise—did Jim Feenstra. Behind the bench, Judge Clark listened expressionlessly, but the spectators' faces were intent and sympathetic.

Continuing, Ben added with a concerned shake of his head, "That happens real fast in a climate like this when it gets down to a foot below zero. Without any repairs at all, the snowfall over a couple of winters can take down a roof, and after that everything else goes quickly. Wood rots, animals move in, and the forest overruns the place.''

Even in this spacious paneled chamber, the still air was unusually hot for the beginning of summer. Like a blanket of feathers, it seemed to press down on everyone in the room. But all that heat lost its impact for a moment with Ben's words. A shiver ran over Verity's skin, and behind her the soft sound of fanning papers fell silent. Desolation echoed in that simple description. Ben hadn't quite finished, either.

"Anyone like Pierre, whose place was dismantled and who was trying to manage by moving from one building to the next as each rotted away, would have to tolerate conditions that went from bad to worse. Except in winter, it wouldn't be a whole lot better than living outside. And even that old man, who's got to know every survival trick there is, can't get by like that indefinitely."

The ranger stopped speaking, and a ripple of sympathy swept the spectators. Rising to face the judge again herself, Verity picked up from Ben while that murmur was still audible.

"No," she agreed vehemently, "even he can get sick and be too ill to fend for himself—too ill to use the tricks he knows, or to go for food when he's run out, or even to move his bed from under the leak that's giving him pneumonia—"

"Point taken, Counselor." Looking over the tops of his glasses, Judge Clark cut off her impassioned speech. "You can stop now."

She bit back any more words, while the judge addressed Ben again. "And Mr. Dumont's original property, Chief Ranger Hall, was located where?"

"Right along the lakeshore, Your Honor, in the heart of the park and on some of the most ecologically vulnerable land. The government did consider offering a lifetime lease, but the site was just too important. And Mr. Dumont did consent to sell out."

"Thank you. You may step down now."

As Ben stood up and walked quietly back to sit in one of the carved pews Judge Clark consulted a sheaf of papers before him. Glancing up, he asked, "And this, Mr. Feenstra, is the correct amount of the payment Mr. Dumont received?"

"Yes, Your Honor."

"A respectable sum, it would seem."

"The government appraiser thought so," he agreed, and Verity rose to cut in swiftly.

"Perhaps, Your Honor, but as you can see from the comparative property values presented below, it isn't anywhere near the cost of the same size piece of land farther along the shoreline, even without allowing for the unusual beauty of the property he gave up."

Tilting his head to look through his glasses for a change, the judge surveyed Verity's figures on the pages he held. "Why, then, did he accept it?"

"Because he had no idea there was any alternative! That, too, the government somehow *neglected* to tell him." She let indignation infuse her tone, and Jim Feenstra began to look ill at ease again.

"Is that the case?" Judge Clark glanced at him for confirmation.

"Yes, Your Honor. Unfortunately, it seems to be."

"And he didn't think to ask, Ms. Brandon?"

"No, Your Honor, he didn't."

"Hmmmm."

Judge Clark looked thoughtful, and Verity brushed her notes aside, stepping out from behind her table so she could stand facing him.

"Your Honor, if I may explain—"

He nodded permission, and she took a deep breath.

"Pierre Dumont is a simple man, Your Honor, and he has always led a simple life. Born and raised in Grand Marais, he has hardly ever left that area. A cottage and a few possessions—besides the beauty of the lake he loved, those were all he needed, and all he knew. If he thought about the federal government, it was only to feel a wordless thanksgiving that this was a country where a man could live as he liked in such a place."

Judge Clark's face was unreadable, but a quick look sideways told her that she had the spectators' complete attention. More than half of them were leaning forward, caught up by the rhythm and passion of her words. Both hands extended palms up, she continued.

"And when that government came to him—when that

government said it needed his land—when that government talked of 'eminent domain' and 'condemnation'—'' Shrugging, she let her listeners feel Pierre's bewilderment and dropped her hands. ''Then all he understood was that his country had called on him and he must pay at last for all those years of freedom—pay with the only thing he had—his home.''

She stopped speaking, and a few seconds later the court stenographer's tapping ceased as well. Motionless in the quiet room, Verity let her words have their last echo.

''I gather, then, Ms. Brandon,'' Judge Clark broke the silence for a summary, ''that your contention before this court is that although your client accepted the government's first offer, it was only because he hadn't been informed he could refuse if he thought that offer was too low?''

More expert than the spectators at resisting appeals like hers, his voice was a shade dry. Verity turned to face him alone. ''Yes, Your Honor,'' she answered simply.

''And if this bench were to rule in your client's favor and increase the payment to him, perhaps as a kind of belated relocation assistance, what would he do with it? Would he agree to buy land farther along the lakeshore and leave the park property?''

On his second question the judge gave her another shrewd look over those spectacles, and meeting it, Verity gave her answer more slowly this time. ''Yes, Your Honor, I believe so.''

But *would* he? her thoughts demanded. That was the solution to Pierre's problem that his niece had suggested when she hired Verity and Verity had agreed then that it seemed like the best one. But that was before she knew Pierre and knew how he could blend stubbornness with gallantry, good manners with iron determination. It was before she realized, as she was doing right here and now, that he'd never actually promised to do any such thing.

Only last night she'd made a point of reminding him

again why it was that she had come north in the first place. Sitting with him after supper when Toby and Brock had gone out to give the sloop a bedtime check, she had poured them each a last cup of coffee and brought up the case.

"Well, Pierre"—she set her cup back in the saucer and glanced across the kitchen table at him—"tomorrow is our day in court."

"Is it, my dear?" Finished with tamping the old pipe Brock had retrieved for him, Pierre drew on it and then exhaled a cloud of aromatic smoke that hovered between them.

"Yes, and I'm almost positive the judge is going to agree with us that your land was worth more than the government paid you."

"Perhaps." She couldn't see his face clearly, but his voice expressed only a polite interest. It warmed, however, when he went on. "But whatever happens I want you to understand, Verity, how much I appreciate all you've done for my sake." Reaching across the table, he patted her free hand, and she turned it up to clasp his. "You're very dear to me now, you know."

"And you to me," she managed, meaning every word. Her throat was suddenly tight, though, and before she could recover enough to say any more about the case, he'd given her fingers a last squeeze and pulled his own hand away.

"And since I care so much about you, child, I think I'm going to take this smelly old pipe of mine outdoors before I poison you completely with it." Then, he rose and was gone out the back door a moment later, and she was left to notice that he hadn't really said anything at all about the case.

Maybe he didn't expect her to win it? That thought had just made her more determined to do it, concentrating all her energies on convincing Judge Clark today. But now, standing in front of the judge with her thoughts racing,

Verity realized that she hadn't ever actually looked past a ruling in their favor.

Horrified by the oversight, she tried now to analyze whether in fact her answer was right. While he was sick, Pierre had refused to go even as far as Grand Marais, much less to the east side of the village, where land might be available. But that must have been the fever talking. He hadn't mentioned it since then, or said any more about "Marie."

Judge Clark was speaking again, and Verity dragged her attention back to the sound of his voice.

". . . have about enough information on this case, but it's getting late, so you may have my decision tomorrow, Ms. Brandon, Mr. Feenstra." Banging the gavel on his bench, he intoned, "This court is recessed until ten o'clock tomorrow morning."

"Thank you, Your Honor—"

In spite of the disarray of her thoughts, Verity made her tone coolly professional.

"And thank you for your testimony." Outside the courtroom five minutes later, she smiled into Ben Hall's pleasant, rugged face as they walked down the corridor together. "Coming from the park itself, that was a powerful picture of the life Pierre was leading, and I really appreciate your fairness."

Ben agreed with a slight answering smile.

"Well, the government obviously doesn't manage to do everything right— I'm afraid its failure to tell Pierre what options and help he could have is ample proof of that. But we do try to see both sides of things, and old Pierre *is* a pretty special case, too. He probably knows more about the history of this area than the rest of us put together, and when he gets a notion to refuse to leave you can't help but respect his determination."

Verity nodded, and Ben's forehead creased in worry as he added, "That's why my people haven't made any real effort to find him and see that he's put out of the park for good. But at the same time his own place was taken down long ago, and he can't very well go on trying to get by like this.''

''No, it certainly wasn't working out when I caught up with him!''

''How is he now, by the way?'' Ben asked, holding the door to the stairs for her.

''Much better, thanks. That four-hour round trip here and back would still be a bit much for him, but otherwise he seems to have most of his strength back and be in top form again.''

''And Brock? How are he and the restoration doing?''

Ben evidently knew they'd been staying at the lighthouse. But Verity still chose to answer just the second part of that question as she walked down the steps at his side.

''Well, he's got the embankment shored up and the tower's painted,'' she told the ranger. ''In fact, everything looks so good I can't imagine there's too much more he can do.''

That realization brought a pang with it, but Ben kept on talking, and she didn't have time to wonder what would happen when Brock was finished at the station.

''Good.'' Ben sounded satisfied with his decision to let Brock live there while he worked on the restoration. ''And that little sloop of his? How's it coming along?''

''He's been laying down boat ways for launching her sometime soon,'' Verity said, and Ben looked thoughtful.

''Probably the best thing his grandfather ever did, teaching that man to build boats. It's got to be one of the most tranquil things going.''

Opening a lower door from the stairwell, the ranger gazed off across the spacious post office lobby on the ground floor of this federal building, almost as if he could see Brock's boat there in front of him and study its trim lines. ''Wonder if he's going to name it Serena?'' he murmured absentmindedly.

''I beg your pardon?'' Passing through the door as he

held it, Verity didn't think she'd caught his words, which were said more to himself than her.

But Ben didn't repeat them. "I'm sorry."

He came up beside her again and spoke more quickly than usual, almost as if he were realizing he'd forgotten that she was there. "I seem to be starting to talk to myself—pretty poor habit, and in such charming company!"

It was a graceful compliment, and she smiled as he obviously meant her to do. But at the same time she was urgently aware that he was trying to distract her from those murmured words. What was it he'd said?— something about Brock naming his boat "Serena"?

Ben Hall went on speaking, ignoring her abstraction. "Wish I could stay and mend my ways," he went on lightly, "but I've got to be off to check on some other cases we've got coming through here. You take care now, Ms. Brandon, and let me know if there's anything else we can do for Pierre—"

His warm handshake brought Verity back to the moment, but it was too late. Ben put on his peaked hat, gave her a last smile and strode away, vanishing down the steps that led to the outer door.

Her curiosity stirred but not satisfied, Verity stared after him in frustration. This was the man Sam said probably knew more about Brock's life in the last few years than anyone. But he'd just beaten a quick retreat before she could ask him anything at all about Brock's past—or Serena.

Who was she? Like the post office around her, every other question Verity had about Brock's background faded away. Only that one remained, repeating itself again and again as the lovely name tolled in her mind. Who was Serena?

Without warning, pure jealousy surged through Verity, souring her mouth and prickling her skin. Whoever Serena was, wherever she was, if she was someone Brock cared about, how dared she leave him alone at his lighthouse? Or maybe she was the reason he'd gone there in the first place. Well, just let her try coming near him now!

Primitive dislike and anger seething inside her for endless seconds, Verity didn't even see the contradiction in that. Totally absorbed, she didn't see anything at all. The huge room around her was only a pale blur, and the clear thinking she'd prided herself on for years was in complete abeyance while her hostility focused like a laser on the unknown Serena.

"Excuse me—"

Someone brushed past, and Verity's reason finally returned and she realized what was happening to her. She slowed her hurried breath and uncurled her fingers that had grown stiff like claws, shocked at the strength of her reaction. If this was jealousy, she decided ruefully, she'd rather not find out anything more about it.

Walking outside into the hot air to find her car on the street, she almost welcomed the distraction of the heat. At least that was a cauldron made by nature and not the darker side of her own emotions! She flung her briefcase in and followed it onto the scalding seat.

Even with the windows down and the vents wide open, the drive home seemed miles longer than ever before, but with a sense of escape she finally reached the shoreline trail, taking deep breaths of cooler air off the water. Near the kitchen door the air turned even more appealing, too, rich with some savory unfamiliar smell. Hunger pushed everything else aside, and she followed her nose, sniffing eagerly as she wondered what could have moved Brock to take over the cooking again.

It wasn't Brock, though, but Pierre who turned from the stove as she walked in.

"Ah, Verity—good. Home at last."

"Pierre, *what* is that fantastic smell?"

All thought of the case fled from her mind for the moment as Verity dumped her briefcase on the table and hurried to stand beside him over the huge cast-iron frying pan. He turned the contents with a long-handled wooden spatula, and the smell rose on a cloud of steam, richer than ever.

"So you think you'll be able to settle for fresh brook trout from Hurricane River, eh?" he asked.

"Settle for?" Her voice climbed the scale before she caught a twinkle in his dark eyes. Smothering an answering smile, she dropped her tone again and made it elaborately thoughtful. "Well, I think so," she opined. "But of course I'll have to run a thorough taste test before I know for sure. . . ."

She did, too; before the evening was over, she'd had four of the delectable fish. By the time she knew she couldn't possibly eat another bite, she had confirmed that they were the best she'd ever tasted. Given that enticing smell, of course, she wasn't surprised. But the thing that did surprise her was the evening itself, because it was warm and relaxed, comfortable and laughing, the way no time at the lighthouse had ever been before.

Most of that was because Pierre appointed himself as chef and host for the evening, and he was in his element. Repaying some of the kindness he'd found here, he dressed for the occasion in his own clothes Brock had brought him. In his black vest, with a collarless white shirt and scarlet neckerchief, he was a splendid sight, his mustache trimmed and curled into a magnificent handlebar. Looking at him by the soft light of a kerosene lamp, Verity could almost see the turn of the century come to life again.

And it was lively. Serving them with a lavish hand, Pierre kept both the food and the talk going. The only thing he wouldn't discuss, though, was the case.

Verity tried right away when they first sat down.

"Pierre," she began eagerly as he passed over the first plate, "I think we might have done it today in court."

On the far side of the table Brock glanced up, his face

bronzed by the lamplight, but Pierre simply kept on serving. "That one's yours, Toby," was all he said, handing over the second plate.

Verity went on anyway. "The government's lawyer admitted no one had told you anything about your rights, and that was really the thing we needed most."

"Yes?" Pierre asked and added without waiting for an answer, "—yours, Brock."

"Mmm-hmmm. And tomorrow we'll have a ruling."

"Is that so? Eat, everyone, before it's cold."

Setting down his own plate, Pierre commanded them with a raised fork. He didn't offer any other comment on her news, and behind a curl of steam, his seamed face was about as expressive as old wood. Gazing at it in frustration, Verity realized that he simply didn't want to talk about the case. Like last night, tonight too he was ducking the issue. But maybe it was just that he didn't want to think too much about it for fear the ruling might go against them after all.

Whether that was the reason or not, Verity gave up and let the subject drop. And on every other one, Pierre was more than willing to talk, starting with stories of the old days at the lighthouse.

"Well, yes and no."

Having finished eating, he sat pipe in hand and answered Toby's latest question as he tamped down a bowlful of fresh tobacco, glancing around the kitchen.

"This room *is* pretty much the way I remember it from visits out here when I was a kid, but I do know that icebox was added a bit later on. Before that, they used to keep things stored in big crocks under the porch on the north side during warm weather."

"Right under the porch?" Toby asked eagerly, and Verity knew that he'd be out at sun-up tomorrow to check for any long-lost bits and pieces.

"Right there," Pierre confirmed. "Things like eggs and butter did just fine that way, too."

Striking a wooden match, he drew down the flame and added, "Matter of fact, that reminds me of the story one keeper's wife used to tell about the summer she decided she wanted an icebox."

"Uh-huh?" Toby encouraged, and from under bushy brows Pierre gave him a look that glinted, accepting the lure. Exhaling, he grinned reminiscently through the smoke and looked back into a past he made them see as clearly as he could.

"As I remember it," he began with relish, "that was the year she kept noticing the napkin she left over the top of the butter crock had been moved every time she went down there. She didn't really think much about it at first, but after a while she got to paying real close attention, and then she was sure. Somebody else was moving that napkin and stealing from her five pounds of butter besides. She got madder and madder about it, and the day the whole crock vanished outright she just about decided to accuse one of the new assistant keepers of sending his wife over to pilfer it. But, you know, that very same day her husband found that missing crock out in the woods."

Letting the suspense build, he paused and glanced around at each of them in turn. Brock slouched comfortably, but Toby was perched on the edge of his chair, and even Verity found herself inclining forward.

"*Licked* clean as a whistle, it was. Right beside it on the ground was the napkin, and on it was the biggest bear track ever seen in these parts."

"Wow!" Toby breathed happily. Satisfied, Pierre puffed on his pipe for a minute.

Rather than let him wind down, though, Brock spoke up. "Wasn't there some story too, Pierre, about an animal *bringing* food out here instead of taking it? Seems to me my grandfather used to tell me one like that."

One white eyebrow rising thoughtfully, Pierre met his glance and then grunted his agreement past the stem of his pipe. "Mmmmph. Right." He nodded, twinkling.

"*Bringing* food?" Toby repeated hopefully, looking from one man to the other.

Taking the pipestem from his lips a moment, Pierre pointed it at Brock. To Verity's surprise and delight he took the cue.

"Well, apparently it did happen at least one time," Brock told Toby with a grin. "Once years ago when the keeper himself got tossed up on the rocks out here with a full boat load of winter supplies, the only things he ever recovered were a few apples that floated in—and a string of sausage the dog brought home."

Toby's delighted giggle had an echo from Verity, and even Pierre laughed in fresh amusement at an old story.

"Sometimes a loss like that had some pretty far-reaching effects, too," he chimed in again. "When the freighter *Kiowa* went down west of here with a whole cargo of flax seed, fishing in these parts got better for years."

He waited a beat and added dryly, "They did say, though, down in those fancy restaurants in Chicago, that all our catch tasted like linseed oil."

Verity decided that Brock's rich bass chuckle beneath her own laughter and Toby's was the perfect harmony. Pierre didn't need any more encouragement, either. While the lamplight grew yellower and Lake Superior calmed beyond their windows, he regaled them with stories of great ships foundering and their crews all dead, frozen in glassy tombs along the cliffs; "Cousin Jack" Cornishmen working the copper with hot pasties in hand, as their fathers did in Britain for two thousand years before them; voyageurs in long canoes, singing with the tongues of France; Indians fishing off the banks, then storing their catch in permafrost that lay below the sand. . . .

Caught up in the magic, Toby listened with eyes alight and his fork in slack fingers. The last fish cooled unnoticed before him, and for once his appetite was forgotten. Verity, too, forgot almost everything outside the enchanted realm of Pierre's storytelling. As she listened, spellbound, the quiet kitchen around her dissolved and she seemed to slip farther and farther back in history. Only Brock stayed in focus for her, a touchstone in time.

Involved in stories of the past too, he had let down his guard against the present, and she was aware of him in every cell of her body, feeling him at ease for once. Pushed back from the table, with one long leg crossed over the other knee and an elbow hooked around the arm of his chair, he listened with a smile, his expression open and relaxed. Warm golden lamplight fell across his face, melting away the iron control and softening the steel-sharp angles. Off his guard at last, he egged Pierre on with reminders of other tales and even added a few more of his own.

For Verity, it was like catching a glimpse of the man Brock must have been once. Easy-going and witty, low-key and laughing, he was another completely different person from the man who chose isolation at the lighthouse, scarred in body and evidently in mind as well. This wasn't the hostile stranger of their first meeting, the skillful man who brought Pierre through his delirium, or even the good-natured one who let Toby trail him around. This was someone else entirely, and if she had loved the other Brocks, she loved this one even more.

Chapter Eleven

$\mathcal{I}$t was nearly midnight when Pierre stopped to pour out the last coffee in the pot, and Verity returned to reality to find Toby practically asleep. Propped on one hand, his fair head sagged so low that it was almost in his plate. Laughing softly, she shook his shoulder.

"Toby—come on, tadpole. Let's get you upstairs to bed before you turn into a pumpkin."

"Uhnn?" he inquired sleepily.

"A pumpkin, my love," she repeated. "Right on the stroke of twelve, when the princess goes back to being Cinderella and the footmen turn to rats. You've got about five minutes to avoid winding up in the pumpkin patch."

He chuckled sleepily, stumbling to his feet and letting her guide him toward the door with a hand at the small of his back.

"G'nigh'," he mumbled in the general direction of Brock and Pierre, and over his drooping head Verity echoed, "Good night from me too—and thank you both for a wonderful evening. I never knew before that so many centuries could come to life in a single room, and not even be crowded!''

Pierre nodded an answer. "You're most welcome, my dear. It's been a long time since I thought of all those stories, but it was good to rediscover them and a pleasure to have such an audience.''

Still leaning back in his chair, Brock was watching Pierre. Oddly intent, he was looking at the old man with a kind of satisfaction. He must have felt Verity's laughing gaze move to him, though, because he glanced her way and gave her a sudden smile. Without all the tension that usually marked any contact between them, it was curiously sweet. It lighted his lean face, and all the way across the room she felt its warmth, like a friend's touch. Leaving was suddenly hard; like a moth she wanted to stay near that small flame, but Toby gave a great grimace of a yawn, and she recollected herself.

"I didn't say a *Halloween* pumpkin,'' she objected teasingly, and he belatedly stuck a fist in front of the cavern as she guided him away.

Upstairs she shucked him neatly out of his jeans and jersey, replacing them with red pajamas, and well before the fateful stroke from the clock on Brock's desk, Toby was sound asleep. His breathing deep and regular, he curled like a caterpillar and slept with the same enthusiasm as he did everything else. Folding those small cast-off clothes, Verity lingered for a few minutes in the nighttime serenity of her son's room—so different from the turmoil that followed Toby by day! But finally she straightened the covers around him and dropped a light kiss on his sun-scented skin, slipping away to her own room.

Two hours later she was still awake. Deep voices had rumbled below her in the kitchen until Pierre went to his room and Brock came quietly up the stairs. Outside her door his steps almost seemed to hesitate, but before she could rise and run to open it they passed by. In his own room she could hear him moving around softly for a time, then the bedsprings creaked beneath his weight, and the cottage was still.

Except for the sounds of Verity's own springs, that was. Unable to sleep, she tossed and turned while Brock's image floated before her every time she shut her eyes. She saw him a hundred different ways: remote and aloof or hot and dirt-stained, his eyes flat and cold or alive with passion. But most of all she saw him as he'd looked just now in the lamplit kitchen. That open, smiling face drifted in the peaceful darkness of her room, and she didn't know whether to feel despair or delight—despair that something had transformed him so drastically, or delight that at least a little of the old self remained. By turns both emotions filled her, and she lay restlessly awake, wishing wildly that she could go to Brock and ask him outright what had changed his life.

She couldn't, of course. At least, not ordinarily. But that revelation of the Brock who used to be seemed to cost him dearly, and in the quietest hours of the night he began to pay. Still sleepless herself, Verity heard a muffled sound and then another, gradually penetrating the confusion in her mind. Sitting up, she listened, wondering if Pierre had somehow fallen ill again—or Toby.

Sliding from her tumbled bed, she hurried barefoot across the room and into the hall, cocking her head to hear. At first there was only silence, except for the faint murmur of the lake outside and the soft sighing of the wind. Then it came again, a stifled desperate sound, and it came from Brock's room, not Toby's or Pierre's.

The door was closed, and she rested her fingertips on it, hesitating. Did loving him give her any right just to walk in on him in the middle of the night? The light tower, the boatshed—one by one, his retreats had been ceded to the rest of them. And now she was going to barge into the last small sanctuary he had?

Gently, she tapped at the door, but the only response was a few muttered words, followed by another of those noises, this time recognizable as a groan. It was a heart-wrenching sound, and privacy was trivial compared to pain. She slipped through the door.

Moonlight streamed between the curtains, washing the room with a tide of cold light that illuminated Brock in his bed. His eyes closed, he was evidently dreaming—or having nightmares. The covers around him had been yanked into a wild tangle, and he lay on his stomach in the heap, partly on the bare mattress. Where they were visible between the knotted sheets, the scars carving his left side seemed almost black in the dim light, and his legs were sprawled at awkward angles in their thin pajama trousers.

Softly, she shut the door behind her, and at the tiny click it made he began to fight the sheets that bound him. Face turned against the mattress, he struggled as though the fabric were far stronger than it could really be, fighting to free himself while sweat beaded his forehead and upper lip.

"No!" The one explosive syllable was clear, even though he spoke in a harsh broken voice she had never heard before. It cracked as he went on wildly, "Oh, God, NO! Let me through—help me! Don't—" The rest of the words were lost, choked off by dry, wracking gulps, and his lean cheeks were wet.

Stabbed by love and pity, she dropped to her knees beside the bed, setting one hand gently on his shoulder. She was desperate to reach him through the nightmare, but he just twisted violently away from her touch, throwing her fingers off and spitting out curses in some guttural language she didn't know.

Letting her hand fall, she spoke to him instead. "Brock —Brock, listen. It's all right—never mind."

Kneeling so her lips were near his ear, she made her voice insistent and low to reach whatever private hell engulfed him. "Brock, come back. Listen to me. It's me— I'm here—"

He didn't react at first. Reliving the unbearable past, he was blind and deaf to the present. But finally her words began to get through to him. His own slowed and broke off. Eyes still closed, he seemed at least to hear her, as if she had spoken in his dream. Lying motionless, his whole body taut as a bowstring, he listened to her.

"It's all right, Brock. I'm here—"

Without warning, he flung himself around and reached for her, dragging her up from the floor and into a crushing embrace. Startled, she struggled in surprise until the meaning of his words caught up with her, and she went soft in his arms.

"You're all right!! Thank God—oh, thank God, you're all right! They told me you were—"

He bit back the word. Holding her against his heaving chest, he kissed her with a wild thankfulness that broke her heart, running his hands over her face and arms, her neck and throat, as if he couldn't believe that she was there with him.

He wasn't really kissing her at all, and she knew it now. She had walked into his nightmare, and he thought that she was some other woman—Serena?—lost to him in whatever tragedy had brought him to the lighthouse. But she didn't speak again, and she didn't try to free herself from his crushing hold. She just lay in his arms and welcomed him, giving him kiss for kiss as she met him with lips that tasted of salt.

Finally the urgency went out of his touch. Her flimsy nightgown long since pushed aside, he lay with his head on the satin skin of her breast and one big hand on the creamy roundness of her belly. Desire checked by tenderness and sorrow, she ran her fingers lightly through the springy hair at his temple, stroking it back in a steady rhythm while his breathing slowed and deepened. He stirred, turning to kiss her fingers once, then lay still in her arms.

Uncounted heartbeats passed, his or hers, and she didn't move. She stayed where she was while the moon set and the first faint trace of dawn began to lighten his room. Like the ghosts of lovers past, she could see the pale gleam of their intertwined bodies materialize in his mirror. Eyes wide and dark, she looked at it for a long time. Then she shifted him gently onto his side and slipped from his bed. Turning back, she set a lingering kiss on his lips and stole away to her own room.

Surprisingly, she did sleep at last, only waking long after her usual hour to find her room filled with a fitful play of sun and shadow. Clouds swept across the sky, and through her window she could see a few of them. Beginning near the horizon with bands of gray, they rose to towering white heights, tall ships with snowy sails and darker hulls. Racing on a sea vaster than even the great lake below, they sailed in stately armadas that blocked the sun and then revealed it.

Watching as they changed the air from light to dark and light again, Verity was half-aware of a sense of kinship. This morning her emotions were in every bit as much of a turmoil as last night: She had finally learned that Brock must have come here because he lost the woman he loved. But even if he didn't remember it today, she had broken through his nightmare to let him escape that pain for a while at least, and there was a kind of bittersweet joy in the knowledge, like sun in shade.

She rolled on her side and propped her head on one hand, her eyes still following the clouds as she came to terms with the inescapable limits. She couldn't *be* that woman he had loved, but she could let him mistake her in a dream; for a few hours she could release him from a memory that had caused him so much grief. Even though the past was out of her control, in the present she could love him enough to help him find a brief forgetfulness and ask for nothing more than he could give.

That wasn't very much—only a few fleeting, broken kisses and an occasional hour of companionship when he forgot to keep her at a distance. But it was a little, and more than she had known for years now. Even within these limits, loving Brock brought her to life at last, like sunlight falling on a dormant seed, and if shadows came with the sun, then she would learn to live with the shade. And simply hope for better weather some day!

With a rueful half-smile, she accepted it all but left herself room for hope. The time might come when Brock would have more to give and would take more that she wanted to give. But for now—

A glance at the small alarm clock on her dresser sent Verity jumping out of bed. She must have forgotten to set it last night, because now it said she had barely more than two hours to get to court in Marquette for the judge's decision. And she was expected to arrive there decently clothed and alert, without a sheaf of speeding tickets in her hand!

Snatching up her washcloth and toothbrush, she took a few swipes at herself and pulled on her clothes—a cream-colored suit and navy blouse. One hand fastened her wristwatch onto the other, then both fluffed her hair into shape while her toes searched for shoes. With her earrings and necklace clipped on, she touched a bit of color to her mouth and eyes, thanking heaven for skin that needed nothing else.

Ready in record time, she swept up her briefcase and bag and rushed down the stairs. There were no signs of life in the kitchen. Apparently everyone else had already eaten and gone, leaving her to sleep in—on this, of all mornings!

Gulping a cup of tepid coffee, she couldn't decide if they'd done her a favor or not. Sleep was all very well, but now she was going to have to fly to make it to Marquette.

Granted, Pierre and Brock didn't know what time she was supposed to be in court, but she did wonder hastily what diversion could have kept Toby from his usual morning rounds with an overflowing cup. Only the most enticing of distractions lured him away.

Outside, she found out. His back to her, Brock was busy with a pile of lumber, while Pierre consulted and Toby flailed the air in practice strokes with a hammer and saw.

"Look, Mom," he announced gleefully, "it's going to be a chicken coop! There was one here in the old days, so we have to put it back."

"Fine, Chicken Little." She nodded agreeably. "We'll move your things in as soon as it's done."

He studied the boards consideringly before he realized that she was teasing. "Aw, Mo-om!"

Sophisticated scorn couldn't quite cover up a trace of disappointment in his voice, and she laughed. "Sorry, Toby! Build the most luxurious hen house ever, and I'll come join you in it. But in the meantime, how about a quick kiss? I'm about to be late to court."

Abandoning the tools for a minute, he swooped over to meet her and wrapped her in a bearhug, disengaging almost as fast after she touched a kiss to the top of his tousled head. Then he charged back to talk hen houses with Pierre, while she hastily balanced her load, briefcase for one hand and purse for the other.

"Verity."

Her bent head snapping upright, she found Brock only three feet away. But it wasn't just his unexpected nearness that parted her lips in surprise. Even more, it was his appearance.

"You shaved—" she whispered.

He had indeed. His thick reddish beard and the mustache above were both gone, and it was as if Brock Randall, international correspondent, had stepped from her television screen. Or as if the face that looked up at her from the photograph in his desk drawer had come to life. The hard clear line of his jaw, the cleft in his square chin, the smooth bare skin she knew would be warm and firm to her touch—eyes wide, she recognized them all. They were all just as they had been before he grew a beard, before he came to the lighthouse, before he gave up broadcast journalism.

And yet, they weren't completely the same. As she went on searching his features, she also recognized small differences. Leaner and more angular, almost honed down, his face had added lines at the eyes and mouth. The old openness was gone, too, and with it a kind of brash confidence. But in their place was a new endurance, and even an added strength. Overall, the change was as if the face from his past had been modeled easily out of clay, while this present one was cast in bronze, newly made from fire.

"Yes," he confirmed the obvious. "This morning."

He didn't offer any explanation but just shifted the length of board he was carrying, almost awkwardly. Tearing her gaze from his face, she realized that he was probably heading toward his tools in the boatshed, although that would mean he'd come out of his way to speak to her, and he'd always been far more likely to go out of his way to avoid speaking to her.

But he was still standing there in front of her, and her surprise that he had shaved grew into an even stronger curiosity. Without knowing whether she was hopeful or fearful, she started to wonder if he *could* have detoured especially to say something—if he *had* shaved today of all days for any particular reason—if he *could* remember last night's dream and its ending. . . .

But that wasn't likely. After all, he never really woke up, only exchanged a nightmare for sleep. He couldn't know she was there. To remember her would be to lose the other woman again, so she couldn't let him recall that he lay in her arms with his head on her breast.

The stabbing sweetness of that memory pierced through her, and she caught her breath in a tiny gasp. Her laden hands stirred, as if to reach for him again of their own will, but the weight of her briefcase and bag held them down. That burden reminded her too that she had to think of today, not last night, of the law and settlements, not love and remembrance.

"Oh. Well, I'm late," she blurted. "I was supposed to be in court early today, and somehow I overslept, so I've really got to run to make it on time—"

Struggling against the sweet pain of last night's memory, she fought to sound normal and wound up sounding brusque. The words spilled out like little pebbles, and she turned away, missing the rare uncertainty that opened up his shuttered face. Walking quickly down the forest trail, she didn't see him stare after her; hurrying away from last night's memory, she didn't know that doubt slowly darkened his features where light had been before.

"Before I issue a decision, Ms. Brandon, I understand Mr. Feenstra wants to offer your client an out-of-court settlement on behalf of the government."

In the spacious courtroom again, Judge Clark lowered his papers and peered through his silver spectacles. "Mr. Feenstra?"

Thanking heaven that she'd managed to get there on time for a development of this sort, Verity turned to look at the man standing at her side before Judge Clark's bench.

"Given that the government hasn't handled Mr. Dumont's situation quite as well as it could have, Ms. Brandon, I'm authorized to offer him a payment of thirty-five hundred dollars, as a ten percent increase on the original appraisal of his property, and an additional two thousand dollars as relocation assistance."

Listening, Verity fought the impulse to dance an unprofessional jig. That might not sound like a great deal of money, but it would be enough so that Pierre really could buy a cottage along the shore east of the village and be less than ten miles from the place he'd spent his whole life—

"Would you accept that as a final cash settlement of all claims on your client's behalf?" Judge Clark asked her.

"Yes, Your Honor, I would, with thanks to the government and this court on his behalf as well."

Now she smiled warmly at both men, beginning to gather her papers into her briefcase. On the far side of his wide bench, however, the judge returned it with a twitch of his lips but then rattled the sheaf of pages in his own hands, so that she looked up again.

"Harr-umph." He cleared his throat impressively. "After all this, Ms. Brandon, perhaps you can delay your exit until Mr. Feenstra can add the second part of the government's offer?"

"Yes, of course, Your Honor— Excuse me, Mr. Feenstra."

Even as she apologized, Verity's mind was racing. Second part of the offer? Her only request on Pierre's behalf had been for the additional cash settlement, and the judge had just made it very clear that that was to be the end of any such efforts on her part. So what else—

Judge Clark was waiting for her attention with exaggerated patience, and Jim Feenstra wore a slight smile. Having let all her papers fall on the table in front of her, Verity rested her fingertips there too. Giving the two men her total attention, she tried to mask her puzzlement with professional calm.

She was only partway successful. "You must study poker, Ms. Brandon," Judge Clark murmured with the ghost of a twinkle in his shrewd blue eyes, steepling his fingertips while Jim Feenstra's grin widened.

"Yes, Your Honor," she returned in the same tone. "Shall I bet too?"

She gave him a demure nod of her head as she inquired

if the judge were recommending that she break Michigan's gambling laws.

"Ha!" A single crack of mirth escaped Judge Clark, and she realized that he had laugh lines at the corners of his penetrating eyes. "Only on yourself, Counselor," he retorted deftly, reminding her how he got to be a federal judge.

The three of them exchanged a smile off the record, then Jim got back down to business.

"The other part of the government's offer, Ms. Brandon," he told her, "is the suggestion that your client be offered the opportunity to take seasonal employment with the National Park Service each year, filling the position of interpreter at the Au Sable Lighthouse Visitors' Center."

Professional sangfroid forgotten, Verity stared. Employment for Pierre, with the Park Service? And at the lighthouse?

Enjoying her surprise, Judge Clark shot her another look over his glasses, and Jim Feenstra went on.

"If he chooses to accept such a position, he'll be quartered in the restored keeper's cottage, living and working there in the style of the turn of the century, so that park visitors could learn first-hand about the unique history of such sites. At his discretion, the job could begin as of the first of July, too, since the government's understanding is that the Visitors' Center is almost completely restored to its original condition now and will be ready to open officially by that date."

"Well, Ms. Brandon?" Judge Clark asked, breaking the silence that fell with Jim's last words.

"Your Honor, Mr. Feenstra—" Caught completely off guard by this second part of the verdict, Verity hesitated, and the judge's eyes began that faint twinkling again.

"I was given to understand your client might find an offer of this sort acceptable," he suggested, deadpan.

Verity made herself find her words again. "It's far more

than acceptable, Your Honor," she said, abandoning any attempt to keep her expression properly neutral. Face alight, she added, "It's wonderful! Mr. Feenstra, it's the most kindly, creative solution—"

"I gather you feel you can accept on his behalf," Judge Clark interposed with a dry smile. Not all the settlements in his experience were greeted with this kind of enthusiasm.

"Yes, Your Honor, I believe I can. It's an inspired answer to his problems, and my client will be grateful to Mr. Feenstra for thinking of it—"

Looking at the man beside her, she returned his grin with the full power of one of her own, and he blinked, then concealed it by rubbing his forehead. "As a matter of fact," he allowed with careful regard for accuracy, "the lighthouse idea came from the Park Service."

"The Park Service?" Verity repeated in surprise.

"Yes," the judge confirmed. "This morning before you reached the court. Chief Ranger Hall brought it to Mr. Feenstra in my chambers, acting on a recommendation phoned in to him from Grand Marais from—"

He paused, and Jim Feenstra shook his head, unable to help. Glancing off into space as he searched his memory, Judge Clark muttered, "Let me think—" Then he snapped his fingers. "From that fellow who's been finishing the restoration out there. Brock Randall, his name is."

Chapter Twelve

 $\mathcal{A}$ fterward, Verity never recollected how she got out of Judge Clark's courtroom that last time. She must have said and done approximately the right things, because Jim Feenstra didn't comment and the judge made no further suggestions about poker. But if the judge's keen eyes noted how distracted she was, he drew his own conclusions about it and she didn't know.

Utterly absorbed in the discovery that Brock had intervened in Pierre's case, she was a robot with a briefcase, hardly conscious of making her way along the corridor outside the courtroom. Her high heels clicked on the stone floor, but she noticed only that her steps seemed to have a voice. "Brock's idea," it said over and over again. "Brock's idea."

She was heading absentmindedly toward the stairs when the elevator door opened to her left and her name rang out.

"Verity!" a rich baritone said. "Verity, wait."

Even her own name didn't really get through the first

time, but the second time she slowed her steps and turned vaguely. Then her abstracted gaze took in the lean, elegant figure approaching her, and astonished, she dropped her briefcase to hold out both hands.

"Mark! How good to see you!" As he gathered in those hands, she kissed him and added, "But what on earth are you doing way up here?"

Before he answered, Mark Patterson dropped a graceful kiss in each of her palms; it was a gesture that would have seemed theatrical in any other man, but Mark made it perfectly natural, maybe because everything else he did was equally dramatic. And for all that, he was completely sincere.

It showed in the gaze he slanted her, humorous but still intent. "As a matter of fact," he said, "I came up to ask you the same thing."

Smiling, she answered literally, "Getting a settlement on my case."

"Yes, I know that. I called the court clerk to find out when you'd be in again."

She glanced at him again in mild surprise. As partners, they'd always worked separately, equal but independent, with each going his own way. So why was Mark checking up on her at this late date?

This time he didn't meet her eyes, though. He retrieved her briefcase and put an arm under her elbow to turn her toward the stairs again.

"Where can we go for a cup of coffee?" he asked.

Verity thought a moment. "I still don't know Marquette very well," she admitted, "but I think there's a coffee shop somewhere right around here."

There was, too, and in five minutes they had dropped her briefcase in her car and were facing each other across a small cafe table. While Mark ordered coffee and a sandwich for each of them, she studied those dark handsome features less than three feet away. She'd known them since law school; they were almost as familiar as her

own. The sleek black hair, the aristocratic good looks—
they were just as they'd always been. But as she surveyed
them, Verity realized that she hadn't actually *looked* at
Mark in months.

Deliberately blind for all those years to everything but
her cases, she had accepted him without really seeing him.
He was just an old friend, a partner, an occasional
companion for some concert or Bar Association dinner.
And whenever he made one of his repeated proposals, she
evaded him teasingly. He was simply trying to cement the
partnership, but it was fine just as it was.

But now, as if the thaw in her heart these last few weeks
had somehow reached her eyes as well, she saw Mark all
over again, rediscovering aspects of him she'd let herself
forget. She'd always known that, like a rapier hidden in a
velvet case, he kept a lethal genius for cross-examination
concealed beneath his playboy pose. Below that, too,
were a single-minded commitment and the sensitivity of a
seismograph. Watching him, she found them again in the
faint creases on his forehead, the intensity of his jet black
eyes, the restlessness of his long-fingered hands.

But the hands were still now, linked deliberately on the
orange Formica tabletop in front of him, and his eyes were
fixed on her. Verity realized that the waitress had left with
their order, and Mark was giving her the same evaluation
she'd just given him. Their glances met, and they both
smiled.

His black eyes warm, he said, "You're looking good,
Counselor."

"So are you," she returned promptly.

He was, too. The crisp navy blazer and immaculate
white slacks made him look as though he'd just stepped
off a luxury yacht. As a matter of fact, he almost might
have. His family kept a fifty-foot cruiser at Harbor
Springs, and he'd probably driven up from there, even
though she still didn't know why. He wasn't volunteering
an answer either.

"How did it go?" He inquired about her case instead and, long used to his habit of starting a conversation again in the middle, she followed him with ease.

"We got everything we'd hoped for, and then some."

"Of course."

She gave him a quick delighted grin. One of the things she'd always loved about Mark was his calm certainty that she was an excellent lawyer.

"Tell me about it," he invited now.

She didn't need a second bidding. Over turkey sandwiches and several cups of coffee, she brought him up to date on the case since her call the day after she and Toby found Pierre: the old man's dramatic relapses and slow recovery; Ben Hall's vivid testimony; the government's cash offer and that inspired idea of making Pierre a turn-of-the-century lighthouse keeper for the Park Service. And, inevitably, she told him about Brock Randall.

It wasn't that she meant to. She intended to tell Mark only about the progress of her case, but she couldn't leave Brock out. Giving them shelter, caring for Pierre, contacting Ben with his suggestion about the lighthouse—Brock was woven into everything that had happened. In her mind every moment, waking or sleeping, he had to be in her words too.

Asking an occasional question, Mark listened to her answers and watched her mobile face across their narrow table. Worry, relief, hope, satisfaction, delight—her voice was lively and her features alight, the way they always were when she got deeply involved in a case. But this time was different. This time an extra vitality animated her, so that her expressions sparkled in her face like sunlight on waves whenever she mentioned Brock Randall.

Seeing her, hearing her, Mark abandoned the rest of his sandwich. His thin fingers clenched around his coffee cup; he drained it as if he wished it held something stronger. A refill went the same way, too, but Verity didn't notice because he kept a slight smile on his lips. Wound up, she went on talking and didn't see the crease deepening across his forehead or the tiny lines etching themselves from nose to mouth.

Finally, though, she checked herself, apologizing on a little laugh. "I'm sorry, Mark—that was probably a good deal more detail than you really needed to hear! Why didn't you stop me?"

He shrugged, a continental gesture that had most of its usual grace. "I can stand it. We've been out of touch," he excused her, "and I hadn't heard anything at all about it in weeks."

There was nothing particular in his tone, except maybe that it sounded a bit less expressive than usual. But Verity found herself unexpectedly fidgeting with her coffee spoon and made herself set it aside.

"I didn't realize it had been so long."

"Four weeks and a day."

He answered immediately, without needing any time to figure that out, and afterward an odd silence fell between them as their eyes connected across the table. The last echoes of his words faded into the pop music around them, the laughter and clinking plates, and Verity really looked at Mark again, the way she had when they first sat down.

He was gazing directly at her, with an intensity that vibrated like a bowstring, and as she met that gaze she saw what he meant her to see in it. The languid playboy pose was gone, and so was the astute lawyer, the partner and the friend. One thing only remained, and that was the man who had loved her for years while she refused to acknowledge it.

"Mark—"

She leaned across the table to set both hands on his, as recognition and regret made her voice catch on that single syllable. He heard them, but as if he had to have her say it in words—had to be absolutely, irrevocably sure—he asked, "You're in love with this Brock Randall, aren't you?"

It was more a statement than a question, but she answered it anyway. "Yes."

He shook his head very slightly, his eyes closing for a second or two, and when he opened them again they almost seemed to have changed from a brilliant jet black to a flat, dull ebony. He gave her a twisted smile. "Congratulations. He's a lucky man."

Freeing his fingers from hers, he glanced at the fine gold watch he wore on one wrist and stood up, dropping a few bills on the table. "I won't keep you any longer, then. You'll be wanting to get back."

"I have time—" she began, rising slowly.

But he cut her off, sweeping her out the door with a hand under her elbow.

"You've never had time," he contradicted her. "It's always been the wrong time for us."

Just for a moment, real anger crackled in his voice, and they stared at each other, face to face on the sidewalk outside the coffeeshop. One last time they searched each other's eyes, and at the dismay in her expression the anger faded from his.

"Oh, hell!" he muttered. "I'm a sore loser."

"You're a very dear man," she disagreed with a break in her voice.

"But not quite dear enough!" he pointed out dryly on a reluctant, lopsided grin. Setting both hands on her shoulders, he went on, "Remember, though, if you ever *do* need me—for anything else, that is!—I'll always be there."

Mute, she nodded, and he drew her in against him for a single blistering kiss. Then she was free.

"Good-bye," he said thickly. "I'll miss my partner in crime."

It was the oldest of their puns, and she made a strangled sound between laughter and tears. When her eyes had cleared, he was halfway down the block, striding rapidly away. At the corner, he lifted one hand in a brief salute and was gone.

In her car the seats were scorching again and the steering wheel so hot she could only hold it with her fingertips, even though she'd left the windows cracked. Still, she started the engine, rolled her windows down all the way and drove out of town without paying much attention, because Mark was so much on her mind.

He loved her, and maybe he always had. Thinking back to their first semester in law school, when they had found themselves together in a study group, she remembered the endless hours they had spent working side by side. His wit and determination had never flagged, and he'd made sure she was always as well prepared as he was. But she'd been too wrapped up in starting her life over, too busy keeping her heart carefully numb, to realize why he cared so much. Later she'd overlooked the way he worried about her exhausting work in the Public Defender's office, and still later she'd missed the underlying seriousness to his proposals that they make their partnership complete. Only now, when she'd fallen in love with Brock, could she see how Mark had always felt—now, when it was too late.

Ruefully, Verity noted how unfair a heart could be. Coming to life at last, hers had ignored the love nearby and fixed on someone else instead. Mark was steady where Brock was changeable, open where Brock was shuttered—and a dear friend where Brock was the man she loved.

And she loved him so much that even Mark's image gradually faded away as she drove on toward the lighthouse. Brock was there, and he had suggested Pierre as lighthouse keeper. Astonishment and delight flooded through her again, and her attention, her mind and heart focused on him while she tried harder than ever to understand him.

He was the person who came up with that wonderfully

sensitive solution to Pierre's problems? Brock, who accepted the government's policy of condemning private land where need be, in order to create a public park? Brock, who believed only in the greatest good for the greatest number, even if that meant individuals had to suffer?

Trying to reconcile his proposal to the jury with their first quarrel about the park, she failed miserably. The cold-blooded pragmatist he had claimed to be then simply wouldn't have thought of any plan so humane. All she accomplished by remembering that quarrel was reminding herself how angry he had made her. Wild all over again at an attitude so callous and defeatist, she had to take a couple of deep breaths to cool down, unclenching her hands on the car's steering wheel while the long miles passed.

But the truth was that no matter what he claimed to be—no matter what, perhaps, he tried to be—even now Brock Randall was neither callous nor defeatist. He might try to deny any concern or compassion, but weighed against what he said was what he did, and the scales tipped decisively.

The man who had always reported the human side of any conflict still cared about people. The man who had used his strength to share someone else's pain in that picture Toby found still shared himself the same way. No matter what he might say he meant to do, he sheltered all the motley arrivals at his door, lending them his strength through illness, injury or uncertainty. Pierre and she, Toby and Nick—they had all found him a rock to cling to, even for the uninvited. That was what mattered. Only what he did counted, not what he said of himself thanks to whatever horror it was that haunted his nightmares.

She could feel again the tired weight of his body finally relaxing against her the night before. Under her fingers, his thick hair curled with an energy of its own, while his hands clung wearily to her shoulder and belly, heavy with exhaustion but afraid to let her go. Pressed to her bare breast, the salty dampness of his face dried slowly while his breath crept softly over her skin. . . .

"Cock-a-doodle-doo!"

Ahead of her Toby's exuberant attempt to be a rooster called Verity out of her trance, and she realized that she was nearly at the lighthouse. Driving and then walking, she'd come back like a homing pigeon without even minding the two-hour trip. Walking into the sunny clearing behind the keeper's cottage, she found Brock nowhere in sight but Pierre just picking up the last scraps of leftover lumber while Toby strutted around the new hen house, his arms akimbo and elbows flapping.

Returned abruptly from the sublime to the ridiculous, Verity couldn't help a wry grin. "Hello, you two!" she called laughingly.

"Mom!" At the sound of her voice, Toby stopped being a rooster and scampered over to meet her. "It's done. Isn't it the greatest chicken coop you ever saw?"

"Yes, love, it is," she agreed, setting down her things to give him a quick hug. "And one of the few, frankly! But it's certainly far and away the best."

Keeping one hand on Toby's shoulder, she took a deep breath and then made her voice casual. "What sort of hens are you thinking of keeping, Pierre?"

Hands full of scrap lumber, he stopped, his leathery forehead creasing. "White leghorns would be good, I think," he decided and then shrugged. "But it doesn't matter anyway. This hen house is only part of the restoration. It has to be here, but there won't be any chickens in it."

"There could be if you felt like it," she suggested while Toby twisted to peer up at the odd tone in her voice.

"Eh?" Pierre was looking at her about the same way.

"You might decide you wanted fresh eggs in the

summertime, while you were working out here in the lighthouse and running everything the old way—for park visitors to see.''

The scraps of wood fell slowly from Pierre's hands as he stared at her unbelievingly.

"Mom! You mean Pierre's going to be allowed to *live* here?" Never speechless himself, Toby spoke for Pierre, perched on his tiptoes with excitement.

"If he wants to." Verity replied over her son's bobbing head, her eyes locked on Pierre's in answer to his mute inquiry.

"Officially and everything?" Toby persisted.

"Absolutely—he'll be working for the Park Service."

"The whole summer?"

"All summer, every summer, as long as he wants to. And then in winter he can get a piece of land to live on just east of the village, out by the lake. I found out in Marquette this morning.''

"Whooppee!" Toby danced away to circle the hen house and crow in delight.

Behind him, Pierre and Verity stared at each other. Into her gaze she put every bit of conviction she could muster, and gradually an answering certainty dawned in his. For just a second his shoulders bowed in relief, then he squared them proudly. Walking over to Verity with a measured step, he gave her a slight old-fashioned bow and caught her hand in his to kiss it, while his luxuriant mustache brushed softly against her skin. As he straightened again, she glimpsed the moisture sparkling on his brown cheeks, like spring rains on ancient stone.

"Thank you, my dear," he said quietly.

"You're welcome." Speaking in the same tone, she curled her fingers tightly around his, and they stood together while Toby's happy racket came to them only faintly.

Finally a hint of reckless mischief crept into Pierre's

expression, and he released her hand. With a gleam of laughter, he swung around.

"Like this, Toby—leghorn style." And dropping into a ridiculous crouching strut, he hooked his thumbs into his red suspenders, flapped his elbows and bobbed his head up and down, letting loose with the most accurate chicken cackle Verity had ever heard.

The emotion of a minute earlier evaporated. While Toby fell excitedly into line behind Pierre and tried to match him strut for strut, Verity laughed until she had to sit on the ground, mopping her eyes. That joyous, absurd crowing wasn't the last she heard from Pierre on the subject, however.

Late that afternoon she climbed the lighthouse tower. She hadn't gone up it again after that one tranquil meeting there with Brock; she wouldn't risk trying to repeat that halcyon hour in their usually stormy relationship. But now she was almost halfway up before she recognized the source of her impulse, before she let herself admit that she was hoping against hope that Brock might be there again.

It was Pierre, though, who stood already on the narrow catwalk, gazing out across the lake. Hearing her approach, he turned slightly and made a small gesture of welcome at his side. Instead of climbing quietly back down, she stood by him.

A tall graceful woman and a sturdy old man, they stood side by side, watching in companionable silence while the waves approached the shore. An endless procession, they rose from the depths of the lake in rolling green swells that quickly reached their full height, then bowed to the land in a flurry of white spray before retreating again to the chilly deep.

Mesmerized as always by that age-old rhythm, Verity watched it in mindless contentment for long minutes. When she finally spoke, it was as natural and unpremeditated as the waves.

"*Is* it a good solution, Pierre?" she asked quietly, still watching the water.

"Yes, my dear," he answered slowly. "It really is, more than even you could know."

She kept her eyes on the lake and maintained a receptive silence, counting to see if every seventh wave really would be larger than the others, the way some people claimed. Two whole flotillas had gone past before he spoke again.

"I had a daughter once, you see," he explained, letting out a long breath and linking his gnarled hands carefully around the railing in front of them. "Her mother died when she was born, and she was all I had. Air and sunlight, fire and lakewater, Marie was everything beautiful in the world."

Soundlessly, Verity caught her breath, while Pierre's fingers tightened on the thin railing.

"When she was sixteen, she fell in love with a boy from town. They came to me and asked for my permission to marry, but I said no. He wasn't good enough for her—he had no job to support her—they were too young. I said it all, but what I meant was that I couldn't give her up yet."

Knuckles white, he stared out over the water, but Verity knew achingly that he saw only his daughter's face.

"She pleaded with me and I got angry, because I was afraid I'd weaken and say yes. So I shouted at her and said she couldn't ever see him again as long as she lived under my roof. And in the morning, she wasn't under my roof anymore. They were both gone from Grand Marais, and they haven't ever come back."

When he finished speaking, his eyes were closed and his whole face was stiff with pain. Her own eyes filled, Verity tucked a warm young hand in the crook of his elbow, clasping tightly until Pierre finally patted it with his other hand.

His face under control again, he went on with just a

trace of hoarseness. "So you see, that's why I can't leave this area. I let love go once, and I can't ever make that mistake again. I have to stay as near the old property as I can."

Verity didn't understand right away. Blinking away her tears, she still looked puzzled, so he explained simply. "Because Marie may come back some day to find me. I have to be there to meet her."

"I see." She could only get two syllables past the lump in her throat, but she leaned over and kissed the lined cheek beside her.

"And you, my dear—" In a minute Pierre went on, patting her hand again. "You mustn't make my mistake. Don't let love go."

Swift color flushed her expressive face, and he noted it with wise old eyes. "It's far too precious," he insisted gently. "Never let it go, and never give up hope."

As she met his intense gaze, her color receded, and dodges and denials died on her lips. The time for those was long past, if there had ever been a time. "No," she breathed, "I won't."

"Good." Satisfied, he nodded his head once. "And now, my dear Verity, you go ahead down and leave an old man up here to think about his good fortune in having such a job ahead—and such friends."

With a last affectionate look, he turned his back, gazing out across the lake again. His advice in mind, Verity slipped away down the tower.

At the bottom, however, Brock was still nowhere in sight; short of instituting an out-and-out search for him, she couldn't very well heed Pierre's advice right now. Stymied, she had to settle for fixing supper instead, hanging over a hot stove on an evening that was surprisingly warm. And then Brock didn't appear to eat. Fluffing her damp hair away from her face, Verity set his plate on the back of the stove.

He didn't come for it until sundown, and it was the longest day of the year. Pulling their green window-shades, Toby and Pierre had gone to bed before he walked through the late northern sunset, from the direction of the boatshed. At the kitchen table Verity was idly sorting out her papers on Pierre's case for the final time—a job she could have done in her own room but chose to do near the back door instead.

Seeing her, Brock broke his stride, almost as if he would have retreated if he'd known in time that she was there. She hadn't stayed to speak to him this morning, and now he seemed to have no interest in speaking to her. But the door was already open, so he passed on through, while her heart started its usual pounding.

To her carefully calm "Hello" he returned a brusque "Good evening," picking up his plate and going right on through the kitchen to his desk in the living room. There he set it down within easy reach and dropped into his big chair, fishing out a sheaf of papers from the desk drawer. Obviously, he meant to lose himself in his work on those articles and ignore her presence entirely.

Finishing with her own papers, Verity thought about that. She had promised herself that she wouldn't ask for more than he could give; she would simply wait and hope. But Pierre was right too. She couldn't just let love go—not when the lighthouse restoration was nearly through and her reason for being there almost ended. And not when she'd only come to life herself these last weeks; she couldn't go back to existing in the old frozen way. As if he were a bonfire in the Arctic, fear of that sent her after Brock.

She spoke as she walked through the doorway. "Brock—"

Looking up coolly as she halted by the desk, he raised one eyebrow but didn't answer.

"I want to thank you."

The eyebrow stayed up skeptically. "For what?"

"Pierre. It's such a good solution!"

"Yes, he told me about the settlement." His eyes were shallow, giving away nothing.

"And the judge told me who suggested the lighthouse part of it! I want to thank you for coming up with a plan that's so perfect for Pierre. It lets him stay where he feels he must and gives him back his dignity at the same time."

Enthusiasm filled her face, but he looked down at the papers on the desk. "Glad you like it," he said tersely, in the tone of someone who wasn't glad about anything. This morning, his freshly shaved face had made him look at least a little like the old Brock, almost as if that open candid picture in his drawer had come to life. But tonight his face was as cold and closed as a steel vault, and the photo might as well have shown a stranger.

Eyes on the nape of his neck, she pushed her hot hair off her forehead impatiently. This was not one of their more successful conversations. But stubbornly she persisted.

"I want to apologize too."

That brought his head up again.

"Oh?" he said on a rising note and leaned back in his chair, idly tapping a pen. His tone made it more than clear that he considered that she had plenty of scope for that project.

Nettled, she gave him a heated look. He was right, of course—starting with her first assault on his door, there was a whole list of similar infractions she could be apologizing for. But she had let herself slip into the comfortable assumption they were at least past that sort of record keeping. It seemed that he hadn't done the same.

Stuffing her hands in the pockets of her shorts, she set her chin and went on. "I made the mistake of thinking that because you accepted the government's policy of acquiring land for the park any way it had to, you didn't care who got caught in the works. When you said you believed in the greatest good for the greatest number, I thought that proved you couldn't care for a single individual like Pierre, and I'm sorry.''

It seemed like an adequate apology, but something she said must have struck a nerve. Instead of accepting her regrets, Brock snapped, ''Don't be. You were perfectly correct in your original assessment of my character. I suggested Pierre as lighthouse keeper for the Visitors' Center only because it would offer the public more information about the area than they could get any other way, and not because I had some noble motive in mind.''

It was as if, having started, he couldn't stop. His long mouth twisted sardonically and his eyes were dark with anger as he added, ''Not that there *are* any noble motives. If there ever were, they went out with fairy tales and knights in armor. All that's left now is greed, fear and a lust for violence, which you as a lawyer ought to know better than most.''

She stared at him, shaken by the breadth of his cynicism and the utter disillusionment that had to have created it. Again she seemed to feel him lying in her arms after she walked into his nightmare, and sure instinct told her that it was remembered agony putting the raw anger and pain in his voice now. But he was still wrong.

Whatever it had been, however cruel it had been, that tragedy wasn't everything. It wasn't all there was, any more than greed, fear and violence were the only remaining motives. Locking stares with him, she fought back.

''I don't,'' she said decisively. ''I don't, because they aren't all that's left. Compassion is left, and generosity, and affection. I've seen them too in the courts, and I've seen them here as well—''

Slapping the pen down on the desk, he cut her off. ''Then your eyesight's off,'' he grated, ''either because you simply keep your head in the sand, or because you're such a Pollyanna you can't recognize rottenness when you see it!''

Suddenly she was past her limits. Love for this man, pain for his suffering, and anger that he wouldn't let it go combined like air and embers, erupting into flame.

''Oh, I've seen it,'' she said, barely leashed rage making her voice tremble. ''I've seen it, and I've lived with it.''

She swung away for an instant, taking a deep breath to get her voice under control again. But before he could respond, she spun around, going on with furious fluency as she told him what she'd never told anyone.

''I've lived with a man so rotten he could marry me in a cold-blooded scheme to keep his job with my father's company—so arrogant that he didn't even conceal the plan past our first anniversary—so depraved that when I told him about Toby, he asked if I knew who the father was. Then he went laughing to his mistress, as soon as he was sure I understood he'd been with her during all those 'business trips' and late hours at the office!''

Like a flame-thrower, she shot out the scorching words. ''He got himself killed with her too, flying a private plane that same night when he was drunk. And I got to spend my first wedding anniversary at the cemetery, while everyone tried to comfort the bereaved young wife—and I tried to control my nausea!''

Her cheeks scarlet and her hands clenched at her sides, she stormed across the room and back, stopping by Brock's chair again. He had bent his head again, but the desk in front of him was bare. She kept right on raging.

''I've seen my share of rottenness, all right, thank you just the same! I've hurt, and I've cried, and I've had to live with the memories. But at least I had the sense not to make my own tragedy grounds for condemning the whole human race out of hand. I went on somehow, instead of

clutching the bitterness to me until it froze me into a block
of ice forever!''

Brock still sat motionless. She stood poised beside him,
breathing hard, but he neither moved nor spoke. With an
incoherent sound, she whirled and charged out of the
room, too torn by love and anger to stay near him. Behind
her the kitchen door banged shut.

Chapter Thirteen

*O*utside, she turned east for the sand banks. The trail to her car was too familiar, so she headed in the other direction, charging along the shore at a furious pace. Without even noticing, she passed near the rocks where she'd found Nick so recently and yet so many years ago.

Around her the twilight crept on. Among the trees, shadows deepened with infinite slowness while a few last insects buzzed. Old leaves rustled on the ground beside the trail, as some small night creature began to stir, and overhead, birds called lazily, settling to sleep. Everything was calm and serene around her, but Verity rushed by in her own private whirlwind.

She couldn't even remember being this angry before, but at least some lingering trace of common sense was making her work it through by burning out that pent-up energy. There was plenty to burn, too. Even when the path started to climb steeply toward the banks themselves, she wouldn't have slowed her stride. But because the fading light was better now along the water's edge, she veered down to the sand and picked her way along there at almost the same speed.

By the time she finally reached the base of the banks themselves, though, her sense of proportion was beginning to return. For a few minutes, she just stood there with that majestic backdrop behind her, catching her breath and gazing out over the ghostly lake. Then she walked on, strolling now at a much slower pace, while her mind began to operate rationally again.

The first thing it did was to replay everything she and Brock had said. He'd sounded so bitter and cynical that she had blown up and railed at him, telling him off for the easy assumption that she couldn't understand his disillusionment. Wild to get through to him, she'd said—

What she'd said was exactly what Mark would have said outright ages ago, if he'd known why she was so blind to his feelings—why she guarded her emotions— why she went along behaving very much like Brock for all those empty years. Over and over Mark had tried to warn her against keeping her heart on ice. Instead of listening and loving him, she had turned around to fall in love with Brock and tell him that his was likely to freeze forever!

That was one danger, at least, she didn't face anymore. Whatever else happened to her heart, it certainly wasn't frozen. Her wandering steps slowed still more as Verity realized that David's vicious legacy to her was all used up at last. She had dared to fall in love again, with a man who was his opposite in every way that mattered. Brock was direct instead of devious and compassionate instead of cruel.

A sense of catharsis cleansed her. She was finally free of David. She had spoken of him and with only remembered pain. She loved Brock, and telling him about David had finished exorcising that malign influence from her life.

But this last quarrel with Brock was so much worse

than the ones they'd had before that she was at a loss to know how she could salvage anything between them. Once she'd wondered which was worse, quarrelling or silence, and now she knew. Brock's stubborn silences were a wall around him, but a quarrel like this could only be a fortress between them.

Sinking to the sand in discouragement, Verity linked her arms around her knees and gazed out over the lake. To the east a full moon was rising out of the water like a giant golden coin, and soft light spilled across everything around her. The first stars sparkled overhead, and suddenly she heard Pierre as if he sat by her side, telling again the most beautiful of all his Indian legends.

Only son of the Evening Star, Osseo had grown old and frail before at last he found Oweenee, fair and young and full of graces. But all the same she gave him back his love whole-hearted, in full measure, and ignored the laughs of friends. Osseo heard the jeers, however, and finally begged his father for help, finding himself a minute later once again a strong young brave. But Oweenee, standing beside him, now was bent and white with age. Still he loved her, staying with her, kissing still her pale thin lips. And for all their staunch devotion, both were lifted to the stars, young and strong and true forever.

Pierre's remembered voice fell silent, and Verity found her hands locked tightly around her knees. Above her, the stars seemed to shimmer through a mist of tears in her eyes. But near her feet tiny wavelets lapped at the shore, as if to offer comfort, and finally their whispered consolations lulled her racing thoughts.

Behind her wind breathed across the clay, and separate grains of sand talked with tiny voices, so that the very air seemed alive. Ages old and wise, it welcomed her like the countless others who had come before. Here by these mighty banks Indians had come to fast and dream, and now she sat here too. Just another little mortal, she too could think her thoughts and see her visions crouching below these towering heights until her own small self was swept up into the rushing tide of life around her.

Serene again, she lay back on the dry sand and stared at the moon, letting herself drift mindlessly now until an impulse stirred her into motion again. Beneath her, the sand still held the day's unseasonable heat, and it was seeping into her. The evening air was warm too, even at this hour. Sitting up, Verity glanced around the empty shore and then came smoothly to her feet, kicking off her shoes. Stripping off her shorts and jersey too, she folded them on the sand, dropping her bra and panties on top of the little pile. Stepping free of everything, she was as graceful as the first woman in an empty world.

Only a few feet away, a tree lay fallen from the side of the banks, rolled until it was half in and half out of the water where a little stream ran down. Still thick and fresh, the leaves shone platinum in the moonlight, rustling softly and offering a dappled screen, and Verity waded into the lake in their shadow.

After the first few inches the water turned chill, shocking her heated skin. But she kept on going, invigorated, not stopping until it rose nearly to her breasts. She didn't have any intention of swimming alone, but she could simply stand here until Superior washed away the last of the heat and turmoil, doubt and confusion of the day.

The lake rippled around her, looking like molten metal glittering in the moonlight, and she splashed idly, shooting sprays into the air to watch them rain down like diamonds. Moon gems dripped from her fingers, and more adorned her arms and shoulders, while Verity let herself think only of the night and its beauty, not of Brock and their quarrel.

Preoccupied, she didn't see him walk along the shore or notice the unfamiliar crooked smile on his face as he followed her footsteps. His own steps silent in the sand, he

came around the fallen tree without warning; only then did
Verity see his tall figure and duck reflexively. Before he
could recognize the heap of clothes nearby and glance out
into the lake for her, she had registered just that she was
no longer alone, dropping into the water until only her
head was visible.

He caught sight of her then, her hair a pale cap of curls
and her neck rising gracefully from the waves as if she
were in over her head. Too far away for her to see, his
once empty face ran through a rapid series of expressions,
and she missed them all. Bemused apology gave way to
startled concern, and then that turned into anger.

"What in blazes do you think you're doing?" he
demanded furiously, his voice ringing over the water.
"Haven't you got any better sense than to swim alone, and
at night besides? Get the hell out of there!"

Not some passing stranger walking late on the lakeshore
trail, it was definitely Brock. Her first surge of joy faded
right away, though. They'd come full circle. After tonight's quarrel, this was probably about the last thing he'd
ever say to her. And it was almost exactly the same thing
he'd said the first time he ever spoke to her; the words
were neatly imprinted on her mind, like everything else
he'd ever said.

But then he had had some reason for his irritation. After
all, she *had* been trying to break into his cottage. Now,
however, he was simply assuming that because he could
just see her head above water, she must really be swimming alone at night; an understandable mistake, maybe,
but only if he believed that she really *was* that much of an
idiot.

Busy leaping to conclusions herself, she missed several
interesting points. She didn't stop to wonder why he'd
come after her, or why he might overreact to the chance
she was in danger. Hurt, she hastily took refuge in anger
herself, flaming up again the way she had only two hours
ago.

In spite of the cold lake water, heat poured through her body, and recklessness accompanied it. Instead of telling him that she was standing firmly on the bottom, or that she'd come out as soon as he wasn't between her and her clothes, she said something quite different.

Her voice dangerously sweet and clearly audible across the water, she invited, "Why don't you just try making me do it?"

It might have been a childish response, but his was no better. Kicking off his shoes, he charged into the lake after her. Still fully dressed otherwise, he reached hip-deep water in a couple of strides, then flung himself forward into a smooth, expert crawl.

Jolted, Verity had retreated a few steps the instant he swung into motion. As he came on, a burst of irrational, atavistic fear filled her, and she took off in front of him, swimming away along the shore at top speed. Behind her, the lighthouse beacon was only a faraway marker.

She was a strong swimmer, but after a few hundred feet she began to tire. He was gaining on her; she could hear him churning along in her wake. But for the second time tonight a burst of energy had worked out both her anger and that sudden fear. Her sense of humor came back, and she realized how absurd this silly, childish chase was. Laughing breathlessly, she touched her toes to the sandy bottom and turned to face him.

The lake behind her was empty, and the laughter choked in her throat. The ripples of her passage made a faint, spreading vee, but otherwise there was nothing but lazy swells of black water, featureless and implacable now under the remote, uncaring moon. Raw terror sliced through her, so that she stumbled brokenly.

Then Brock erupted from the dark water right beside her, rising in a fountain of spray. A shriek was ripped from her, and it was still echoing when he dragged her into his arms. Boneless with relief, she was easy prey for him to catch at knees and shoulders, holding her crosswise against his hard chest while he strode splashing toward the shore.

"One way or another," he growled, "you're coming out."

The absolute certainty in his tone put life back into her—and resistance. Stiffening in his hold, she set both palms against the soggy shirt plastered to his body and pushed, kicking her feet and wriggling like a fish. His big hands slipped, then tightened their grip on her wet bare flesh as he reached the shallows.

While waves lapped around his ankles, the hand circling her knees began to trace patterns on her smooth, cool thigh. The one beneath her shoulders stirred against her breast, and resistance melted from her mind. Turning her head to him, she found his lips only an inch away. She neither knew nor cared which of them it was that closed the gap.

As her eyes fell shut, she only knew that their lips met with a sense of inevitability, of sweet and welcome fate. One hand rose to hold his face to hers, stroking the lean, smooth cheek as she opened to him like a flower in the sun, greeting him with a tiny croon that died inside his mouth.

Tasting her, his tongue searched gently, then with growing urgency as she took him in, leading him deeper. His arms went slack, and she slid down his body to stand on her tiptoes in the lake, pressed against him eagerly. While her hips met his, soft against the hardness of his need, she arched her spine away from him so her hasty fingers could undo the buttons of his shirt.

The action freed her breasts for his touch, and his hands cupped them, lifting the ivory fullness to his lips with an incoherent murmur of wonder. Caressing the soft weight, he ran his thumbs over her nipples, again and again, until those shadowed peaks were taut and anxious and a flame leaped up somewhere deep inside her. Bending his head, he took first one nipple and then the other into his mouth, drawing her into him and out of herself, imploringly, demandingly. Her hands flew to cradle him to her, and she gasped at the sweetness of his entreaty.

"Yes," she breathed raggedly, "yes," and didn't know she spoke.

He moved then, raining kisses on her breasts, her arms, her shoulders, while his hands roamed down her sides. They paused at her narrow waist, holding her while she pressed her face to the matted hair on his chest and felt a vibrant quaking through his tall body. It grew stronger as she stripped the shirt from his wide shoulders, letting it drop into the water, and found the snap on his jeans. Tugging it open, she pushed the worn denim down over his hips, stroking the hard untanned flesh of his flanks after he kicked off the jeans and let them float away.

Naked at last, he took her lips again, a bruising kiss she gloried in while his hands slid lower and gripped her buttocks, holding her tight against him and kneading the soft flesh until it melted in his grasp as the flames shot through her. Trembling already, her legs buckled beneath her, so she slipped down in his hold. He followed her, keeping his mouth on hers and his hands on her hips, until they lay together in the shallow water just where it met the shore.

Faint and faraway, she heard the slight waves lapping at them and felt the water's light touch. Nearer, she saw the moonlight pouring over his body, turning the clean strong grace of him to something magical and unknown. But the universe had contracted around them, and all she really sensed was the pulsing core of it here in his arms.

He had drawn her up onto his chest, so that she lay silhouetted against the stars, with her breasts crushed against him and her slim legs tangled with his, feeling the deep tremor throughout his body. His hands still stirred slowly up and down her slender back, tracing the curve of her spine, rising over the swell of her buttocks, and flowing down her thighs, while she arched hungrily into his touch. His mouth fusing with hers, his tongue began a rhythmic probing. Accepting it, answering it, her body moved on his, rocking in a sinuous pattern, and he tore his lips away, his breathing labored.

Eyes open, he looked up at her and fire seemed to simmer along the strong planes of his face, blurring and melting them with desire.

"Verity?"

His voice was rough with passion, and she gazed down into the face so near her heart. Once it had been blank, but now it was alive with desire and longing that turned his eyes dark and flared his nostrils. His whole body was taut beneath her, held in check by an iron control; only a faint quiver betrayed how much it was costing him.

But he waited while she stared, motionless in the moonlight as she studied his face. Even passion dissipated for a few heartbeats, letting her think clearly about this man who held her in his arms and gave her one more chance to draw back. Wide open now, all defenses down, he met her searching look, and she found everything she had ever dreamed of but long ago despaired of finding. Honesty was there and quick intelligence, strength and a steadfast compassion.

The lake rippled along her sides in tiny waves, and love flooded through her, washing away the last remnants of old grief and disillusion. Unbearably moved, she let her head sink until her lips just brushed his. They stirred and were still again until she whispered, "Yes, Brock, yes." Then his mouth took hers in a fierce and joyous possession, as his arms clamped around her convulsively.

They lay like that while the lake murmured around them and the moon sailed serenely overhead. But finally, passion rose again. Slowly, deliberately, his tongue began its steady probing, the rhythm accelerating as she answered it. Their breathing grew harsh and the water swirled around them, until he pulled back a quarter inch from her lips.

She gave a little incoherent cry of disappointment, but he murmured hoarsely, "I think I'd rather drown in your arms than the lake."

Laughter gleamed beside the hot white flame in his eyes, and she nodded with a breathless chuckle. Letting her slip down beside him, he circled her knees and shoulders again and then rose powerfully to his feet with her in his arms. A few long strides took him out of the water at last, and he crossed the sand to the foot of the banks.

Rainwater washing down those steep slopes had worn deep gullies, and in one of them, a patch of hardy grass had found a toehold. Silky and luxuriant, it made a small green dell, and he laid her gently down there, standing straight again for a moment while urgency gave way to sweet, slow certainty.

Tall and hard-muscled, he was a perfect pagan statue, ancient marble in the white moonlight. Gazing up at him as the light and shadow played over his magnificent body, she caught her breath at the primitive beauty of him. He was the only man in the world, and she the only woman, and time stood still around them.

But then he dropped to his knees beside her in the grass, and time began again with her hurrying heartbeats. With a kind of homage in his touch, he bent to set a lingering kiss on her lips and then set out quite deliberately to kiss every other inch of her as well.

Her cheeks, her eyelids, even the tip of her nose all thoroughly kissed, he trailed his mouth down the column of her throat, pressing his lips to the quickening pulse he found and then tracing her collarbone to each arm. At her right elbow his lips found a faint pink thread, all that remained of the cut he'd tended so gently, and his breath paused to soothe away the last dim memory of pain. Then kisses savored the satin skin on the inside of her arms and drifted downward to acknowledge each separate finger and pause in each palm. Both hands clenched around the lingering warmth, and he went on with his dallying, maddening progress while tendrils of fire stirred between her thighs.

As his big hands circled each breast, faintly blue-veined in the moonlight, he ringed it with kisses. Rising to each quivering summit, he caught it in his mouth again, tugging and pulling gently while his tongue flickered against the budded tip. Pleasure so keen it was almost painful lanced through her, and her back arched into his caress. Pale gold in the white light, her hair spilled across the grass as she rolled her head wildly from side to side.

Her hands clutched at him, catching at his shoulders, reaching for him, to draw him in to her until the raging hunger he had awakened should be satisfied. But he slipped from her grasp, dropping a kiss on her fingers as he set them aside. Cool air rushed across her heated flesh as he pulled back, and a choking cry of loss burst from her lips. Blindly, like some primitive thing stretching toward the sun, she groped for him, but he was gone.

Agonized, she went limp, collapsing in the bruised grasses while their cool, pungent scent rose around her. Then she felt his lips again, giving her back her life. He had moved down her body, and now he caught her feet in his warm hands, pressing kisses to the tender skin inside each ankle.

All over again, he began the maddening progress along her body, this time dawdling up each leg. Idly, he traced the bones with his mouth, while shivers raced over her skin. Bending each knee, he kissed the pulse that hammered behind it as her muscles turned to water.

And at last he came to her, moving up to cover her with himself as the sky covers the sea. The stars behind him were blacked out, and there was only Brock. His eyes blazed, almost mad with need, and his breath tore in and out of his heaving chest. Utterly open, she received him eagerly, welcoming him into her with elemental joy as he gave an inchoate cry and they moved in a wild ageless rhythm. Asking and answering, giving and taking, they fused together into a single glowing, searing entity, like two suns falling into each other's orbit. The cataclysm rocked them both, and a high keening cry trembled on the night. Then they were still.

Chapter Fourteen

Sunshine moved across her room and touched the slight smile lingering on Verity's face. Rosy heat seeped through her eyelids, warm as a kiss, and woke her gently. She shifted against her pillow, and the sheet slid down one bare shoulder as her hand reached across the tumbled bed and found only cool cotton.

Her eyes fluttered open and she curled up on her side, gazing bemusedly at a newly created world. Every color seemed fresh, every detail sharp and unworn. Against the pure cream expanse of the walls, her furniture had a rich brown patina, catching the light on its carved surfaces. The curtains at her windows were snowy sails, snapping and billowing, while lake-scented air filled the room.

Brock was gone, of course, and with him almost every trace of his presence in her room. Now only her own clothes lay on the floor, damp and sandy, heaped where his eager hands had let them fall at the end of a moonlit walk back from that enchanted green bower in the banks.

But the far side of her bed was rumpled, and beside her, a second pillow still bore the imprint of his head.

Delicate, wondering, her fingers traced the faint outline of his body while a pink color rose in her cheeks and a smile shadowed her eyes. He had lain here with her when passion flung them both across the sky like arcing meteors. And when its searing heat sank again to embers, he had cradled her against his wide chest. Drifting into sleep, with his arms locked around her and his heartbeat the rhythm of the universe, she had known happiness beyond longing, even beyond imagining.

As a girl she'd dreamed of the man she would someday love; as a woman she'd thought that she found him in David; as a widow she'd given up hope that he could exist. But Brock was all she'd ever imagined, and so much more. More than a knight on a white horse, more than a handsome charmer, more than even a man of honor—he made her old dreams pale by comparison. All those things and others, he was no cardboard hero but a real one: a man whose strength and compassion, courage and integrity had been tried by fire and come out true.

Sunshine falling on her like a blessing, Verity rested her cheek where Brock had lain. Awed to learn such joy could be, she didn't even hear at first when shouts from the boatshed drifted down an east wind. She didn't know that Brock had slipped away as soon as she fell asleep. While she slept, she'd missed the lights burning there the rest of the night, and now she missed Pierre and Toby yelling encouragement.

"Ready to go!"

"Yippee!"

But when Brock's voice ordered, "Hold it!" her daydreams melted away. That sound could call her from a coma. Lifting her head, she listened for his part in the confusion of comments and commands that floated in her direction now.

"Once more—let's go through it. Toby?"

"Pull out the chocks."

"—*with* the ropes."

"And then?"

"Stand clear!"

"Got it!"

The three voices twined and wove around each other, each loved in its own way, and something in her sang with the harmony. But there was also a peculiar squeaking noise, resonant and piercing, and passive pleasure gave way to active curiosity. Even memories of Brock's presence here last night couldn't keep her from his presence out there now.

Quick and light as air, she sprang out of bed and ran to splash her face at the washstand. Jeans and a coral tee shirt came to hand, and she yanked them on, sliding into sandals only an instant before she darted down the stairs and out into a radiant morning. Feet barely touching the ground, she ran along the walkway to the shed and Brock.

She saw him last, though, as she skidded to a halt in astonishment and delight. The shed doors to the lake stood wide, and poised just outside the opening was his sloop, her varnished deck glittering in the sunlight above a snowy hull. Already moved ten feet, the wheeled cradle Brock had built his boat in now perched at the top of the tracks he'd laid to the water, just where they began to slope. On the far side, Toby hovered near a set of wheel chocks, and in the doorway Pierre had both hands raised to the boat's trim bow. Farther into the dim interior, Brock was only a tall shape, bending to adjust something she couldn't see.

"Mom, Brock's finished his boat, and we're gonna launch her! Isn't it great?!"

Toby's voice was hoarse with excitement, and Verity knew why her morning coffee hadn't arrived this morning. What routine could possibly compete with the thrill of launching a boat? It made even building a chicken coop dull by comparison!

"Perfect!" she agreed readily, but she meant more than Toby heard. Launching that lovely sloop was the perfect celebration for a perfect day in a perfect place. Happiness bubbled in her like champagne, and her voice was alive with it.

Caught by the sound, Pierre tossed a quick glance over his shoulder at Verity's glowing face, and his own creased in reflected pleasure. "Just in time, Verity," he smiled. "You can give us a hand with the launch—"

"Okay, Toby!" Brock's voice interrupted. "Give 'em a yank!"

"Wait!"

Face intent, Toby was already beginning to pull on the ropes that ran from his small paws to the wheel chocks, but he halted at her command, gazing at her in surprise while his mouth made a round O.

"Just a minute—"

Glancing around, Verity's eyes fell on a half-full coffee cup on the ground near Pierre.

"May I?" She shot him a laughing, eager look.

"Of course." He nodded once. "It seems only right."

Chuckling, he watched as she flung the coffee into the bushes and flew down to the dock, dropping on one knee to scoop up a cup of water.

"What—" Toby began in bewilderment.

"You'll see."

While Verity leaped to her feet and ran back up to them, balancing the extended cup so that hardly a drop spilled, Pierre held up a delaying finger. He let his hand fall as she reached the bow of the sloop and took a position beside it, across from Toby's puzzled face.

"Brock—" She peered into the shed and called, blinded by the brilliance of the day outside so that she could barely see him straighten and turn her way. "What's her name?"

Sunshine turned her hair into a glittering halo, and poised with one arm extended, she could almost have been the figurehead of some fine old square-rigged ship. But a gilded carving wouldn't have breathed fast or spoken in a voice that brimmed with excitement and laughter.

"I don't know." Brock's answer finally came from the shadows, but she still couldn't see his face.

"How about Sea Bird?" Toby offered eagerly. "Or Gull? Or White Sails? Or—"

Serena, Verity's own mind suggested over Toby's next inspiration, and she heard Ben Hall's voice in her memory. But she pushed the thought aside; that name belonged to Brock's past, and last night he had finally stopped living in it. Fresh color glowed in her cheeks, and to hide it she turned back to the boat.

"For now," she told it solemnly, splashing its bow with lake water, "I christen you *Sailboat.*"

Toby giggled and Pierre let out an amused laugh at her efforts, so Verity hastened to soothe any ruffled feelings. "May you find only fair winds," she added to the boat by way of apology for the lack of a real name, as Toby yelled "Here goes!" and yanked out the chocks.

"Ready?" Pierre asked, and Brock shouted back, "Ready!"

His gnarled hands on the bow again, Pierre leaned into the hull and let his weight rest against it until the cradled boat inched forward, tilting down the inclined ways and beginning to move on her own. Hooked to the upper end of the cradle was a cable running back into the shed, slack until now but growing taut as gravity pulled at the boat and Brock used a winch to keep it from sliding down too fast. Slowly, deliberately, the sloop made her way to the water.

"She's moving!"

"Steady, steady—" Pierre watched the process intently, while Toby cavorted around, whooping, and Verity paced beside the hull.

"Here she comes!"

"Just like that—keep coming, keep coming—"

"How far?" Brock called from the shed.

"Eight feet to water . . . four feet . . ." Verity counted down the distance.

"The cradle's under!"

"A little more?"

"That's it—she'll float now."

Pierre's voice rang with quiet satisfaction as he cast off the lines that lashed the sloop to her cradle. She floated free, taking to water like a land-born swan. An empty eggshell, the cradle rose dripping from the lake as Brock winched it back into the shed. Meanwhile, with Toby for an escort Pierre walked the boat along the dock, looping her sternline around a cleat and then fastening the bow as well. Obediently, the sloop bobbed gently on each incoming swell.

"She's beautiful," Verity murmured, and for a minute all three just stood admiring the sleek grace that had come of shavings and sawdust. For once, even Toby held still in amazement.

Then the shed doors slammed behind them, and Brock loped down to the dock.

"You do good work, young man," Pierre commented, helping him step the mast.

"Thanks, Pierre." The men's eyes met. "I had a good teacher."

Pierre nodded decisively, and they worked intently for several hours until the mast and boom were in place and Toby's long unnatural silence vanished in a barrage of questions.

"Is she all set to go now?" he asked incredulously, firing the first shot.

"Not quite, but we're getting there."

"Gosh! Can I come on board for a look?" Toby danced from one foot to the other as he begged for permission.

At work on the rigging, Brock tossed him a quick understanding grin. "Hop in—but step carefully."

"Yessir!" Toby leaped over the rail and disappeared below. Behind him, a faint "Wow!" drifted back.

On the dock where she'd sat to watch the whole procedure so far, Verity was still gazing at the sloop that came from that dark shed where Brock had gone so often to exorcise his private demons. Marveling how beauty could come from such humble beginnings, she murmured, "What a lovely thing!"

Coiling lines, Brock gave her a long look, his eyes intent and dark above an old black fisherman's sweater. Pierre had finally strolled off along the dock, and he stepped toward her. But Toby popped up through the companionway.

"Boy, is this neat!" he caroled, and laughing, Verity stood up and walked over to watch him scramble out. Eyes fixed on the boat in front of her, she didn't see Brock's movement. He went back to checking the rigging, and within a surprisingly short time, Toby's last question got answered.

"When are you going to take her out for a sail?"

"Now, as a matter of fact. I've got to go out by myself to make sure she's seaworthy."

Startled, Verity looked his way, but, his back to her, Brock bent to cast off at the stern and stepped aboard. "Pierre?" he asked.

"Right."

At hand again, the old man released the bowline, giving the boat a push toward open water, and Brock began to raise the mainsail. It fluttered up the mast, then caught the wind and held it.

"Back in a few hours!" he shouted, waving one hand before he looked away. He trimmed the sail, and graceful as a gull, the sloop heeled and ran before the wind toward the west. In minutes, it was only a small white triangle against the blue-green vastness of the lake.

"Boy, is that neat!"

"A fine little boat, eh?"

Pierre and Toby strolled away together, talking, but Verity stayed where she was, hardly aware of their receding voices. One hand shielding her forehead, she peered after Brock until her eyes watered; she blinked and couldn't find him again.

He was only sailing along the shore, out of her sight. But as she strained to see him again and failed, the day seemed to lose its luster. She let her hand fall at last and realized that a cloud had blocked the sun. The air—so warm for the last week or two—was cool against her skin, and a faint chill invaded her temporary paradise.

Brock had gone. He'd launched that lovely sloop and sailed away up the shoreline—and in all the commotion of launching the boat, rigging it and seeing it off, he hadn't once spoken directly to her. He'd given orders to them all, answered Toby's questions, and responded to Pierre, but he hadn't said anything to her alone. No private good morning, no murmured endearment, nothing about last night—not a word the rest of the world couldn't hear. No passing touch, or even a meeting of the eyes—

Verity's fingers clenched and her shoulders began to hunch against the pain, as her own eyes squeezed shut. The darkness behind her eyelids was lit by occasional flares of light, but the darkness that settled in her heart was absolute. Alone and motionless on the dock that he had left, she stood frozen while long minutes passed and she hurt too much even to think.

Finally she moved. Stiff as a statue, she walked slowly and awkwardly back along the dock, following the metal ways up to the boatshed without any of her usual grace. At the double doors, she fumbled with the latch, her fingers increasingly desperate as they tore at it. It gave way at last, and she clawed one door open far enough to slip through. Inside, she tugged it shut behind her until the latch clicked, as final as a knell.

The shed was dim and shadowy around her, its only

light from two small dusty windows. The air was rich with the scent of wood shavings that lay heaped in all the corners, but otherwise the shed was almost empty. Just Brock's tools and the abandoned cradle remained to tell her of all the hours he had spent here.

Searching uncontrollably, she peered around the shed, moved by an irrational hope that tried to tell her some essence of him had to linger in a place where he had spent so much time. But there was nothing, nothing at all to make her feel his presence. She was completely alone, and the tears finally started to fall. Her knees buckled as the sobs racked her, and she slid down the door jamb she'd leaned on to land in a heap on a pile of shavings, writhing there while she wept for a perfect joy that ended as soon as it began.

After all the passion and beauty of last night, all the communion and delight, he'd gone away this morning without a sign that anything whatsoever had changed between them. Coolly efficient, calm and practical as usual, he'd been the same today as a dozen other days after their open warfare had ended. And not a look, a touch, a word had shown her that what happened between them meant something to him.

Twisting wildly, she still couldn't hide from it. If Brock wanted to tell her she misunderstood, that last night had been nothing more than physical satisfaction, brief and meaningless—if he wanted to deny the chance of anything committed and lasting between them—then he had found out how to do it. His silence, even louder than words, was the easiest and clearest way to tell her. And the cruelest.

She cried until her eyes ran dry at last and the fragrant wood curls beneath her were damp. At last, tears exhausted and muscles limp, she lay until her gasping breath grew smooth. Very slowly then she sat up, brushing off the sawdust and combing away the shavings with careful, deliberate hands. Even agony can grow familiar, and as it did her mind began to work.

She had done just exactly what she swore on David's death she would never do again. She had let herself care about a man; she had fallen in love with him and committed herself to him utterly, daring to expect a future. And apparently there wasn't going to be one.

Last night she'd been too eager to love him, throwing aside all those years of caution, and now she would have to live with the consequences. Whatever drove him to do it, Brock had made that brutally clear this morning. She loved where she wasn't equally loved in return, and so she would have to learn to live with the pain of it.

Eight years ago a paler pain than this had made her retreat into herself and hide her heart. She'd stored it away, far out of reach of any further hurt, and had managed to get by without it until now. She could do the same again, too: She could withdraw into herself again, and—however long this pain took to wear away—make more certain than ever that it would never be repeated.

But this wasn't eight years ago. She wasn't the same person she'd been then, reacting like a shocked and frightened child to the first suffering in a sheltered life. She was someone quite different now, and as her fingers stirred idly in the scented shavings she finally recognized what the difference was.

She was a gambler now. Then she'd lost the game and vowed to quit playing forever, but now she understood the stakes better and knew that—no matter what the odds—it was better to play than to quit. At stake was a life worth living—full of risks, open to joy and to pain as well—instead of a safe, cold, empty one.

She loved Brock Randall, and he didn't love her. A handful of shavings crumpled as her fingers clenched spasmodically. But she made herself go on thinking it all through, learning what she had lost and what she had gained.

The pain was only too obvious. But before that pain had come so much laughter and anticipation, delight and passion that she'd felt alive for the first time in years. The price for it was high, but it was still well worth the cost. This time, she *wasn't* going to retreat again into self-imposed isolation. Brock might not dare to love and be loved, but she was going to go right on doing it anyway.

For one thing there was Toby. Having found that sturdy, sunny character at last, how could she possibly shut him out of her heart again? How could she do that to him, or to herself?

She couldn't, and she wouldn't, but she was going to have to take her son and leave here. Climbing to her feet, Verity flung back her tangled hair and brushed off her clothes, picking her way to the nearer window and looking out beyond the fog signal house to the lake. As always, the waves rolled serenely to the shore, and even though they brought no sleek small sailboat, she was able to watch them calmly again at last.

The truth was that much as she loved Brock, she could hardly build a relationship with a man who only acknowledged her at night! And without him, there was nothing else to keep her here. This remote and beautiful place would always be dear to her, because Brock had been here, because she'd come back to life here. But her case was closed, and Pierre would soon be opening the lighthouse to the public. She might as well pack and go; at least at home she had her practice. And Mark wouldn't be losing a partner after all.

Casting a last look around the shed, she composed herself and walked out the door, pulling it neatly to behind her.

"By the way, we're all set to leave in the morning."

Handing Brock his coffee at supper, Verity made herself speak casually and didn't meet his eyes. He'd waited so long to hear those words, he was bound to look pleased and—firmly under control as she might be—she still wasn't eager to watch his relief at their parting.

By the time he sailed back, late in the afternoon, she had gathered up everything belonging to herself and Toby, packing it away neatly in the suitcases they'd carried out there so long ago, that day in May. While Pierre sat nearby in silence, she'd explained, too, telling Toby that with Pierre's case all wrapped up, it was time they went home.

Now both the old man and the boy listened to her impassively, continuing with their meal. Her attention fixed on Toby's head bent over a bowl of chowder, Verity watched the way his cornsilk hair fell across his forehead. But she still heard Brock's spoon clatter against his bowl, and she heard the abrupt way he answered.

"You can't go. Not yet."

Toby glanced up at him curiously, and Verity forced herself to keep watching her son's round face, instead of looking at the angular one beside it. But fighting that temptation took an enormous effort, and it left her nothing to calm her racing pulse. They couldn't go? He wouldn't let them leave?

"Remember that ride I promised you, Toby, as soon as I knew the boat was safe? You've still got that coming to you."

But before her skyrocketing hopes could clear the launch pad, Brock kept talking and she realized that he didn't want to keep her here, only to delay her long enough for him to take Toby out for a sail.

"As a matter of fact, before we all go our separate ways I thought we could go down through the Soo Locks and along to Mackinac Island—you and Pierre, and Verity—as a last adventure."

That final word had to be aimed at Toby—Verity could hear the quotation marks around it—and she and Pierre sounded very much like afterthoughts. But Verity discovered that she didn't have any pride left where Brock was concerned, only relief and a feeling of reprieve that she needn't say good-bye to him forever quite yet. She could have at least a few more days with him first—

"What a marvellous idea!" she said impulsively. "We'd love to come!"

Delighted, she let herself stop watching Toby, just as an odd sequence of expressions passed over his face. An instant of pure small-boy relish gave way to doubt, as he flicked a questioning look at Pierre. A tiny nod there, and Toby's transparent face mirrored indecision, then resolution. The faintest trace of regret lingered a few seconds, but vanished before Verity could see it.

"Wait a little," Pierre interposed. "Why don't you three go without me, eh? If I'm going to be opening this lighthouse as a Visitors' Center for those park folks, seems like I'd better be getting busy with them to find out just what they want done. But you go have a fine time."

"Me too," Toby blurted, before either Brock or Verity had a chance to react to Pierre's statement.

"What—" Verity began, but he rushed on.

"I'll stay here too. Please, Mom?" Without quite meeting her eyes, Toby looked at his mother with an expression of earnest entreaty. "I mean, boats are great and all, I guess—sailing and everything—but I bet I'd get seasick or something."

Brock gave him an intent, evaluating look, but Toby didn't react. Instead, the grim prospect of seasickness seemed to catch his attention for a minute. "I'd prob'ly have to spend all my time hanging off the end of the boat, and you'd make me walk the plank or something—"

"Chicken Little, I hardly think—"

Verity's laughing interruption stopped him from embroidering on the horrible possibilities. But Toby just charged off in another direction, while Brock turned his stare to Pierre. Almost as if to avoid it, the old man blew a thick cloud of smoke that rose and hid his face.

"Besides, if I stayed here, I could spend some more

time with Pierre before we have to go." Standing up, Toby moved a couple of steps to crowd against Pierre's chair. "Couldn't I?"

"You'd be welcome, of course. The company is good, eh?"

Pierre's voice drifted out of the cloud a little hoarsely, and Verity remembered he hadn't been well all that long. Maybe he really shouldn't be entirely alone yet. He and Toby could take care of each other—

"Can I stay, Mom? Please?" Toby's whole body seemed to incline toward her eagerly, and Verity recognized the full force of a "special please." He never used it for a minor wheedle but only for something he wanted very badly. She had a hard time resisting it, and he knew it.

"Please?"

"All right, Toby," she capitulated. "If you really want it, then you two stay and look after each other."

"Yaaaay!"

Short arms locked around her in a breathtaking hug, then Toby darted off while Brock observed, "Well, that settles it. You two can hold the fort here for a couple of days, and the two of us will leave in the morning."

Trying to still her racing pulse, Verity told herself that it was just as much because Toby'd squeezed the wind out of her as because she was going to have two more days with Brock. Just the chance to be with him didn't mean she'd be able to break through those walls of his at last—

But her heart kept pounding, and it also kept her from seeing the laughing, conspiratorial look that passed between Toby and Pierre. Or from seeing that Brock caught it too.

Chapter Fifteen

$\int$tubby fingers scratched at her door, and Toby's voice penetrated it in a hoarse stage whisper. "Mom? It's time—"

Hazily, Verity checked her clock with one eye—6:00 A.M. What on earth?— The eye closed, but then she leaped awake as she remembered that they were setting sail at 7:00.

"All right, Toby—I'm awake."

Long after midnight she'd still been restless. Half of her wanted to hold back the time, clinging with both hands to these last remaining hours, because in the morning her life at the lighthouse would be over. She'd come back from Mackinac to pick up Toby, of course, but that would be a flying visit, and she would already be a stranger again to this simple turn-of-the-century life. She would go back to the outside world of modern gadgets—and modern fidgets. Instead of the ageless rhythms of the lake, she'd have only coffee spoons and traffic lights to measure out her days, only the trivial instead of the elemental. And it was hard to give up a life so free for one so confined.

But at the same time, half of her found each minute endless because it lay between herself and the morning's sail with Brock. At dawn they'd head into the rising sun, setting out for Mackinac, and she'd have two days alone with Brock: two days to store up memories enough to last forever, or to break through to him once and for all.

Over and over again last night she had checked the carry-all that held what little she'd need for a two-day sail. Substituting one sweater for another, she had repacked it and then decided to add an extra jersey, repacking yet again. The clock hands had barely moved. She had sorted out the papers on Pierre's case again, arranging them in a new order when the old one had been perfectly good. Only a few minutes had passed when she was done. Finally she had paced from window to window, gazing out into the night. And time crawled by. Not until well past one did she even go to bed, and it was past two before she fell into a heavy, dreamless sleep.

"Want some coffee?"

Brock and Pierre must both have been awake already, but Toby's voice was still impressed at the hour.

"Love it, Toby—thanks!"

Even today, early morning wasn't going to be her shining moment, especially after a late night. But swinging long legs out of bed with considerably more than her usual energy, Verity rushed to get ready. For better or worse, the time had come to leave the lighthouse.

Right on schedule, Brock hoisted the mainsail at 7:00, while Verity held the tiller. Around them, the mist on the lake was just beginning to lift, as the wind stirred the air and water to life for the day. At the horizon, silvery swells met a cotton sky, but overhead white gave way to palest blue. On the dock Toby and Pierre were bright notes of color, waving farewell, and their voices carried clearly over the water.

"Good-bye and good sailing!"

"Bye, Mom! Bye, Brock!"

"Have a good time together, land-lubbers!"

That was Brock, with a sudden laugh that made her heart beat faster, even while it puzzled her. Why that flash of amusement? But the expanse of empty water between boat and shore was widening, and she raised one hand from the tiller to wave.

"Good-bye, Pierre. Tadpole, remember—"

"I know!" Verity could hear Toby's grin, even if she could no longer see it at this distance. "Eat, sleep, wash and behave!"

"Right!" In spite of the lump in her throat, she couldn't help laughing at that succinct summary of maternal commandments. So much for the ten minutes they spent alone together over her coffee! But as the luffing sail began to pull and Toby's sturdy little figure grew even smaller, the ever-present baseball cap only a scarlet dot, she added recklessly across the water between them, "And remember I love you!"

"Me too!"

"Take care—"

"Have a super time!"

Fainter and fainter, their voices drifted over the lake, finally lost in the soft rush of water along the sailboat's hull. Verity waved once more and let her hand fall to the tiller, where it locked tightly into the other one.

Checking the sheets, Brock gave her a quick look. It took in her trim yellow sweater, hair curling around her face, slender hands clamped on the tiller, and an unusual lack of expression on her clear face.

"Steer into the sun, would you?" he suggested, and she nodded, heading east toward Grand Marais.

Above, the horizon mist had turned to melted silver as the sun began to burn through, and she had to blink rapidly. Watching, he gave a private nod of satisfaction as she concentrated on his instructions; her features started to lose their set look without her understanding what he'd done.

In a few minutes she could say dispassionately, "I'm sorry they both decided not to come."

Brock didn't comment directly. Instead, he asked from the bow, "How long has Toby been down on sailing?"

Verity's puzzlement creased her forehead as she stared thoughtfully at the tiller. "I'm not sure," she admitted. "He never even hinted at it before. He's been out on powerboats once or twice, but—"

Looking up, she tried to find some tactful excuse for her son's abrupt refusal to join them. "Maybe he really did think Pierre needed him."

"Mmmm."

In the bow Brock moved around the mast so the sail hid his reaction to that idea. Verity might have missed the conspiratorial glances the old man and the boy had taken to exchanging, but Brock hadn't and her answer confirmed a guess of his. He said nothing else about it, though, and a minute later the sound of a small powerboat floated toward them, its engine a ragged putt-putt in the haze. As the boat itself took shape, Verity's face came to life even more. Side by side again, Sam and Nick were heading out to fish.

"Hallo!" Sam hollered with a mighty wave, and Verity waved back enthusiastically while Brock raised one hand.

"Where's Toby?" Nick piped.

"Back at the lighthouse with Pierre." Verity cupped her hands to her mouth and called. "We're off sailing for a couple of days, and he didn't want to come."

At her words Brock laughed to himself, but he was just far enough up in the bow so that Verity missed the small sound. She was watching Nick shake his head wildly to show he hadn't heard.

"What?" he shouted.

Verity gave up on details at this distance. "Back at the lighthouse!"

Nick said something else that was swallowed up as Sam's old engine gave a series of choking coughs. With a broad shrug of amusement and disgust, Sam himself waved them on. "Have a good time!"

"Get a sail!" Verity suggested, teasing, and heard Sam laugh. In a couple of minutes he and Nick had vanished into the last of the mist.

But eastward in their direction were blue sky and bright sun. The sail pulled strongly now, heeling the boat at an exhilarating angle and—far more exhilarating—Brock had settled beside her to take the tiller, one foot braced casually against the far side of the cockpit.

His eyes narrowed to peer ahead of them, he had turned his head from her so that she could see only his cheek and the solid line of his jaw. One arm lay along the rail, but the other held the tiller easily. He'd rolled up his sleeve along a hard forearm, where wiry bleached hairs ran down onto the back of his hand, a hand whose long sensitive fingers had caressed and stroked her, learning every intimate detail of her body. . . .

Heat flooded her, sending color into her cheeks. This was the man she loved with every particle of her being, and she had one last chance to find a way to tell him so, to find a way to pass beyond the barriers around him. But she quickly discovered that mere words weren't going to do it.

"It was good to see Sam and Nick out fishing together again." She broke the short silence that had fallen.

"Mmmm-hmmm."

"Especially when Sam thought he'd lost everything in that storm—"

"Right," Brock agreed absentmindedly.

Tilting his head back, he checked the top of the mast with one eye, while she hunted for words to tell him that she'd lose everything too if . . .

"Glad I rigged the jib sheets," he observed. "We can hoist the jib any time."

"Oh—"

"In fact, why don't you take the tiller again, and I'll do it now."

He turned away, and with him went her conversational opener.

Determinedly, she tried again as they finished the second round of sandwiches she'd made in the tiny galley down below.

"Brock—"

Back at her side, he turned to look inquiringly. Fringed by those thick lashes, his eyes had picked up the green of the lake, and they were so beautiful that her carefully planned sentence went completely out of her mind. One of his eyebrows rose, and she made herself concentrate, the words tumbling out.

"Brock, do you think Marie ever *will* come back to Pierre?"

"I don't know." Shifting his gaze out into the lake, he answered slowly. "I suppose she still might, but it's been a long time. She left when I was only a kid, and that's a lot of years ago. She could be halfway around the world, or even dead by now. Or she could think that Pierre must be dead by now."

"He said he let love go," she remembered. "But that he could still hope—"

He'd also warned her not to make the same mistake, and she had promised not to let her own love go. But before she could figure out how to tell Brock that—how to tell him her love was enough for them both, even if he didn't dare to love—a gust of wind snapped the sails with a sharp cracking sound.

"The wind's shifting," Brock noted. "There's a storm coming."

"But it's a beautiful day!" Verity protested, her attention still fixed on ways to reach him.

"Pierre and I both thought we were in for at least two days of clear sailing, too, but you've seen how fast the weather can change on Superior."

She had, like the night of that sudden storm when they met half-dressed at Pierre's door, and he carried her back to her room with passion flaming on his face. . . . But Brock was speaking again.

"There it is," he commented, his narrowed eyes scanning the horizon to the north and west of them.

"What?" she asked absently.

"Look over there." Holding the tiller in his right hand, he stretched his left arm around behind her so she could sight down its length. "See that haze on the horizon?"

"Yes—"

"That's the storm. The only question," he added calmly, "is how long we've got."

Verity was only a fair-weather sailor. A chill passed over her, and he had her full attention at last. Hardly noticing what she was doing, she zipped up the parka that had been fluttering open over her sweater, while he stared intently behind them, estimating the storm's distance from them and the wind's speed.

"Two hours," he decided. "Maybe."

She moved closer to him as he kept on talking matter-of-factly.

"We're far enough past Little Lake Harbor so it doesn't make much sense to try beating back upwind to take shelter there, so that leaves Whitefish Point. The shoreline to the east of us is empty—if we capsized or got driven aground, there'd be no one to lend a hand. We'll just have to run for cover in the lee of the point."

In spite of the ordinary tone, he was telling her that there wasn't a thing they could do except try to keep ahead of the storm until they could find shelter. Dimly, Verity remembered a map showing an enormous stretch of nothing at all between Little Lake Harbor and Whitefish Point, miles away. They really *didn't* have a choice.

Pierre had told them that the Indians said a fish god ate the white men's boats. Wood or steel, they were crushed by storms on the lake. It had already happened countless times, and it would happen as many times again. Like some old and tragic newsreel, images flickered through her mind. Schooners and steamers, barges, tugs, and freighters—they'd all gone down along this graveyard coast, and even modern man's technology was no protection. Only a few years ago the seven hundred foot *Edmund Fitzgerald* had vanished in a storm off Whitefish Point, taking her whole crew with her to Superior's crystal tombs.

She shivered, and Brock turned to look squarely at her. "All right?" he asked.

Searchingly, she stared back. His eyes were clear and steady, and the corners of his mouth quirked up. In the face of his confidence, her burgeoning fear withered again.

"All right," she answered, and he gave her that oddly sweet smile she'd only seen once or twice before.

"Good! Then let's get going."

On those words, he swung into action. Fastening a separate safety line around each of them, he clipped it at one end to their life jackets and at the other to the boat. Then while he took the tiller, Verity followed his instructions to make what preparations they could. Moving her line from one spot to the next so she could make her way around the boat, she clambered back down below to the neat cabin Toby admired so much. But there was no time for admiration now as she lashed down everything she could reach.

Beneath the boat the swells grew larger, and she bumped around, bouncing off the chart table and catching herself on the edge of the double berth. But Brock kept one eye on her, calling encouragement, and finally she'd done the best she could. Scrambling up the companionway, she struggled out the hatch and closed it tightly behind her, wedging herself into the cockpit beside him again.

As long as he could, Brock sailed aggressively, heading

almost straight down the rising wind while miles of shoreline slipped past them. Like some wild and wary sea bird they ran ahead of the storm, but eventually it caught up with them, greenish black and livid.

Almost between one breath and the next, the visibility dropped abruptly; they were confined in a narrow world of howling wind and boiling water. Thunder rumbled like the lake itself groaning, and lightning flickered eerily in the gloom. Torrential rain swept almost sideways to lash them with its stinging force, while enormous waves pounded the hull and broke over the combing, again and again, until the cockpit was awash. In seconds they were both soaked to the skin. The boat heeled sharply, so they had to brace themselves against the steep angle, and overhead the sails heaved and strained while the rigging shrieked.

"Verity!"

Right beside her, Brock had to shout in Verity's ear to make himself heard above the uproar.

"We've got way too much sail up for this now. Can you manage the tiller again?"

He pulled back a few inches for her response, and she could see his face, taut with concentration. His hair was plastered to his head, and drops of water ran down his lean cheeks; she felt more of them dripping down her own skin. Tension honed his face, but his expression was as calm as if he were asking her to pass the coffee.

She nodded, and he added, "Steer by the shoreline, but don't worry about trying to hold a steady course. Okay?"

"Okay."

Wind tore the syllables from her mouth, but he read her lips. With a quick grin, he dropped a kiss on her wet cheek. "Good girl!"

The contact lasted only a second. But without illusions Verity knew that for another of those easy intimate gestures she'd willingly steer this boat through the worst storm ever seen on the lake—or anywhere else.

His hands steadied hers on the tiller, warm and solid,

then they were gone and she fought to control a boat that leaped and twisted like a mad thing. Everywhere was hissing water, as the lake roiled beneath them, while rain and spray saturated the heavy gray air. Waves seemed to come from all directions at once, towering over them as they fell into a trough, then lifting to drop them again with another jarring crash.

Braced between the two sides of the cockpit, Verity felt each jolt in every bone of her body, and her jaw ached from clamping her teeth together. Soaked, her clothes clung to her skin, and her hair hung in her face in damp tendrils; she could hardly spare a second to push it aside with stiff fingers so she could peer forward again. Overhead, thunder and lightning still raged, but she hardly noticed them anymore. They at least stayed outside the confines of this little sloop, where all of her attention was fixed on Brock.

"Be careful—" she called. But even to herself her voice was barely audible. His back to her, he couldn't possibly have heard the useless, loving words. She could only breathe a hasty prayer.

Her heart in her mouth, she watched him inch forward, moving his lifeline ahead a few feet at a time. Over and over again, huge waves smashed into him and tried to sweep him from the deck. Solid walls of water hid him from her anxious eyes, then crumbled and broke on his broad shoulders, cascading away before the next onslaught. But somehow he kept his balance, catlike and stubborn, to reach the bow. Feet planted wide, he rolled there with the boat's frantic heaving, bracing himself to ride it while he hauled in the jib. Released on his signal, the sail whipped around him, buffeting him between waves, but finally he had it stuffed into its bag.

"Got it!" he shouted, grabbing the rail so he could toss her a lopsided grin.

The words blew away downwind, but she was focused so intently on him that his voice seemed to ring in her mind when it couldn't reach her ears. It was a sound of simple triumph, and on a flash of intuition she realized that at least part of him was enjoying this elemental fight against the storm. She smiled in answer, and even the strain of holding the tiller seemed less. Only a minute later, though, relief gave way to worry again as he lurched a few steps aft to the mast.

Blinking the rain from her eyes, she watched him reef the mainsail now, balancing precariously on the pitching deck so he could use both hands again. With each new jolt it seemed that he had to be thrown into the seething water, and every muscle in her body tightened as if that could help him; unconsciously, she bit her lower lip until her teeth almost met. But somehow he managed it, leaving a smaller triangle of straining canvas.

She let out a long breath she didn't know she'd been holding, while he steadied himself on the mast, peering ahead of them into the turbulent grayness. It was all a blank and featureless wall to her, but he must have spotted something because he called to her over his shoulder.

"Point . . . not far now."

She tried without any luck to find what he'd caught sight of, rising to a precarious half-crouch to strain her eyes until they burned, before she gave up. His satisfaction reached back to her like a ray of sunshine, though. She sent him a smiling nod, lifting one stiff hand from the tiller for a thumbs-up sign. With another grin, he started to mirror her gesture; she saw his hand begin to move. And then everything went black.

Chapter Sixteen

She came to slowly, returning to consciousness like a traveller who savors his homecoming. Familiar landmarks, she recognized sensations without any particular surprise that they should be reappearing one by one after an absence. Content to stay where she was, she greeted them calmly and without question, her eyes still closed.

Sound came back first. In the distance she heard a hollow-toned foghorn and closer, the familiar soft slapping of little waves. Movement was the next sensation to return. Everything was in motion, a gentle rocking that was comfortable rather than disturbing. Touch was there again, too—her hands lay loosely on something wet. Her clothes? They clung damply to her body and more moisture dewed her face. But she wasn't cold.

Idly curious now, she wondered how she could be so soaked and not feel chilled. She made an effort to concentrate and discovered that there was something warm and solid underneath her. In fact, it almost surrounded her, cradling her carefully. That must be why she felt so safe and secure. Letting her concentration drift away again, she lay still, limp and contented.

Awareness kept expanding, though, and gradually she noticed a few odd things. Once in a while, as if it had a separate existence of its own, the warmth around her shifted; at the same time, contradictorily, a patch above one ear seemed to be numb with cold. With a murmur of protest, she raised a hand to it just as she realized that another voice was rumbling nearby—and had been all along.

Her fingers collided with other fingers, and a wet cloth dropped away.

"Verity!"

Her name sounded even while the earlier words faded. For an instant they had seemed almost recognizable, but then their sound dissipated and she let them go. After all, they couldn't really have been words like "darling."

Cautiously, her hand slid past her temple, feeling its way through the wet curls until it found an enormous bump.

"Ouch!"

Her eyes flew open at last, just as hard bands of warmth tightened around her.

"Verity, thank God!"

Those were Brock's arms encircling her. She lay across his lap and he bent above her.

"What happened?" she asked him.

"A last freak gust of wind slammed the boom over, and it caught you across the side of the head."

"Oh." That explained the lump over her ear. Her hand fell. "But—

Her mind was working very slowly. There was another question, but she couldn't seem to gather up enough words to ask it. He answered anyway.

"We're in the lee of Whitefish Point. We'd almost made it to safe harbor when you got hurt."

More wistful than she knew, she said the words over to herself. "Safe harbor?"

"Yes."

He had cleared his throat before he spoke this time, but even so his deep voice was husky. The planes of his face seemed blurred, too, and she blinked to make her eyes focus better. But those hard angles were still softer than usual.

As she stared, his face filling her vision, a single drop of water slipped down a cheek that was pale beneath his tan. Laying one fingertip against his skin for a moment, she caught it and gazed at the little bead of moisture. Not tears—

Wondering, almost afraid, she looked back up at him, her hand still raised. A crooked smile flickered and faded at the corner of his mouth. Luminous silver, his eyes met hers, steady but somehow unfamiliar.

Searching them, searching his face, she found no barriers, no masks, no retreats, only emotions that lay perfectly open for her to read. A deep thanksgiving was there, and she felt its echo begin to sing inside her, clear and small at first but gaining strength. Passion was there, and she knew it by the answering heat that coursed through her. And one more emotion shone there, too, waiting quietly and unafraid for her to recognize it at last.

Finally, tremulously, she did, finding it everywhere. In the slight tremor that shook his arms around her, in the softening of his hard face and the pallor of his skin, in the bottomless candor of his eyes, and most of all in the droplet that still glistened on her fingertip—loving vulnerability was in them all.

"Brock?" The most fundamental courage of all—the courage to risk love, with full knowledge of its dangers—glowed in her own face too as she whispered his name.

"Yes," he repeated, and they gazed at each other in complete understanding.

In loving each other they would risk everything. For

each other's sake, they would lay open heart and mind and soul to the pain that time and change, separation and death might one day bring. But while every instinct for self-preservation shouted at them both to run, to return to the colorless safety of loving no one, they stayed as they were. And finally Brock spoke again, so that they could repeat in words all they had just said with their eyes.

"I love you, Verity Brandon," he said steadily. "Will you marry me?"

"I will."

Steadying herself with both hands on his chest, she reached up and set her lips on his as a seal. He took them that same way, and across the separateness of self from self they exchanged a kiss of affirmation and promise. But as their mouths warmed to each other, the separation seemed to vanish and promise for the future became desire in the present.

Carrying her with him, he surged to his feet so suddenly the boat rocked, even at its mooring in safe harbor, and she was crushed against his body. As if the iron bands of his arms could end any distance between them and make them one forever, he held her to him. Clinging with all her strength, she met him at chest and hip and thigh, fusing to him as she matched his need with her own, and passion exploded in them.

A groan shook them, bursting from one throat or both, and then he shifted his grip to draw her up into his arms again. Eyes closed, she lay in his embrace, hardly conscious of her changed position. His lips still held hers, his tongue still searched her mouth and she barely knew or cared when he began to walk with her.

She just accepted it when he edged down the companionway and into the cabin, to lay her across the double berth and follow her down without breaking the kiss that joined them. Moving now to instincts that were older even than the lake beneath them, she helped him pull away the fabric that was a last thin limit between them. Then it was gone, and nothing whatsoever kept them from each other. With a glad cry she welcomed the pale shadow that arched above her; he descended to her and entered, so that their union was complete.

A long time later the boat rode quietly at its mooring. On the lake the storm had rolled away to the east, and in the snug cabin Verity and Brock lay quietly in each other's arms in perfect harmony. With their bodies and with their words they had said almost everything. But one thing remained to be said.

"Verity."

He spoke her name, and the word rumbled deep in his chest so that she felt it beneath her cheek as well as hearing it. Lifting her head slightly, she pressed a kiss against the salty dampness of his skin and then rolled to look into his face. It was filled with love, and a certainty she had never seen before in him humbled her. But there was also a seriousness that made her pay attention instead of dissolving again in delight.

"May I tell you about Serena Morrison?"

Serena. The name Ben Hall had mentioned. The woman Brock had lost?

"Yes, please," Verity agreed, knowing that if he could finally talk about the past, then it truly *was* past.

Settling her more comfortably against him, he cupped her face in his caressing fingers before letting his hand fall and looking beyond her into distances far outside the warm world of their embrace.

"Before I came back to the Upper Peninsula, my last assignment as a reporter was in Pretoria." He began thoughtfully, but after the first few words his voice took on a professional detachment. "My job was to cover the growing unrest that was sparking riots against the apartheid government, but it ended abruptly when a car bomb went off only twenty feet from where we were filming. It blasted me half way down the block, and it killed Serena instantly—she was my camerawoman as well as my fiancée.''

He moved spasmodically beneath her, and for a split second Verity's breathing was suspended as the full impact of it all hit her. *That* was what had changed him so, scarring his mind and body and making him cut off both his career and his emotions. His pain tore at her with a force beyond bearing, and she knew it was only a faint echo of the original agony.

But even though his face was taut, it was only remembered suffering, not fresh. As well as seeing the past again, he saw her too, and there were no new shadows in his eyes. Instead, there was acceptance at last, and understanding.

He went on speaking, and now clipped professionalism gave way in turn to a slower searching for words, as he tried to say out loud what he'd only just realized for himself.

''She was brilliant with a camera. Even before I loved her for herself, I loved her work. As well as a talent for living life to the hilt, she had a gift for capturing simple images that said more than all my reports could do.''

One after another, the sheaf of photographs in his desk drawer flashed before Verity's eyes. Serena's work, she knew, and knew also that Brock spoke no more than the truth about that work. But he was still talking.

''She had an instinct for the right place to be and the right moment to be there, to catch the most telling and poignant pictures. It was only a matter of time before she won a Pulitzer Prize for photo-journalism of that caliber. And when it was all wiped out in an instant's senseless brutality—all that brilliance and vibrant life splattered with her blood across a narrow alley, by an explosion so useless that even the most fanatical groups didn't claim responsibility—''

His voice cracked, and he paused to draw a deep steadying breath. Even so, old bitterness and disgust rang as he went on.

"When they finally let me out of the hospital, I was still so full of grief and rage I could hardly think. I came back to Grand Marais because taking a familiar route was easier than figuring out where else to go. And besides, it was the remotest place I knew. The network wanted me back at work as soon as I was up to it—"

Suddenly, a cold white light lit her mind, and she saw him standing again in other bloodstained streets, other war-torn cities, other crumbling countries. Fiercely, her hands tightened on him, as if she'd keep him away from danger like that by holding him to her if she had to. But then she made herself relax that stranglehold.

She couldn't do it. She couldn't bind him to her like that, not even to keep him safe. The very things she loved about him—his compassion, his honesty, his clear thinking—were the things that gave his voice weight when it spoke about chaos and disorder. She couldn't try to silence that voice when the world needed to hear it; she could only accept the possible danger to him as another of the risks of loving.

Fear and determination, knowledge and acceptance, they all flashed through her thoughts in a second or two while she bowed her head against his body. In loving Brock she had to love his career as well, and she came to terms with that. But she was still relieved to hear his next parenthetical words.

"They offered me a spot as head of the Chicago bureau, and if you agree, I'll take it now—"

She nodded silently, thankfully, and he gave her a quick hard kiss for the future before he went on explaining about the past.

"But all I wanted to do then was to get away. To get so far away from the rest of humanity that I could never be touched by any of that cruelty and viciousness again. Or by anything else, either. I just wanted to stop feeling, and caring, and hurting.''

She made a little involuntary movement of comfort, and he looked full into her eyes. The old anger died out in his own, and he smoothed a strand of her hair away from her loving face with one long finger. When he spoke again, his deep voice was reflective.

''It worked for a while, too. Thanks to the Park Service letting me trade labor for living quarters out at the lighthouse, I was completely isolated from everyone and could cut off any new emotions. There was nothing but work—no people and no more pain; no feelings at all except my body getting back into usable condition again.

''I had empty weeks and months for my muscles to finish mending while I worked on mending those old buildings. I started this sloop too, as a kind of tribute to my grandfather for teaching me everything he knew about boatbuilding back when I still believed that man and his doings could be worth something. I began trying to shape Serena's last photographs into a book as well, all the while telling myself I'd had it for good with the rest of the race.

''That was why I was so disgusted when you showed up. There you were, with Toby and Pierre in tow, and it was like coming out of a cave into the sunshine. But I'd chosen the cave and kept on pig-headedly clinging to it. I was damned if I was going to let that insidious warmth of yours seep into me!''

He let his voice echo the old determination, but at the same time both hands rose to cradle her face again. ''And it wasn't until you blazed up the other night and told me off for my self-pity that I realized that was what grief had dwindled into. Without knowing it, I'd finally gotten over the shock of Serena's death. Even the nightmares have finally stopped—''

He broke off, and she murmured, ''I'm glad.''

She met his look as he searched her eyes. A hint of pink edged up into her cheeks, though, and he kissed her deeply. "I thought so in the morning," he said in a low voice when their lips were a few inches apart again. "But you acted as if nothing had happened, and I started to think I must have dreamed your voice cutting through the terror, your arms holding me together. . . ."

She touched her lips to his for a moment. "I didn't know how else to act," she explained with her breath soft on his mouth. "I was afraid if you remembered I was there, you'd lose Serena again and still have nightmares."

He understood that immediately, gazing into the generous, loving face so close to his own. "When the truth was that losing you is the only loss that would mean anything —everything—to me."

Her kiss was his reassurance, and silence fell while they spoke without words. Some time later he took a deep breath, picking up where he'd left off with an effort at concentration.

"The fact was that I'd been using her image to hold you off, without even realizing the image was only what I wanted Serena to be and not what she ever was. It wasn't until you forced me to see again that I recognized the knowledge that must have been taking shape all those months.

"She *was* a magnificent photographer, but it was a studied, calculated brilliance—missing your warmth. She was fiercely ambitious, and she wanted that Pulitzer more than anything else in the world, including me. If she loved me at all, it took second place to her hell-bent insistence on getting where the stories would be hot. No matter how dangerous a location might be, if there was a chance of good pictures, we had to go there. And so we went into places every other news team had long since pulled out of. That was why she died, because she had more ambition than love."

He fell silent, and Verity finally had all the pieces. At last she knew it all—why he had gone to the lighthouse and why he had so resented her arrival there, why he'd been drawn to her and why he'd fought so hard against caring for her. An hour ago he had given her heart and body; now he'd let her have mind and soul as well, laying before her everything that made him what he was today and holding no secrets in reserve.

And she would do the same. With wisdom that came from nowhere, she knew that she had to match generosity with generosity and honesty with honesty. She owned his entire past, but he was still missing a piece of hers, and it affected how he felt about both her and Serena.

"That might have been because ambition takes less courage than love."

Her voice was uneven, and she had to swallow hard before she could go on. But he waited, his thumbs gently tracing the line of her cheeks. Slowly and awkwardly, the words came out, because she made them come.

"I didn't really tell you the truth when I said I hadn't let David turn me against the whole human race. He did, for years. Ambition was so much safer than love for me that I poured every waking moment of every day into making myself the best trial lawyer around and didn't even dare to love my own son. Toby had to almost die in an accident this spring before I learned enough courage to admit that love is worth all the risks."

As fleeting as a match flame, Mark flickered across her mind, and she gave him a silent apology and good-bye. Then he was gone and only Brock remained. She met his eyes, love brimming in her own, and added steadily, "Toby and you are my second chance, Brock, and I'll always be thankful from the bottom of my heart that fate has given me a second chance. Maybe Serena just didn't get one."

He looked away, and she shut her eyes. It was done. She'd told him the truth about herself—and perhaps about Serena Morrison as well. Whatever his reaction might be now, she'd had to do it, for all their sakes.

His response was a long time coming. He lay motionless and she curled against his chest, her whole being concentrated on him. Desperately, she told herself that this too was one of the risks, and she loved him too much not to take it. But it took all of her hard-won courage to wait for the consequences.

When he finally stirred, it was to set a kiss as homage on her forehead, while her eyes flew open as joy began to flood her.

"Thank you," he said very quietly, "for giving me all of yourself, and for giving me back Serena as well. I said my last good-bye to her yesterday during that solo sail along the rocks, but you've made me understand her better than I ever did before. I haven't been able to finish gathering her last pictures into the book I promised myself I'd do for her, but now I'll be able to wrap it up. Now I can finally see how her own kind of fear could limit her love, but it took a love without limits to show me."

His last word was lost on her lips, and Verity didn't even know how much time passed before he spoke again. But at first it seemed as if he was talking at random.

"Years ago," he said in a low voice that rumbled beneath her, "I read a quotation from Francis Bacon that etched itself into my memory."

"Mmmmm?" she murmured a drowsy inquiry.

"He that hath wife and children," he quoted, "hath given hostages to fortune."

Sleep fled, and she heard the words again and again. That was it. That was why it took such courage to love. She moved until their eyes could meet again, and they looked far into each other's hearts and minds. Lovingly, bravely, they looked at their hostages and dared fortune.

"It's true, of course," he acknowledged for them both. "But love is still the greater verity."

Epilogue

𝒱erity woke softly in a world grown small. The boundaries were Brock's arms, wrapped loosely around her, and his legs, twined with hers. Under her cheek, his chest rose and fell as smoothly as the tides, and a measured thudding beneath her ear was the heartbeat of her universe.

For long minutes she just lay still, marveling that the whole world could be so full of joy. Finally, she opened her eyes in the shadowy room, letting her horizons expand slightly, but the man who held her was still the center of it all. Drawing in the warm male scent of him, she let out her breath to watch it stir the mat of bronze hair near her lips. Idle fingers twisted those damp gold-brown curls, tugging at them gently as she came fully awake, and a moment later Brock was awake too.

Shifting a bit, she saw his eyelids flutter, his eyes instantly aware, and her own eyes filled with mischief. Taking her hand from his chest, she let it lift and light and lift again, airy as a moth wing. It flitted over his skin, brushing across the wide yoke of his collarbone and the hollow of his throat, touching down on the flat male nipples, then tracing the fine hair of his torso. She skimmed around the curve of his navel and wandered on, smoothing over each hipbone in turn and wondering how long he'd let her get away with this sort of teasing.

Moving down his lean belly, she got her answer in his sudden growl and peeped at his face. His eyes burning hot silver, he gave her a stern look. "You'll pay for that, woman," he threatened softly, and deep in her throat she gave a little gurgle of anticipation.

In an instant he'd flipped her neatly on her back, pinning her with the weight of his body. Staring at her from six inches away, he ran those glowing eyes over her, taking in the amber hair already tumbled by his hands, red lips already swollen by his kisses, alabaster breasts already full to his touch.

"Again," he added thickly, the syllables lost against her body, and they came together like fire and air.

When Verity opened her eyes again, it was to find Brock awake first this time, staring at her with an expression of bemused tenderness on his face. Only a little sheepish at being caught like that, admiring his own wife, he leaned over to kiss her and then pushed himself up against the headboard of their bed, drawing her up to lean on him.

"Well, Mrs. Randall?" he asked, savoring the words.
"Yes, Mr. Randall?"

Demure as a nineteenth century heroine, she parried, and on a chuckle he swatted her fanny.

"Lawyers!" he snorted in disgust, while she made much of rubbing the offended spot. But he persisted. "What do you think of married life?"

He was still smiling, but he *had* asked, and intuitively she knew what was behind the question. While his big hand moved gently over her shoulder, she gave the last thirty-six hours or so careful consideration.

They had married in St. Anne's Church on Mackinac Island, hands linked and voices blending in the ancient words of the wedding ceremony. At their sides Pierre and Toby had grinned like a pair of Cheshire cats at the success of their plan. Then, while the other two returned to the lighthouse, they'd come by horse-drawn carriage to the Old World splendor of the Grand Hotel for a few days' honeymoon. The day after tomorrow, they would collect Toby and leave for Chicago—Chicago, and Brock's new job as network bureau chief, Verity's new practice, their new life together.

But right now, when it was all just beginning, he had asked her how she liked it. Tucking her legs up under her so she could turn to face him, she looked into that lean, beloved face and all teasing vanished from her own features.

"I love it," she said directly. "I love it because I love you more each minute of each hour, so that being your wife is more happiness than I ever dreamed of."

Those crystal eyes clung to hers, and she gazed deep into him as if she could see the years ahead of them foretold there in light and shadow. Softly, very surely, she added, "And whatever happens to us in the future, nothing will ever make me regret giving hostages to fortune."

Every question answered, he took her to him again and they fell silent. Outside their window twilight crept over the Straits of Mackinac, and tiny lights winked like a diamond necklace along the graceful span of the Mackinac Bridge. They saw none of it; they only saw each other. But together they had learned a lasting truth: that love conquers fear, and pain, and even time itself. And below them, moored at the water's edge, the *Eternal Verities* rocked softly at her anchor.

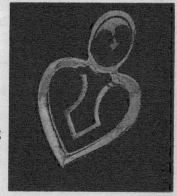

Silhouette Special Edition

MORE ROMANCE FOR
A SPECIAL WAY TO RELAX

$1.95 each

2 ☐ Hastings	21 ☐ Hastings	41 ☐ Halston	60 ☐ Thorne
3 ☐ Dixon	22 ☐ Howard	42 ☐ Drummond	61 ☐ Beckman
4 ☐ Vitek	23 ☐ Charles	43 ☐ Shaw	62 ☐ Bright
5 ☐ Converse	24 ☐ Dixon	44 ☐ Eden	63 ☐ Wallace
6 ☐ Douglass	25 ☐ Hardy	45 ☐ Charles	64 ☐ Converse
7 ☐ Stanford	26 ☐ Scott	46 ☐ Howard	65 ☐ Cates
8 ☐ Halston	27 ☐ Wisdom	47 ☐ Stephens	66 ☐ Mikels
9 ☐ Baxter	28 ☐ Ripy	48 ☐ Ferrell	67 ☐ Shaw
10 ☐ Thiels	29 ☐ Bergen	49 ☐ Hastings	68 ☐ Sinclair
11 ☐ Thornton	30 ☐ Stephens	50 ☐ Browning	69 ☐ Dalton
12 ☐ Sinclair	31 ☐ Baxter	51 ☐ Trent	70 ☐ Clare
13 ☐ Beckman	32 ☐ Douglass	52 ☐ Sinclair	71 ☐ Skillern
14 ☐ Keene	33 ☐ Palmer	53 ☐ Thomas	72 ☐ Belmont
15 ☐ James	35 ☐ James	54 ☐ Hohl	73 ☐ Taylor
16 ☐ Carr	36 ☐ Dailey	55 ☐ Stanford	74 ☐ Wisdom
17 ☐ John	37 ☐ Stanford	56 ☐ Wallace	75 ☐ John
18 ☐ Hamilton	38 ☐ John	57 ☐ Thornton	76 ☐ Ripy
19 ☐ Shaw	39 ☐ Milan	58 ☐ Douglass	77 ☐ Bergen
20 ☐ Musgrave	40 ☐ Converse	59 ☐ Roberts	78 ☐ Gladstone

$2.25 each

79 ☐ Hastings	87 ☐ Dixon	95 ☐ Doyle	103 ☐ Taylor
80 ☐ Douglass	88 ☐ Saxon	96 ☐ Baxter	104 ☐ Wallace
81 ☐ Thornton	89 ☐ Meriwether	97 ☐ Shaw	105 ☐ Sinclair
82 ☐ McKenna	90 ☐ Justin	98 ☐ Hurley	106 ☐ John
83 ☐ Major	91 ☐ Stanford	99 ☐ Dixon	107 ☐ Ross
84 ☐ Stephens	92 ☐ Hamilton	100 ☐ Roberts	108 ☐ Stephens
85 ☐ Beckman	93 ☐ Lacey	101 ☐ Bergen	109 ☐ Beckman
86 ☐ Halston	94 ☐ Barrie	102 ☐ Wallace	110 ☐ Browning

Silhouette Special Edition

$2.25 each

111 ☐ Thorne	133 ☐ Douglass	155 ☐ Lacey	177 ☐ Howard
112 ☐ Belmont	134 ☐ Ripy	156 ☐ Hastings	178 ☐ Bishop
113 ☐ Camp	135 ☐ Seger	157 ☐ Taylor	179 ☐ Meriwether
114 ☐ Ripy	136 ☐ Scott	158 ☐ Charles	180 ☐ Jackson
115 ☐ Halston	137 ☐ Parker	159 ☐ Camp	181 ☐ Browning
116 ☐ Roberts	138 ☐ Thornton	160 ☐ Wisdom	182 ☐ Thornton
117 ☐ Converse	139 ☐ Halston	161 ☐ Stanford	183 ☐ Sinclair
118 ☐ Jackson	140 ☐ Sinclair	162 ☐ Roberts	184 ☐ Daniels
119 ☐ Langan	141 ☐ Saxon	163 ☐ Halston	185 ☐ Gordon
120 ☐ Dixon	142 ☐ Bergen	164 ☐ Ripy	186 ☐ Scott
121 ☐ Shaw	143 ☐ Bright	165 ☐ Lee	187 ☐ Stanford
122 ☐ Walker	144 ☐ Meriwether	166 ☐ John	188 ☐ Lacey
123 ☐ Douglass	145 ☐ Wallace	167 ☐ Hurley	189 ☐ Ripy
124 ☐ Mikels	146 ☐ Thornton	168 ☐ Thornton	190 ☐ Wisdom
125 ☐ Cates	147 ☐ Dalton	169 ☐ Beckman	191 ☐ Hardy
126 ☐ Wildman	148 ☐ Gordon	170 ☐ Paige	192 ☐ Taylor
127 ☐ Taylor	149 ☐ Claire	171 ☐ Gray	193 ☐ John
128 ☐ Macomber	150 ☐ Dailey	172 ☐ Hamilton	194 ☐ Jackson
129 ☐ Rowe	151 ☐ Shaw	173 ☐ Belmont	195 ☐ Griffin
130 ☐ Carr	152 ☐ Adams	174 ☐ Dixon	196 ☐ Cates
131 ☐ Lee	153 ☐ Sinclair	175 ☐ Roberts	197 ☐ Lind
132 ☐ Dailey	154 ☐ Malek	176 ☐ Walker	198 ☐ Bishop

SILHOUETTE SPECIAL EDITION, Department SE/2
1230 Avenue of the Americas
New York, NY 10020

Please send me the books I have checked above. I am enclosing $_____ (please add 75¢ to cover postage and handling. NYS and NYC residents please add appropriate sales tax). Send check or money order—no cash or C.O.D.'s please. Allow six weeks for delivery.

NAME _____

ADDRESS _____

CITY _____ STATE/ZIP _____

Silhouette Special Edition